THEATRE ARTS

Connections

D1611711

Level 3

Columbus, OH

The **McGraw·Hill** Companies

SRAonline.com

 SRA

Send all inquiries to:
SRA/McGraw-Hill
8787 Orion Place
Columbus, OH 43240-4027

ISBN 0-07-601876-8

4 5 6 7 8 9 QPD 10 09 08 07 06 05

The **McGraw·Hill** Companies

SRA THEATRE ARTS

Connections

Arts Education for the 21st Century

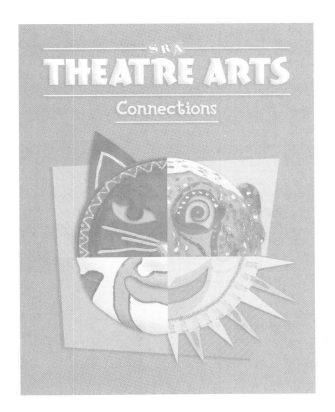

Character   Culture   Plot   Critical Thinking

Creativity   Literature   Personal Expression

**Theatre Arts education encourages different ways
of learning, knowing and communicating.**

THEATRE ARTS
Connections

All the Resources you need for a Total Theatre Arts Curriculum

Theatre Arts Connections **provides everything teachers need to offer meaningful theatre arts education.**

Theatre Arts Connections K–6

Thirty-six 15–30 minute Lessons per grade level develop the elements and principles of theatre arts.

Warm-Up activities focus students on lesson concepts.

Step-by-step teacher instructions promote successful lessons.

Creative Expression quick drama activity in every lesson brings concepts to life.

History and Culture featured in every lesson.

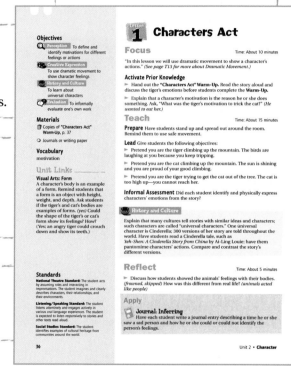

Plus

- **Complete stories and scripts** so teachers have everything they need to be successful

- Unit Openers provide an overview of Unit **concepts and vocabulary** and show theatre's effects across the curriculum.

- Unit Wrap-Up instructions pull unit concepts together as students **create a theatrical production.**

- **Unit Assessments** evaluate understanding.
  - Assessment Rubrics
  - Self-Assessment
  - Quick Quiz

- **Professional Development**

Artsource® Video/DVD

Artsource® Video and DVD offer live performances that apply theatrical elements and principles.

Integrates the four disciplines of art into every lesson

Meet today's standards for theatre arts education.

Perception

Develop concepts about self, human relationships, and the environment using drama elements and theatre conventions.

Creative Expression

Create dramatizations and interpret characters, using voice and body. Apply design, directing, and theatre production concepts and skills.

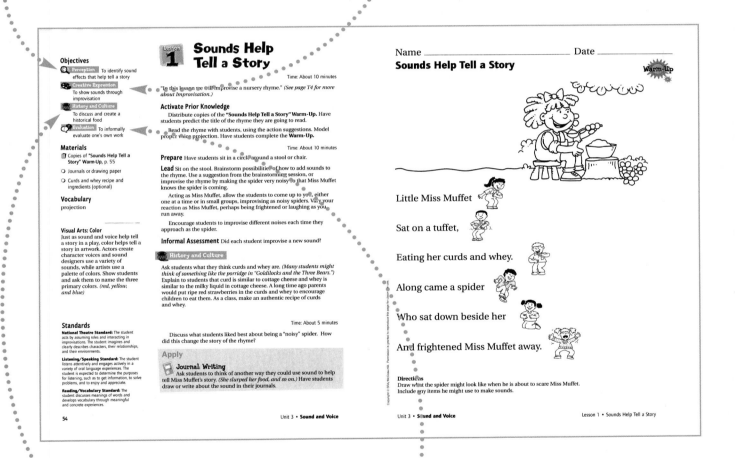

Lesson 1 — Sounds Help Tell a Story

Objectives

- **Perception** To identify sound effects that help tell a story
- **Creative Expression** To show sounds through improvisation
- **History and Culture** To discuss and create a historical food
- **Evaluation** To informally evaluate one's own work

Materials
- Copies of "Sounds Help Tell a Story" Warm-Up, p. 55
- Journals or drawing paper
- Curds and whey recipe and ingredients (optional)

Vocabulary
projection

Visual Arts: Color
Just as sound and voice help tell a story in a play, color helps tell a story in artwork. Actors create character voices and sound designers use a variety of sounds, while artists use a palette of colors. Show students and ask them to name the three primary colors. *(red, yellow, and blue)*

Standards

National Theatre Standard: The student acts by assuming roles and interacting in improvisations. The student imagines and clearly describes characters, their relationships, and their environments.

Listening/Speaking Standard: The student listens attentively and engages actively in a variety of oral language experiences. The student is expected to determine the purposes for listening, such as to get information, to solve problems, and to enjoy and appreciate.

Reading/Vocabulary Standard: The student discusses meanings of words and develops vocabulary through meaningful and concrete experiences.

54

Time: About 10 minutes

"In this lesson we will improvise a nursery rhyme." *(See page T4 for more about Improvisation.)*

Activate Prior Knowledge

Distribute copies of the **"Sounds Help Tell a Story" Warm-Up.** Have students predict the title of the rhyme they are going to read.

Read the rhyme with students, using the action suggestions. Model proper voice projection. Have students complete the **Warm-Up.**

Time: About 10 minutes

Prepare Have students sit in a circle around a stool or chair.

Lead Sit on the stool. Brainstorm possibilities of how to add sounds to the rhyme. Use a suggestion from the brainstorming session, or improvise the rhyme by making the spider very noisy so that Miss Muffet knows the spider is coming.

Acting as Miss Muffet, allow the students to come up to you, either one at a time or in small groups, improvising as noisy spiders. Vary your reaction as Miss Muffet, perhaps being frightened or laughing as you run away.

Encourage students to improvise different noises each time they approach as the spider.

Informal Assessment Did each student improvise a new sound?

History and Culture

Ask students what they think curds and whey are. *(Many students might think of something like the porridge in "Goldilocks and the Three Bears.")* Explain to students that curd is similar to cottage cheese and whey is similar to the milky liquid in cottage cheese. A long time ago parents would put ripe red strawberries in the curds and whey to encourage children to eat them. As a class, make an authentic recipe of curds and whey.

Time: About 5 minutes

Discuss what students liked best about being a "noisy" spider. How did this change the story of the rhyme?

Apply

Journal Writing
Ask students to think of another way they could use sound to help tell Miss Muffet's story. *(She slurped her food, and so on.)* Have students draw or write about the sound in their journals.

Unit 3 • **Sound and Voice**

Name _____ Date _____

Sounds Help Tell a Story

Warm-Up

Little Miss Muffet

Sat on a tuffet,

Eating her curds and whey.

Along came a spider

Who sat down beside her

And frightened Miss Muffet away.

Directions
Draw what the spider might look like when he is about to scare Miss Muffet. Include any items he might use to make sounds.

Unit 3 • **Sound and Voice**

Lesson 1 • Sounds Help Tell a Story

History and Culture

Relate theatre to history, culture, and society.

Evaluation

Respond to and evaluate theatre and theatrical performances.

THEATRE ARTS
Connections

Theatre Arts and ... Math, Science, Social Studies, Reading and Language Arts

Expand understanding and interest in subject-area studies when students explore theatre arts across the curriculum.

Vocabulary Development Key vocabulary terms are identified and defined to develop the language of theatre.

Reading Themes Make reading themes come to life through dramatic play as students explore a common theme in every unit of *Theatre Arts Connections.*

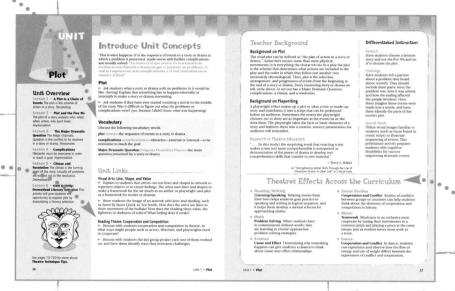

Theatre's Effects Across the Curriculum Show students how theatre concepts relate to science, math, social studies, reading, and language arts in every unit.

History and Culture Develop historical understanding as students explore theatre history and culture in every lesson.

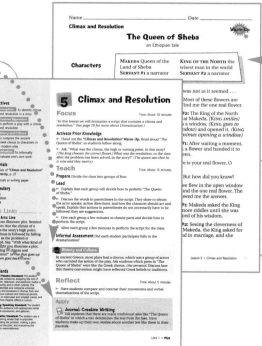

Literature Integration Actively explore literature with stories and scripts from around the world.

Writing Develop writing skills through Journal activities in each lesson.

Integrating the Arts

Expose children to music, dance, and visual arts as they explore the theatre arts.

Music

Artsource® music performances on Video and DVD connect to the elements and principles of theatre.

Visual Arts

Visual Arts connections relate the elements and principles of theatre to the elements and principles of art.

Dance

Artsource® dance performances on Video and DVD help students connect the elements and principles of theatre to professional dance performances.

Case studies have indicated that students perceive "that the arts facilitate their personal and social development." It also appeared that to gain the full benefit of arts education, students should be exposed to all of the arts, including fine arts, dance, theater, and music.

("Arts Education in Secondary School: Effects and Effectiveness" in <u>Critical Links</u>, p. 76)

Author

Betty Jane Wagner

Betty Jane Wagner is an internationally recognized authority on the educational uses of drama in the classroom and on writing instruction. In 1998, she received the Rewey Belle Inglis Award for Outstanding Woman in English Education from the Women in Literature and Life Assembly of the National Council of Teachers of English. She also received the Judith Kase-Polisini Honorary Research Award for International Drama/Theatre Research from the American Alliance for Theatre and Education.

Recently, she completed a revised edition of *Dorothy Heathcote: Drama as a Learning Medium* (Calendar Islands Publishers, 1999), considered a classic in the field. She wrote *Educational Drama and Language Arts: What Research Shows,* (Heinemann, 1998) and edited *Building Moral Communities Through Educational Drama* (Ablex, 1999).

She co-authored with the late James Moffett three editions of *Student-Centered Language Arts, K–12* (1976, 1983, 1992); and with Mark Larson, *Situations: A Case Book of Virtual Realities for the English Teacher* (1995). She has written several curricula, including *Interaction, Language Roundup,* and *Books at Play,* a drama and literacy program. She has also written numerous chapters in books, such as the *Handbook of Research on Teaching the English Language Arts* and *Perspectives on Talk and Learning,* as well as articles for the National Council of Teachers of English journals.

Wagner is a professor in the Language and Literacy Program of the College of Education at Roosevelt University and director of the Chicago Area Writing Project.

McGraw-Hill: Your Fine-Arts Partner for K–12 Art and Music

McGraw-Hill offers textbook programs to build, support, and extend an enriching fine-arts curriculum from Kindergarten through high school.

**Senior Author
Rosalind Ragans**

Start with Art SRA

SRA/McGraw-Hill presents *Art Connections* for Grades K–6. *Art Connections* builds the foundations of the elements and principles of art across the grade levels as the program integrates art history and culture, aesthetic perception, creative expression in art production, and art criticism into every lesson.

Art Connections also develops strong cross-curricular connections and integrates the arts with literature, *Theatre Arts Connections* lessons, *Artsource*® experiences, and integrated music selections from Macmillan/McGraw-Hill's *Spotlight on Music.*

**Author
Rosalind Ragans
and Gene Mittler**

Integrate with Art Glencoe

Glencoe/McGraw-Hill offers comprehensive middle and high school art programs that encourage students to make art a part of their lifelong learning. All Glencoe art programs interweave the elements and principles of art to help students build perceptual skills, promote creative expression, explore historical and cultural heritage, and evaluate artwork.

- Introduce students to the many themes artists express.
- Explore the media, techniques, and processes of art.
- Understand the historical and cultural contexts of art.

**Author
Rosalind Ragans**

ArtTalk offers high school students opportunities to perceive, create, appreciate, and evaluate art as it develops the elements and principles of art.

Motivate with Music Macmillan McGraw-Hill

Macmillan/McGraw-Hill's *Spotlight on Music* offers an exiting and comprehensive exposure to music foundations and appreciation.

Sing with Style Glencoe

Glencoe/McGraw-Hill introduces *Experiencing Choral Music* for Grades 6–12. This multilevel choral music program includes instruction in the basic skills of vocal production and music literacy, and provides expertly recorded music selections in many different styles and from various periods in history.

THEATRE ARTS

Connections

At every grade level units develop...

- Plot
- Character
- Sound and Voice
- Visual Elements
- Movement
- Subject, Theme, and Mood

Activities

- Theatre Games
- Improvisation
- Pantomime
- Tableau
- Puppetry
- Playwriting
- Reader's Theatre
- Costumes
- Props
- Masks
- Direction

Helps students...

- Understand the **elements** of drama and the **conventions** of theatre.
- Explore **history and culture** through dramatic play.
- Experience literary elements of **plot, setting, and character**.
- Apply design, directing, and **theatre production** skills.
- Develop **critical thinking** and analysis.

Standards

- Meets National and State Standards for Theatre Arts
- Reinforces key subject-area standards in Reading and Language Arts, Listening and Speaking, Social Studies, Science, and Mathematics

Getting Started
The very basics...

Here are some tips for Getting Started with Theatre Arts Connections.

Before School Begins

1. Explore the program components.
2. Plan your year.
   - Consider how often you meet with students. *Theatre Arts Connections* is designed to be a rewarding 15–30 minute weekly activity.
   - Decide how many lessons you can present.
   - Examine your curriculum requirements.
   - Select the lessons that best meet your curriculum requirements.

The First Day of School

1. Give an overview of your goals for theatre arts education.
2. Establish and communicate rules for behavior.

Planning a Lesson

1. Review the lesson in the **Teacher's Edition,** including lesson objectives, in-text questions, and *Creative Expression* activities.
2. Make copies of activities or assessments that will be needed for the lesson.
3. Determine how you will assess the lesson.

"I am enough of an artist to draw freely upon my imagination. Imagination is more important than knowledge. Knowledge is limited. Imagination encircles the world."

—Albert Einstein (1879-1955), physicist

Table of Contents

➡️ Indicates Core Lesson

UNIT 3 Visual Elements

Visual Arts: Color and Value • **Reading Theme:** Imagination

UNIT 4 Sound and Voice

Visual Arts: Texture and Balance • **Reading Theme:** Money

UNIT 5 Movement

Visual Arts: Pattern, Rhythm, and Movement • Reading Theme: Storytelling

UNIT 6 Subject, Mood, and Theme

Visual Arts: Harmony, Variety, and Emphasis • Reading Theme: Country Life

➡ Indicates Core Lesson

Teacher's Handbook

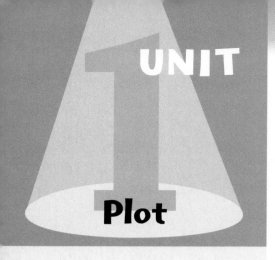

UNIT 1

Plot

Unit Overview

Lesson 1 • A Plot Has Order
Events in a plot are arranged in a certain order. *Storytelling*

Lesson 2 • Plot and the Five Ws
A plot's circumstances can be understood by asking *who, what, where, when,* and *why. Improvisation*

Lesson 3 • A Plot Has a Beginning A plot's beginning events introduce the characters and set up the central problem. *Pantomime*

Lesson 4 • A Problem and Its Complications Problems and complications create interest and excitement in a plot. *Theatre Game*

Lesson 5 • A Plot Has a High Point The problem comes to a head in a plot's climax. *Reader's Theatre*

Lesson 6 • Unit Activity: Dramatized Literary Selection
This activity will give students the opportunity to dramatize the plot of a literary selection using puppetry.

See pages T3–T20 for more about **Theatre Technique Tips.**

Introduce Unit Concepts

"The plot of a story or play is a series of ordered events that presents a problem. Plots have a beginning, middle, and end. Near a plot's end there is a high point; during this part of the plot, the people or animals work the hardest to solve the problem." "La trama de una historia o drama es una serie de eventos ordenados que presenta un problema. Las tramas tienen un principio, un medio y un final. Cerca del final de la trama hay un punto culminante; durante esta parte de la trama, los personajes, personas o animales, trabajan muy duro para resolver el problema."

Plot

▶ Tell students that all stories, including movies, television shows, and nonfiction stories, have events in a certain order. Ask them to briefly describe events, in the correct order, of a movie or show they recently saw. Ask, "What problems did the people or animals face?"

▶ Have students identify the most exciting or suspenseful part of each of the stories that they described.

Vocabulary

Discuss the following vocabulary words.

plot trama—the events that happen in a story

complications complicaciones—new events or people that make a plot's problem more difficult to solve

Unit Links

Visual Arts: Line and Shape

▶ Explain to students that events that happen in a play, especially the high point of the plot, give the audience feelings such as excitement or peacefulness. Similarly artists create feelings in their artwork by using different kinds of lines and shapes.

▶ Show students an image of a painting with clearly defined lines, such as *Mother and Child* by Pablo Picasso. Ask, "What kinds of lines do you see? *(curving)* Does this painting seem exciting and full of movement, or is it peaceful and still? *(peaceful and still)* Have students act out a scene between the mother and child.

Reading Theme: Friendship

▶ Ask, "Can friendships be created or strengthened when people struggle with and solve problems together?" *(yes, because they learn to work together)* Explain that many cultures have stories that show the importance of friendship.

▶ Say, "Think about this situation: one friend is upset because he wasn't invited to a skating party, but his best friend was invited and really wants to go. How could these friends solve their problem?" *(He could decide not to go so his friend wouldn't be sad.)*

Teacher Background

Background on Plot

As in novels, short stories, films, and television shows, the plot in a drama is the sequence of events that occur. Usually, the plot is a development of events that occur as a character or characters encounter a problem, struggle to resolve the problem, and finally resolve it. The climax, or high point, of a plot is the point at which interest, tension, and excitement are highest because this is the point that all the previous events have led up to. It is the turning point in the action of the play.

Background on Acting

Because plays are meant to be performed before an audience, actors and directors must be able to visualize the play's events. To help them do so, play scripts often include stage directions which are set off by italics from the dialogue. These stage directions are often written by the playwright, although sometimes they relate to a particular production of a play. While some stage directions relate to the setting and sound effects, others specify the actions that characters perform to portray the events of the play.

Research in Theatre Education

"... arts-based, project-based learning can assist students in developing higher-order thinking and problem-solving skills."

—Cynthia I. Gersti-Pepin

on "'Stand and Unfold Yourself' A Monograph on the Shakespeare & Company Research Study" in *Critical Links*

Differentiated Instruction

Reteach

Ask students to name exciting experiences they have had, such as the arrival of a new sibling. Have students tell the order of events of each experience.

Challenge

Tell students that a drama's problem can be said in the form of a question known as the Major Dramatic Question. Have students think of a favorite story and express the problem in the form of a question. For example, in "The Tortoise and the Hare," the question is "Who will win the race?"

Special Needs

Successful cooperative learning experiences require teacher modeling. Model appropriate inclusion of students with disabilities by giving each student a chance to speak, waiting patiently, and giving cues and prompts as necessary.

Theatre's Effects Across the Curriculum

★ **Reading/Writing**
Comprehension When students interview other students acting as characters from a story, they learn to retell the order of important events in stories.

★ **Math**
Problem-Solving When students imagine the thought process of a character facing a problem, they select and develop appropriate problem-solving strategies.

★ **Science**
Inquiry When students interview other students acting as characters in a story, they are refining the skill of asking well-defined questions in the process of investigation.

★ **Social Studies**
Human Systems When students pantomime problem situations and complications and discuss ways of solving those problems, they are exploring social situations involving cooperation and conflict.

★ **Music**
Asking Defined Questions When students analyze a plot, they follow a process similar to that used by a songwriter who must consider his or her topic, related words, and rhyming patterns.

★ **Dance**
Characterization When students portray a character, they use gesture and posture to show the characteristics and motivation of that character just as dancers do in classical ballet.

A Plot Has Order

Objectives

 Perception To identify the order of events in a fable

Creative Expression To create a fable as a class with a logical order of events

 History and Culture To learn that the plots of many fables teach morals

Evaluation To informally evaluate one's own work

Materials

- Copies of **"A Plot Has Order" Warm-Up**, p. 19
- Journals or writing paper

Unit Links

Visual Arts: Shape

Shapes in a pattern can illustrate order. Remind students that different shapes repeated in the same order can create a pattern. Ask, "How is a pattern similar to a plot?" *(They both have order.)* Explain that the difference between them is that a plot has a definite beginning, middle, and end, and a pattern can repeat endlessly.

Standards

National Theatre Standard: The student imagines and clearly describes characters, their relationships, and their environment.

Listening/Speaking Standard: The student uses listening and speaking strategies effectively. The student interacts with peers to develop and present familiar ideas for a group activity.

Language Arts Standard: The student recognizes story problems or plot.

Focus

Time: About 10 minutes

"In this lesson we will work together to create the order of events for a new fable." *(See page T11 for more about Storytelling.)*

Activate Prior Knowledge

▶ Hand out the **"A Plot Has Order" Warm-Up** to students. Have them complete the exercise. *(Correct order: 2, 1, 5, 3, 4, 6)*

▶ Have volunteers read the sentences in the correct order. Ask, "What clues helped you choose the correct order?" *(The ant had to be in the river before he was saved, and so on.)*

Teach

Time: About 10 minutes

Prepare Have students remain in their seats.

Lead Say, "We are going to create a class fable that teaches the same lesson as 'The Ant and the Dove': 'A small friend can be a great friend.'"

▶ Say the following sentence: "One day when two crabs were scurrying along a beach, they saw a bottle with a message inside it."

▶ Ask students, "What happened next?" Have volunteers continue the story. Guide any remaining students to provide responses that lead to a conclusion with the correct moral.

Informal Assessment Did each student contribute an event to the story that continued the plot's sequence?

History and Culture

Tell students that fables are very old forms of stories created by people from many parts of the world. Explain that fables are usually very short stories that are intended to teach lessons about life. Point out that most fables do not include elaborate descriptions. Instead, many fables rely almost entirely on a simple sequence of events to teach their lessons.

Reflect

Time: About 5 minutes

▶ Ask students whether it was easy or difficult to think of what would happen next in their class fable. *(It was easy because I knew the crabs would open the bottle next, and so on.)*

Apply

Journal: Sequencing

Ask students to describe some activities they do in which steps must be performed in order. *(playing a board game)* Ask students to think of a time when they had fun with a friend. Have them write a journal entry explaining the order of events of this time.

A Plot Has Order

Warm-Up

The following sentences tell the plot of a fable, but the sentences are out of order. Read the sentences. Number them so that the events of the fable are in order. The first one has been done for you.

The Ant and the Dove

_____ A dove saw the drowning ant. She dropped a leaf in the water. The ant climbed onto the leaf and floated to safety.

___1___ One day, an ant was drinking from a river. While he was drinking, the ant fell into the river.

_____ The ant bit the bird catcher.

_____ "Thank you for saving me," said the ant to the dove. "Maybe someday I will be able to help you."

_____ A few days later, a bird catcher was trying to catch the dove. The ant came by and saw the bird catcher chasing the dove.

_____ With the ant's help, the dove was saved from the bird catcher. "A small friend," said the ant, "can be a great friend."

Objectives

 Perception To identify the five *W*s in a story

 Creative Expression To use the five *W*s while acting as or interviewing characters from a story

 History and Culture To learn about the storytelling tradition of *troubadours* and *minnesingers*

 Evaluation To informally evaluate one's own work

Materials

○ Journals or writing paper

Vocabulary

five *W*s

Standards

National Theatre Standard: The student improvises dialogue to tell stories.

Listening/Speaking Standard: The student asks and responds to questions and makes comments and observations.

Science Standard: The student implements an investigation including asking well-defined questions.

Lesson 2 # Plot and the Five Ws

Focus

Time: About 10 minutes

"In this lesson some of you will pretend to be people or animals from a story, while others will interview these people or animals using the five *W*s." *(See page T4 for more about Improvisation.)*

Activate Prior Knowledge

▶ Read **"Snow White and Rose Red"** to the class.

▶ Ask, "*Who* is the story about? *What* happened in the story? *Where* did the events happen? *Why* did each event happen?" Explain that the question "*When* did the story happen?" does not have one, correct answer because the story happened in an imagined time.

Teach

Time: About 15 minutes

Prepare Assign five students the roles of Snow White, Rose Red, their mother, the Bear/Prince, and the Elf. Have these students sit at the front of the classroom. The remaining students will act as reporters and interview them.

Lead

▶ Say, "I will act as the head of this news conference. If you want to ask one of these people or animals from the story a question, quietly raise your hand and I will call on you. News reporters ask questions that answer the five *W*s."

▶ Point to different "student reporters," giving each student a chance to ask questions.

Informal Assessment Did each student either act as a character or ask a question related to the five *W*s?

History and Culture

Tell students that long ago in Germany and the rest of Europe, most people did not know how to read. Wandering singer-storytellers, called *troubadours* in France and *minnesingers* in Germany, would recite long poems and sing love songs. In the days before television and movies were invented, the arrival of such a storyteller was very exciting.

Reflect

Time: About 5 minutes

▶ Ask students whether the interviews helped them think about the five *W*s of "Snow White and Rose Red." *(yes, because I got to hear about the story from a person or animal in the story)*

Apply

Journal: Summarizing

Tell students that the five *W*s can be applied to many events, stories, or performances. Have students use the five *W*s to write in their journals a brief synopsis of a movie or TV show they saw recently.

Snow White and Rose Red

from *Grimm's Folk Tales* by the Brothers Grimm (Adapted)

There once was a poor woman who lived in a lonely little house in the middle of the woods. The woman had two children who were like rosebushes. One was called Snow White, and the other was called Rose Red.

One winter's evening, someone knocked at their door. When Rose Red opened the door, a great black bear pushed his head in. The girls screamed and hid.

But the bear told them not to be afraid—he only wanted to warm himself by their fire. The woman felt sorry for him, and told her daughters to have no fear.

Soon Snow White and Rose Red were joking and playing with the bear, and they brushed the snow from his fur. The bear slept by their fire that night, and from then on he came back every night to visit his new friends.

When spring came, the bear said that he must leave. "I have to guard my treasure from the evil elves," he said. "When the ground is frozen, the elves stay in their caves, but soon they will try to steal what they can."

Soon afterward, Snow White and Rose Red came upon a little elf. He was jumping up and down in the grass, his beard caught in a log. They offered to help him, but he told them to go away. Finally, Snow White took out her scissors and cut off the end of his beard.

The elf began to yell and scream, saying, "How could you cut off a piece of my beautiful beard?" He ran away in a huff.

Some time later, Snow White and Rose Red were fishing, and they saw the same little elf with his beard tangled in his fishing line.

He was being pulled into the water by a fish he had caught. The two girls tried to untangle his beard, but finally, there was nothing else to do but snip off the piece.

"You stupid girls!" he cried, "You've cut the best part," and he stamped off into the woods.

Soon afterward, the girls came upon this same elf yet again. This time, he was looking into a bag of sparkling jewels. The elf began to yell at them, but suddenly a big black bear leaped out of the woods.

The elf screamed and said, "Please, Mr. Bear, do not hurt me. I would not make a good meal—eat these two girls instead!"

But the bear gave the elf one great swipe of his paw, and the elf fell to the ground. "Snow White, Rose Red," the bear said, "do not be afraid." The girls recognized the voice of their friend.

Suddenly, the bear's fur coat fell from him, and he was a handsome young man dressed all in gold.

"I am a king's son," he said, "and this elf turned me into a bear so he could steal all my treasures. Only his death could release me from the spell."

Little Snow White, Rose Red, and their mother went to live with the prince, and their mother planted two rosebushes nearby. Every year they were covered with the most beautiful red and white roses that ever were seen.

Objectives

Perception To identify how the beginning of a plot introduces a problem

Creative Expression To create and pantomime the beginning of a story

History and Culture To learn about the role of certain phrases used at the beginning of fairy tales

Evaluation To informally evaluate one's own work

Materials

- Copies of "A Plot Has a Beginning" Warm-Up, p. 23
- Journals or writing paper

Vocabulary

rising action
pantomime

Unit Links

Visual Arts: Line
Lines can help illustrate parts of a plot. Remind students that there are many kinds of lines, including zigzag, horizontal, and diagonal. Tell students that the beginning part of a play is often called the *rising action*. Ask them what kind of line could illustrate rising action. *(a diagonal line that slants up to the right)*

Standards

National Theatre Standard: The student acts by assuming roles and interacting in an improvisation. The student assumes a role that exhibits concentration and contributes to the action of classroom dramatizations based on imagination.

Listening/Speaking Standard: The student prepares for and gives presentations for specific occasions, audiences, and purposes (including but not limited to group discussions, informational or dramatic presentations).

Writing Standard: The student generates ideas for writing by using the prewriting technique of drawing.

Lesson 3 · A Plot Has a Beginning

Focus

Time: About 10 minutes

"In this lesson we will pantomime different beginnings for a fairy tale." *(See page T3 for more about Pantomime.)*

Activate Prior Knowledge

▶ Hand out the **"A Plot Has a Beginning" Warm-Up** to students, and have them follow the directions and complete the missing pictures. Tell students to add one new person.

▶ Have volunteers share their pictures and explain how their beginnings lead to the princess's problem.

Teach

Time: About 20 minutes

Prepare Divide students into groups of three.

Lead Have group members compare their ideas from the **Warm-Up.**

▶ Tell students they are going to pantomime the beginning events of the story for the class. The pantomimes should be one minute long. Remind students to use safe movements.

▶ Give each group three minutes to choose one of their three beginnings. Encourage them to choose the beginning that most clearly leads to the princess's problem. Allow groups time to divide roles and rehearse their pantomimes.

▶ Have groups perform their pantomimes for the class.

Informal Assessment Did each student pantomime his or her character's part in the story beginning?

History and Culture

Many cultures have special phrases that begin fairy tales. Remind students that English fairy tales often begin with, "Once upon a time"; in some parts of Africa, storytellers begin with, "We do not really mean that what we will say is true. A story, a story, let it come, let it go." Explain to students that by using these kinds of beginnings, a storyteller lets listeners know that he or she is about to tell an imaginary story.

Reflect

Time: About 5 minutes

▶ Ask students what was challenging about pantomiming the beginning of the story. *(We didn't have much time to plan; we couldn't use words.)*

Apply

Journal: Describing

Ask each student to think of a good friend. When did each student first meet his or her friend? How did the friendship begin? Did the student know right away they would be friends? Have students write journal entries that describe the beginning of a friendship.

A Plot Has a Beginning

The three pictures below show the middle and end of a story. Look at the pictures and imagine the story that they tell. Then imagine what could have happened at the beginning of the story. Draw your story beginning in the two empty boxes.

Objectives

 Perception To identify ways in which people may express emotions that result from problems

 Creative Expression To play a theatre game in which a problem and its complications are portrayed

 History and Culture To learn about mimes in ancient Greece

 Evaluation To informally evaluate one's own work

Materials

📄 Copies of **"A Problem and Its Complications" Warm-Up**, p.25

○ Slips of paper with problem situations, such as disagreeing about a television show or being caught in the rain without an umbrella

○ Journals or writing paper

Vocabulary

complications

Unit Links

Visual Arts: Line
Lines can help illustrate a plot's complications. Remind students that lines can be used to create different types of feelings. For example, zigzag lines can create excitement. Ask students if zigzag lines could illustrate a plot's complications. Why? (*yes, because complications make a plot interesting*)

Standards

National Theatre Standard: The student assumes a role that exhibits concentration and contributes to the action of classroom dramatizations based on imagination.

Listening/Speaking Standard: The student connects experiences and ideas with those of others through speaking and listening.

Social Studies Standard: The student uses a problem-solving process to identify a problem, consider options, consider advantages and disadvantages, and choose a solution.

A Problem and Its Complications

Lesson 4

Focus

Time: About 10 minutes

"In this lesson we will play a theatre game illustrating a problem and complications." (*See page T5 for more about Theatre Games.*)

Activate Prior Knowledge

▶ Hand out the **"A Problem and Its Complications" Warm-Up** and have students complete it.

▶ Ask students to describe how problems make them feel. (*angry, sad*) Say, "When problems build up in a plot, they are called *complications*. People and animals in stories or plays react to complications."

Teach

Time: About 15 minutes

Prepare Put the papers with problem situations in a bowl. Divide students into groups of three.

Lead

▶ Have each group select a slip of paper. Say, "In this game, two students from each group will pantomime the problem from their slip of paper. The third student will then introduce another problem to complicate things even more."

▶ Tell students to use facial expressions and movements. Model this by pantomiming a problem such as spraining your ankle.

▶ Allow each group to perform its pantomime. Have the class guess the group's problem and complication.

Informal Assessment Did each student physically express a problem and a complication?

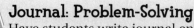 **History and Culture**

Tell students that mimes are actors who use movements and expressions to portray situations. Explain that mimes first performed in ancient Greece about 2,500 years ago. Ask students, "How can a mime express a problem?" (*facial expression , body movements*)

Reflect

Time: About 5 minutes

▶ Discuss ways in which students overcame the problem of silence through specific facial expressions and gestures.

Apply

📱 Journal: Problem-Solving
Have students write journal entries about a time when they encountered a complicated problem and had to work hard to solve it.

A Problem and Its Complications

When a person faces a problem, he or she may feel many different ways. Complete each face below to show two ways a person might feel.

Objectives

 Perception To identify the high point of a plot

 Creative Expression To perform the high point of a play as Reader's Theatre

 History and Culture To learn the significance of some cultures' use of body paint before a hunt

Evaluation To informally evaluate one's own work

Materials

▤ Copies of "A Plot Has a High Point" Warm Up, p.27

○ Journals or writing paper

Standards

National Theatre Standard: The student uses variations of locomotor and nonlocomotor movement and vocal pitch, tempo, and tone for different characters.

Listening/Speaking Standard: The student listens responsively to stories read aloud.

Reading Standard: The student reads to increase knowledge of his or her own culture, the culture of others, and the common elements of culture.

Lesson 5 — A Plot Has a High Point

Focus

Time: About 5 minutes

"In this lesson we will perform the high point of a play as Reader's Theatre." *(See page T9 for more about Reader's Theatre.)*

Activate Prior Knowledge

▶ Tell students, "I am going to tell you the beginning and middle of a story. Some bears catch and are going to eat a lonely man in Alaska. To save himself, he promises them a feast. He paints red stripes on his body. The villagers say 'He's foolish!' because the bears might eat him."

▶ Ask students, "Do you think the next part of the plot will be exciting? Why?" *(yes, because the bears could eat him)* Explain that this part is the high point of the plot.

Teach

Time: About 15 minutes

Prepare Hand out the **"A Plot Has a High Point" Warm-Up.** Have students remain seated.

Lead

▶ Read the lines aloud. Have students close their eyes and imagine what each person or animal is feeling and thinking.

▶ Say, "Now it is your turn to read." Choose volunteers to read the parts of Man, Bear Chief, and Smallest Bear. You will read the stage directions. Everyone else should read the other lines in unison.

▶ Have students read the play in a way that shows feelings.

Informal Assessment Did each student participate in performing the play?

 History and Culture

The Tlingit (pronounced /klink-it/) are a Native Canadian tribe. Tell students that some Native American and Canadian hunters paint their bodies to represent an animal that they are about to hunt. Ask, "Why do you think the bear chief took the stripes off the man's arms? *(neither of them was going to kill the other)*

Reflect

Time: About 5 minutes

▶ Discuss the students' reading. Ask them how they could have made this high point even more exciting. *(make the bears meaner, and so on)*

Apply

Journal: Describing

Have each student briefly describe in their journals his or her favorite story's high point and explain what made it exciting.

A Plot Has a High Point

Inviting the Bears

a Tlingit folktale

Characters | VILLAGERS   BEAR CHIEF   OTHER BEARS   MAN   SMALLEST BEAR

VILLAGERS: Look, look—the bears are coming! They will eat him alive!

(The BEARS come slowly towards the MAN.)

MAN: Welcome to my home, dear guests. Sit and eat.

(The BEARS go inside and eat.)

BEAR CHIEF: *(stands)* Grr, growl, growl, grr, grr.

OTHER BEARS: Grrr, growl, grrr.

(The BEARS stand, form a circle around the MAN, and wash the MAN's red stripes.)

MAN: I feel like you are washing away my sorrows.

(All BEARS except SMALLEST BEAR leave the house.)

SMALLEST BEAR: I used to be a man like you, so I speak your language. The Bear Chief said he knows how it feels to be lonely. He has lost many friends. Think of him when you feel sad.

ALL: *(to audience)* Because of this story, we paint stripes on our skin when we kill a bear. Because of this story, we invite all people, even enemies, to our feasts so we can become friends.

Unit Links   Reading: Friendship

Objectives

 **Perception** To review the parts of a plot and to think about how problems between friends can be resolved in real life

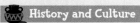 **Creative Expression** To help tell a story's plot in the correct sequence by portraying a puppet character using appropriate hand movements and voice

History and Culture To understand why some cultures have hunted seals and to explore different points of view

Evaluation To thoughtfully and honestly evaluate one's own participation using the four steps of criticism

Materials

- 📄 Copies of "**Kotick Saves the Seals**," pp. 124–126
- ○ Old socks and markers
- ○ Other materials to use for making sock puppets, such as yarn or buttons (optional)
- ○ Table (used as a puppet stage)
- 📄 Copies of the **Unit 1 Self-Criticism Questions**, p. 32
- 📄 Copies of the **Unit 1 Quick Quiz**, p. 33
- ○ *Artsource®* **Performing Arts Resource Package** (optional)

Standards

National Theatre Standard: The student explains how the wants and needs of characters are similar to and different from his or her own.

 Lesson 6 Unit Activity: **Dramatized Literary Section**

Focus

Time: About 10 minutes

Review Unit Concepts

"The plot is what happens in a story. It is the events that happen in order, beginning with a problem that one or more people or animals in the story face. The plot builds to a high point as the people or animals struggle to solve the problem. The plot ends when the problem has been solved." *"La trama es lo que ocurre en una historia. Son los eventos que ocurren en orden, comenzando con un problema o conflicto que una o más personas o animales en la historia tienen que enfrentar. La trama llega a un punto culminante en que los personajes, personas o animales, luchan para resolver el problema. La trama termina cuando se haya resuelto el problema."*

▶ Review with students the ways in which they explored parts of plots in this unit.

▶ Review the unit vocabulary on page 16.

History and Culture

Tell students that many cultures rely or have relied on hunting animals for survival. Some people hunt seals for meat and for skins to make boats, homes, and clothing. Explain that from this cultural point of view, hunting seals is necessary. Point out that the seal's point of view in "Kotick Saves the Seals" is the opposite of that of these humans; however, the seals also have wants and needs in common with humans. Have each student write a paragraph comparing and contrasting three of their own wants and needs to those of the seals in the story.

Classroom Management Tips

The following are tips for managing your classroom during the **Rehearsals** and **Activity:**

✔ **Encourage Creativity** During the **Second Rehearsal** and **Plot Activity,** compliment students on expressive use of the hands in each action portrayed.

✔ **Emphasize Safety** Explain to students that although they will portray fighting, they should not become too rough in their hand movements. In the same way, encourage students to use their voices safely, with no yelling or screaming.

✔ **Take an Active Role** Use your own puppet to guide students to stay within the plot of the story in the form of asides to the audience. For example, to prompt action from the recently married seal, you might say as an aside, "The young seal has been fighting for his nursery this year while Kotick has been away."

Teach

First Rehearsal

▶ Distribute copies of **"Kotick Saves the Seals"** on pages 124 to 126. Have students follow along with you as you read the story aloud. Have them identify the five *W*s of the story.

▶ Say to students, "This story is part of a longer plot. Does this part begin the story and introduce the problem, show complications of the problem, or show the high point of the story and the end of the problem? Why?" *(high point and end; because Kotick has to fight the other seals to save them, but in the end he solves their problem)*

Second Rehearsal

▶ Divide students into groups of seven or eight. Have the group members divide up the roles of the four seals involved in the action and the onlooking seals.

▶ Distribute socks and markers to the groups. *(See pages T8 for more about Puppetry.)* Have them create seal sock puppets by drawing faces on the tips of their socks. If you wish, allow them to use other materials to decorate their puppets.

▶ Make your own sock puppet.

▶ When the puppets are completed, have students practice moving their hands inside their puppets to express various actions, such as talking, jumping, running, laughing, or crying.

Plot Activity

▶ Have students divide into the groups from the **Second Rehearsal.**

▶ Tell students that they are going to use their puppets to act out "Kotick Saves the Seals." Say, "The most important part of this activity is that you show the events of this high point in the order in which they happened."

▶ Discuss appropriate audience behavior, such as being quiet and paying attention. Remind students to apply this behavior during each group's performance.

▶ Allow each group to perform using a table as a puppet stage. Use your own puppet to join each of the performances as an onlooking seal. If necessary, use your character to prompt students to stick to the order of events in the story.

▶ Have students return to their seats.

▶ Discuss what events or problems the seals might encounter on their way along the Sea Cow's tunnel to the new island or after they reach the island. Say, "Even though this was the high point of one story, it could be the beginning of another story. Let's use the question 'What if?' to continue this story."

▶ If you wish, allow one or two groups to use their puppets and act out what might happen next.

Standards

National Theatre Standard: The student imagines and clearly describes characters, their relationships, and their environments. The student uses variations of locomotor movement and vocal pitch, tempo, and tone for different characters.

Visual Arts: Line and Shape

Lines and shapes in artwork can illustrate plots. Tell students that before there was written language, some cultures used simple line and shape drawings to record stories and ideas. One such culture, ancient Egypt, used pictures known as *hieroglyphs*. Bring in some books with pictures of hieroglyphs, or have students visit a Web site such as NOVA's "Pyramids" Web page (go to **www.pbs.org**, and search the site for "pyramid hieroglyph") to learn more about hieroglyphs.

Theatrical Arts Connection

Television Show a cartoon episode. Discuss the order of events that happen in the cartoon. Have students identify the high point.

Film/Video Show part or all of a film that involves characters working together to solve a problem, such as *The Incredible Journey.* Have students identify the problems the characters face and how they resolve them.

Standards

National Theatre Standard: The student analyzes and explains personal preferences and constructs meanings from classroom dramatizations and from theatre, film, television, and electronic media productions.

Reflect

Time: About 10 minutes

Assessment

► Have students evaluate their participation by completing the **Unit 1 Self-Criticism Questions** on page 32.

► Use the assessment rubric to evaluate students' participation in the **Unit Activity** and to assess their understanding of plot.

► Have students complete the **Unit 1 Quick Quiz** on page 33.

	3 Points	2 Points	1 Point
Perception	Has mastered the concept that a plot includes a problem to be resolved, and can connect this to friendships in real life.	Is developing an understanding of the concept that a plot includes a problem to be resolved, and somewhat connects this to friendships in real life.	Has a minimal understanding of the concept that a plot includes a problem to be resolved, and cannot connect this to friendships in real life.
Creative Expression	Fully works to tell a story using a sock puppet. Helps to keep events in their proper sequence.	Somewhat participates in telling a story using a sock puppet. Does not keep all events in their proper sequence.	Shows poor participation in telling a story using a sock puppet. Has difficulty telling events in their proper sequence.
History and Culture	Writes a paragraph that compares and contrasts three of his or her wants and needs with those of the seal characters in the story.	Writes a paragraph that compares and contrasts two of his or her wants and needs with those of the seal characters in the story.	Writes a paragraph that compares and contrasts one of his or her wants and needs with those of the seal characters in the story.
Evaluation	Thoughtfully and honestly evaluates his or her own participation using the four steps of art criticism.	Attempts to evaluate his or her own participation, but shows an incomplete understanding of evaluation criteria.	Makes minimal attempt to evaluate his or her own participation.

Apply

► Ask students, "What kinds of events can happen that cause problems and complications between friends?" *(One of them acts in a way that hurts the other; something happens to one of them that causes the other to feel left out or jealous, and so on.)*

► Ask students what kinds of actions are most likely to help resolve the problems they suggested and what kinds of actions are least likely to resolve the problems.

View a Performance

Plot in Theatre

► Discuss appropriate audience behavior, such as listening quietly, sitting still, and being respectful. Have students agree to apply this behavior during the performance.

► If you have the *Artsource*® videocassette or DVD, have students view the "Bon Marche Dressing Scene" from The Children's Theatre Company's production of *The Story of Babar, the Little Elephant.* Alternatively, you may share a video of another children's theatre performance. Tell students that this excerpt is from the middle of a story about Babar, an elephant who goes into a city to escape being captured by hunters. In the city, Babar becomes friends with a woman named the Old Lady. Babar becomes friends with many city people, but instead of staying, he returns to the forest and becomes King of the Elephants at the story's end. In this scene, Babar goes to a shop to buy his first clothes.

► Discuss the performance with students using the following questions:

Describe What events happened in this scene? *(Babar chooses clothes from a book; he is measured; the clothes are made and brought out; they fit him perfectly.)*

Analyze What are the five Ws of this scene? *(who: Babar, what: he is buying clothing, where: a city store, when: a long time ago, why: so he can fit in with people in the city.)* How did the music make the scene funny? *(Every time they showed his big clothing, funny music played.)* Knowing the rest of the story, which part of a plot is this scene? *(the middle)*

Interpret How was Babar's experience different from times when you have bought clothing? What clues tell you that this is a fantasy story rather than a story taken from real life? *(Babar is an elephant, but he wears clothing and talks to people.)*

Decide What was your favorite part of the scene?

> "The theatre is its continuum, a living muddle of good and bad that takes its vitality from the equally muddled world around it. It's a hand held out to meandering man as he makes his way through swamps and over cloverleafs, now mired, now soaring. . . ."
>
> —Walter Kerr
> (1913–1996), theatre critic

LEARN ABOUT CAREERS IN THEATRE

Tell students that a director is a person who works as a guide for actors. Directors often suggest movements and help actors form ideas about their parts. Explain that most directors are responsible for all aspects of a performance. Have students compare their work as actors with the job of a director. Ask students to imagine that they are all directors for their puppet show of "Kotick Saves the Seals." Discuss with them what they think made the action of the puppets the most believable. As directors, what might they decide to do differently next time?

Standards

National Theatre Standard: The student analyzes and explains personal preferences and constructs meanings from classroom dramatizations and from theatre, film, television, and electronic media productions.

Name _____ Date _____

Unit 1 Self-Criticism Questions

Think about how you used your puppet and voice to show events in the plot from "Kotick Saves the Seals." Then answer the questions below.

1. **Describe** What actions did you perform as your seal puppet?

_____

_____

_____

2. **Analyze** What events of the plot was your seal involved in?

_____

_____

_____

3. **Interpret** How would you act differently from your seal to solve problems in real life?

_____

_____

_____

4. **Decide** If you performed this puppet show again, would you change anything that you did? Why or why not?

_____

_____

_____

Unit 1   Quick Quiz

Completely fill in the bubble of the best answer
for each question below.

1. A plot is
- Ⓐ   the place where a story happens.
- Ⓑ   the events that happen in a story.
- Ⓒ   a person in a story.
- Ⓓ   a person who writes a story.

2. Which of the following is *not* true?
- Ⓕ   People or animals face a problem in the beginning of the plot.
- Ⓖ   Events in a plot can happen in any order.
- Ⓗ   People or animals try to solve a problem in the middle of the plot.
- Ⓙ   A problem is usually solved near the end of the plot.

3.   The high point of the plot is
- Ⓐ   the event that happens first.
- Ⓑ   the most exciting part.
- Ⓒ   the part when someone speaks.
- Ⓓ   the event that happens last.

4.   A complication is
- Ⓕ   something that makes a problem easier to solve.
- Ⓖ   something that solves a problem.
- Ⓗ   something that makes a problem harder to solve.
- Ⓙ   something that makes the problem go away.

Score _____ (Top Score 4)

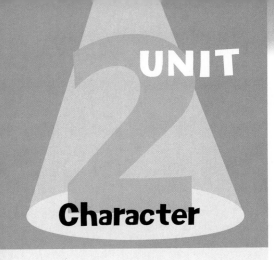

UNIT 2
Character

Unit Overview

Lesson 1 • Characters Act The actions of a character can show his or her identity, feelings, desires, and personality. *Dramatic Movement*

Lesson 2 • Characters Relate Characters relate to one another through speech and actions in a dramatic story. *Tableau*

Lesson 3 • Actions and Reactions The actions and reactions of characters can reveal their feelings and identities. *Theatre Game*

Lesson 4 • Characters Describe Each Other Characters' descriptions of each other help reveal the traits of other characters. *Storytelling*

Lesson 5 • Characters Work Together Actions and dialogue, as characters work together, can reveal characters' relationships with one another. *Improvisation*

Lesson 6 • Unit Activity: Dramatized Folktale This activity will give students the opportunity to show character traits in a dramatized story.

See pages T3–T20 for more about **Theatre Technique Tips.**

Introduce Unit Concepts

"Characters are the people and animals in stories and plays. Actors help bring characters to life." **"Los personajes son las personas y animales en historias y dramas. Los actores dan vida a los personajes."**

Character

▶ Remind students that characters are not always human beings. Have them give examples of nonhuman characters from books they have read. *(pigs, spiders, trees, and so on)*

▶ Ask students which of the five Ws *(who, what, where, when,* and *why)* relates to the dramatic element of character. *(who)*

▶ Have students brainstorm different ways in which an actor can show a character's personality, age, job, physical characteristics, and feelings. *(voice, movement, and so on)*

Vocabulary

Discuss the following vocabulary words.

character personaje—a person or an animal in a book, poem, theatrical work, or story

motivation motivación—a character's reasons for speech or actions

Unit Links

Visual Arts: Space and Form

▶ Explain to students that different kinds of characters in a play can help each character stand out. In the same way, artists use solid forms and empty spaces to make parts of their artwork more noticeable.

▶ Show students the photograph of a sculptural portrait, such as *Little Dancer, Aged Fourteen* by Edgar Degas. Discuss how the character is dressed. What would her voice sound like? How does the negative space—the space surrounding the form—make different parts of the form stand out? How does the dancer seem to feel? Have students compare actual dance with this artwork's representation of a dancer; have them pantomime some of the dancer's possible movements.

Reading Theme: City Wildlife

▶ Ask students to think of plants or animals that live in cities. *(birds, squirrels, trees, and so on)* Discuss and share examples of books in which city animals are prominent characters, such as *Bernelly & Harriet: The Country Mouse and the City Mouse* by Elizabeth Dahlie.

▶ As a class choose a city animal and use it to create a character. Ask students to share ideas about the way this animal character moves and speaks. What kind of personality might this animal have and why? Where does this character live?

Teacher Background

Background on Character

A character can be defined as a person in a drama or novel, but in the context of theatre a character can also be a person or part that an actor portrays. Actors work to show the audience a character's desires, personality, and physical traits.

Background on Acting

Not all actors use the same method of character portrayal. Representational actors approach characterization by seeking to represent a character's movements, behavior, and feelings; actors using an approach called the Method work to experience a character's inner feelings and then allow these to inform the character's movement and actions. This unit draws on both representational and Method acting, as both are valuable in an educational drama setting.

Research in Theatre Education

" . . . when children have been involved in the process of integrating creative drama with reading they are not only able to better comprehend what they've read and acted out, but they are also better able to comprehend what they have read but do not act out, such as the written scenarios they encounter on standardized tests."

—Sherry DuPont

"The Effectiveness of Creative Drama as an Instructional Strategy to Enhance the Reading Comprehension Skills of Fifth-Grade Remedial Readers."

Differentiated Instruction

Reteach
Have students choose a character from a favorite book and ask them to describe the character's personality using only five adjectives. Discuss their answers.

Challenge
Have students make a list of different emotions, such as joy, sorrow, anger, and so on. Challenge them to use body position only (no facial expression) to communicate each emotion so other students may guess it.

Special Needs
Students who are aware of their own emotions and motivations can more successfully identify a character's emotions and motivations. Have students explore their responses to life events, such as completing a difficult task, whenever possible during drama activities.

Theatre's Effects Across the Curriculum

★ **Reading/Writing**
Reading Response Reading a story and then portraying a character from the story gives students another way to practice interpreting a written text.

★ **Math**
Prediction When students improvise characters, they use information, such as a character's desires, to make inferences about the character's actions.

★ **Science**
Inherited Traits Studying animal characters can give students a chance to think about physical characteristics animals inherit from their parents.

★ **Social Studies**
Citizenship Studies of character traits can help students think about positive traits, such as bravery, that great people in history shared.

★ **Music**
Translating Text Musicians have text in the form of symbols, which they interpret and translate into music, just as students read texts and translate them into classroom dramas.

★ **Dance**
Interpreting Text As students dramatize characters based on written texts, they will be able to more effectively interpret other forms of text, such as poetry, through creative dance.

Objectives

 Perception To define and identify motivations for different feelings or actions

 Creative Expression To use dramatic movement to show character feelings

 History and Culture To learn about universal characters

 Evaluation To informally evaluate one's own work

Materials

📄 Copies of "Characters Act" Warm-Up, p. 37

⭕ Journals or writing paper

Vocabulary

motivation

Unit Links

Visual Arts: Form
A character's body is an example of a form. Remind students that a form is an object with height, weight, and depth. Ask students if the tiger's and cat's bodies are examples of forms. *(yes)* Could the shape of the tiger's or cat's form show its feelings? How? *(Yes; an angry tiger could crouch down and show its teeth.)*

Standards

National Theatre Standard: The student acts by assuming roles and interacting in improvisations. The student imagines and clearly describes characters, their relationships, and their environments.

Listening/Speaking Standard: The student listens attentively and engages actively in various oral language experiences. The student is expected to listen responsively to stories and other texts read aloud.

Social Studies Standard: The student identifies examples of cultural heritage from communities around the world.

Lesson 1 — Characters Act

Focus

Time: About 10 minutes

"In this lesson we will use dramatic movement to show a character's actions." *(See page T13 for more about Dramatic Movement.)*

Activate Prior Knowledge

▶ Hand out the **"Characters Act" Warm-Up.** Read the story aloud and discuss the tiger's emotions before students complete the **Warm-Up.**

▶ Explain that a character's motivation is the reason he or she does something. Ask, "What was the tiger's motivation to trick the cat?" *(He wanted to eat her.)*

Teach

Time: About 15 minutes

Prepare Have students stand up and spread out around the room. Remind them to use safe movement.

Lead Give students the following objectives:

▶ Pretend you are the tiger climbing up the mountain. The birds are laughing at you because you keep tripping.

▶ Pretend you are the cat climbing up the mountain. The sun is shining and you are proud of your good climbing.

▶ Pretend you are the tiger trying to get the cat out of the tree. The cat is too high up—you cannot reach her.

Informal Assessment Did each student identify and physically express characters' emotions from the story?

🏺 History and Culture

Explain that many cultures tell stories with similar ideas and characters; such characters are called "universal characters." One universal character is Cinderella; 300 versions of her story are told throughout the world. Have students read a Cinderella tale, such as *Yeh-Shen: A Cinderella Story from China* by Ai-Ling Louie; have them pantomime characters' actions. Compare and contrast the story's different versions.

Reflect

Time: About 5 minutes

▶ Discuss how students showed the animals' feelings with their bodies. *(frowned, skipped)* How was this different from real life? *(animals acted like people)*

Apply

📓 **Journal: Inferring**
Have each student write a journal entry describing a time he or she saw a sad person and how he or she could or could not identify the person's feelings.

Characters Act

Draw a tiger face that shows one of the tiger's feelings in the story below.

The Tiger Finds a Teacher

a Chinese folktale

There was a tiger that tripped over the rocks on his mountain. He asked a cat that never tripped to teach him her tricks. He promised not to eat her.

Soon the tiger knew many tricks. "Now that I know the cat's tricks," he thought, "I will eat her up." But the smart cat gave the tiger a test.

"I have taught you my tricks," the cat told the tiger.

"All of them?" asked the tiger.

"Yes, all of them," said the cat.

"Then you will not escape!" cried the tiger, and he jumped at the cat. But the cat quickly climbed a tall tree.

"I knew I could not trust you," said the cat. "I am glad I did not teach you how to climb, or you would have eaten me." The angry tiger clawed at the tree, but the cat just smiled, and jumped from tree to tree until she was far away.

The tiger could do nothing but walk back up the mountain.

Unit Links Reading: City Wildlife

Characters Relate

Objectives

 Perception To identify relationships among characters in a story

Creative Expression To use body position to show relationships among characters

 History and Culture To learn about a group of moral fables from India

Evaluation To informally evaluate one's own work

Materials

○ Journals or drawing paper

Unit Links

Visual Arts: Space

Overlapping human shapes can illustrate relationships. Remind students that artists use overlapping to create the appearance of distance between and among objects. Say, "If you were planning the staging of a group of characters who were friends, would you place these characters close together or far apart?" *(close together)* Have students note the differences between still artwork and performances in which actors move.

Standards

National Theatre Standard: The student collaborates to select interrelated characters and situations for classroom dramatization. The student identifies and describes the visual elements of classroom dramatizations.

Listening/Speaking Standard: The student connects experiences and ideas with those of others through speaking and listening.

Science Standard: The student identifies characteristics among species that allow each to survive and reproduce.

Focus

Time: About 10 minutes

"In this lesson we will use tableaux to show character relationships." *(See page T7 for more about Tableau.)*

Activate Prior Knowledge

► Read **"Union Is Strength."** Have students stand by their chairs and pantomime in place each character as you read the story a second time.

► Discuss relationships in the story. Who did the doves listen to and follow? *(the queen)* How did the doves relate to the hunter? *(They wanted to escape him.)* What was the hunter trying to do to the doves? *(catch them for his food)*

Teach

Time: About 15 minutes

Prepare Divide students into groups of five or six.

Lead

► Give each group a few minutes to choose a moment from the story and plan a tableau. Tell students to think about how the characters relate to one another; each student's body position should show both the character's feelings as well as the character's relationship with the group. Encourage them to be creative, as each dove might have had a different feeling and reaction, but remind them that all feelings are not equally appropriate.

► Have each group's members arrange themselves in their tableau. Have the other groups politely view and describe the group's scene.

Informal Assessment Did students use body positions to express character relationships?

History and Culture

Tell students that "Union Is Strength" is a part of a group of moral stories called the Panchatantra that have been popular in India for thousands of years. People say that long ago a king had five sons with bad manners, so a wise man came to teach the princes. He made them learn these stories about good living. Have students share examples of stories that could teach people how to relate to each other. *(Aesop's fable "The Ant and the Dove" could teach you to be kind, and so on.)*

Reflect

Time: About 5 minutes

► Discuss how each tableau expressed relationships, as well as what worked. How did each make them feel?

Apply

Journal: Illustrating

Have students draw pictures to show a group of animals living together and working together to survive.

Union Is Strength

a fable from India

A flock of doves went flying far, far from their home looking for food. They flew over lakes and they flew over mountains, but they could find nothing to eat.

"I am so tired," one little dove said as they were flying over a forest. "O queen, may we rest in this forest for a little while?"

"You must be brave," the queen said. "Let us go a little farther and see what we may find."

So the little dove flapped her wings even harder, and the flock kept flying and looking for food. Suddenly the little dove saw something.

"I see food!" the little dove cried. "Down there, below that banyan tree!"

The flock followed the little dove and, white wings flapping, they landed in the grass beneath the tree. Sure enough, rice was scattered across the ground, and the doves began to eat.

But as the birds were eating, a net suddenly fell from the tree onto the doves. They were caught! A big hunter came toward them with a club, and he laughed at them.

"We must do something," the dove queen said.

The net was very strong and the birds could not break free from it. "What do we do, what do we do?" cried the doves.

"I know—let us all fly together," the queen said. "Unity is our only hope."

All at once, each dove held onto a piece of the net and began to flap its wings. Before the hunter could do anything, the doves and the net rose up into the air, and the doves escaped from the hunter.

Objectives

 Perception To identify the ways in which people's actions affect other people and animals

 Creative Expression
To use facial expressions and body movements to express actions of characters

 History and Culture
To consider the effects of television, film, and live theatre

 Evaluation To informally evaluate one's own work

Materials

📄 Copies of **"Actions and Reactions" Warm-Up,** p. 41

○ Slips of paper; write on each paper two characters who are related in a specific way and an action one will perform. (For example: teacher and student; the teacher gives a pop quiz; restaurant waiter and diner; the waiter spills soup on the diner.)

○ Journals or drawing paper

Vocabulary

action
reaction

Standards

National Theatre Standard: The student assumes roles that exhibit concentration and contribute to the action in classroom dramatizations based on personal experience and heritage, imagination, literature, and history.

Listening/Speaking Standard: The student actively participates in class discussions. The student expresses thoughts in an organized manner.

Social Studies Standard: The student analyzes and interprets information to construct reasonable explanations from direct and indirect evidence.

Actions and Reactions

Focus

Time: About 15 minutes

"In this lesson we will play an action-and-reaction theatre game." *(See page T5 for more about Theatre Games.)*

Activate Prior Knowledge

► Hand out the **"Actions and Reactions" Warm-Up,** and have students complete it.

► Discuss students' answers. Have students infer what might happen next. Say, "When characters act a certain way, other characters react."

Teach

Time: About 15 minutes

Prepare Make slips of paper and put them in a box. (See **Materials.**) Divide students into pairs and have each pair draw a slip from the box. Have all students form a circle.

Lead Tell students to think about situations from their own lives similar to those on their papers and use the memory of their feelings to help them act as each character.

► Have each pair divide their listed roles.

► One at a time have each pair stand in the middle of the circle, perform the action along with dialogue, and freeze.

► Say, "Raise your hand if you have ideas about how the other character feels and what he or she will do. I will call on you, and the pair in the middle will choose one idea and act it out." Allow the pair to improvise for one minute, and then say, "Freeze."

Informal Assessment Did each student act as his or her character in the given situation?

 History and Culture

Discuss the roles of television, film, and live theatre in modern America. Say, "The inventions of movies and television caused many Americans to stop depending on live theatre for entertainment." Have students identify actions and reactions in this situation, and compare and contrast their personal reactions to the way each medium tells stories.

Reflect

Time: About 5 minutes

► Discuss the clues in each action that gave students ideas about reactions. *(The hot soup angered the diner, and so on.)*

Apply

 Journal: Describing Cause and Effect
Have students describe in their journals times their actions caused reactions in a pet or wild animal.

Actions and Reactions

Look at the picture below. It shows the middle of
a story. Write the beginning and end of this story
on the lines below.

_____

_____

_____

_____

_____

_____

_____

Objectives

 **Perception** To identify ways in which characters and people perceive one another

Creative Expression To use storytelling to show how characters perceive one another

History and Culture To identify ways culture affects people's descriptions of others in theatre

Evaluation To informally evaluate one's own work

Materials

○ Journals or drawing paper

Standards

National Theatre Standard: The student imagines and clearly describes characters, their relationships, and their environments. The student improvises dialogue to tell stories.

Listening/Speaking Standard: The student makes brief narrative presentations and includes well-chosen details to develop character, setting, and plot. The student organizes ideas chronologically or around major points of information.

English/Language Arts Standard: The student analyzes characters, including their traits, feelings, relationships, and changes.

Lesson 4 Characters Describe Each Other

Focus

Time: About 10 minutes

"In this lesson we will plan and dramatize one character's description of another character." *(See page T11 for more about Storytelling.)*

Activate Prior Knowledge

► Read aloud **"Ben Weatherstaff's Robin,"** and have students perform the passage as narrative pantomime as you read.

► Say, "You can learn about characters by noticing how other characters describe them. For example, how did Ben and Mary describe the robin?" *(curious, friendly, cheerful)*

Teach

Time: About 15 minutes

Prepare Divide students into groups. Have groups sit together.

Lead

► Choose a book that students have read recently; for example, *Charlotte's Web* by E. B. White. Review the book's plot, and then assign each group a minor character from the book, such as Templeton or the goose. Have each group briefly discuss their character's feelings about a major character from the story, such as Wilbur.

► Have group members take turns speaking as their character while other groups listen politely. Have each say one thing about the major character. Prompt them with questions, such as, "Do you like him or her?"

Informal Assessment Did each student participate in group planning and act as the character?

 History and Culture

Discuss ways that culture can affect the ways characters describe each other and what seems realistic in a culture's theatre; for example, in a culture where women do not criticize men, it might not seem realistic for them to do so onstage. Identify ways people change historic stories to match their own cultural values when making movie, book, or play versions of them.

Reflect

Time: About 5 minutes

► Discuss how each character described another character. Would students describe these characters differently?

Apply

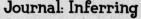 **Journal: Inferring**
Compare and contrast versions of the same characters in books, movies, and plays. How can a movie show a character's thoughts? Compare this with students' understanding of real people. Have students describe a person they know in their journals.

Ben Weatherstaff's Robin

from *The Secret Garden* by Frances Hodgson Burnett

Mary Lennox, a mean and spoiled little orphan, has gone to live with her uncle in England. When Mary finds out there is a locked garden hidden somewhere near her uncle's house, she goes looking for it. While she is searching, she meets gardener Ben Weatherstaff and a friendly little bird.

Mary walked back into the first kitchen-garden she had entered and found Ben Weatherstaff digging there. She went and stood beside him and watched him a few moments in her cold little way. He took no notice of her and so at last she spoke to him.

"There was no door there into the other garden," said Mary.

"What garden?" he said in a rough voice, stopping his digging for a moment.

"The one on the other side of the wall," answered Mistress Mary. "There are trees there—I saw the tops of them. A bird was sitting on one of them and he sang."

To her surprise the surly old weather-beaten face actually changed its expression. A slow smile spread over it and the gardener looked quite different.

He turned about to the orchard side of his garden and began to whistle—a low, soft whistle. She could not understand how such a surly man could make such a coaxing sound. Almost the next moment a wonderful thing happened. She heard a soft little rushing flight through the air—and it was the bird flying to them, and he actually alighted on the big clod of earth quite near to the gardener's foot.

"Here he is," chuckled the old man, and then he spoke to the bird as if he were speaking to a child.

"Where has thou been, thou cheeky little beggar?" he said.

The bird put his tiny head on one side and looked up at him with his soft bright eye which was like a black dewdrop. He seemed quite familiar and not the least afraid. He hopped about and pecked the earth briskly, looking for seeds and insects. It actually gave Mary a queer feeling in her heart, because he was so pretty and cheerful and seemed so like a person.

"Will he always come when you call him?" she asked almost in a whisper.

"Aye, that he will. I've knowed him ever since he was a fledgling."

"What kind of a bird is he?" Mary asked.

"Doesn't thou know? He's a robin an' they're the friendliest, curious-est birds alive. They're almost as friendly as dogs—if you know how to get on with 'em. Watch him peckin' about there an' lookin' round at us now an' again. He knows we're talkin' about him."

It was the queerest thing in the world to see the old fellow. He looked at the plump little scarlet-waistcoated bird as if he were both proud and fond of him.

"He's a conceited one," he chuckled. "He likes to hear folk talk about him. An' curious—bless me, there never was his like for curiosity an' meddling. He's always comin' to see what I'm planting."

The robin hopped about busily pecking the soil and now and then stopped and looked at them a little. Mary thought his black dewdrop eyes gazed at her with great curiosity. It really seemed as if he were finding out all about her.

Objectives

 Perception To recognize the importance of teamwork

 Creative Expression To improvise movements and dialogue that show characters working together

 History and Culture To learn how groups of three animal characters often illustrate teamwork in fairy tales

 Evaluation To informally evaluate one's own work

Materials

📄 Copies of "Characters Work Together" Warm-Up, p. 45

⭘ Journals or writing paper

Unit Links _____

Visual Arts: Form

Forms can illustrate characters working together. Ask students what a statue illustrating teamwork might look like. *(people holding hands, people working hard)* Have students create a teamwork statue with their bodies.

Standards

Lesson 5 — Characters Work Together

Focus

Time: About 10 minutes

"In this lesson we will improvise a scene in which characters use teamwork." *(See page T4 for more about Improvisation.)*

Activate Prior Knowledge

▶ Hand out the **"Characters Work Together" Warm-Up,** and have students complete it.

▶ Discuss the speech students created for the ants.

Teach

Time: About 15 minutes

Prepare Divide students into groups of five or six and clear a space.

Lead

▶ Tell students that each group will make up a scene in which characters work together. Explain that one student from each group will begin performing an assigned activity. A second student should decide on a relationship to the first student's character and join in. The first student will accept and relate to the second student's character. Others in the group should join the activity one at a time.

▶ Say, "The first group will begin with a parent cooking dinner. Other students will add different characters." The second student could enter as the woman's son, while the third enters as a dinner guest, and so on.

▶ To help with focus, make suggestions as they improvise. Encourage other students to enter. Repeat with each group using new scenarios while the class applies appropriate audience behavior.

Informal Assessment Did each student improvise movements and dialogue that showed teamwork?

 History and Culture

Remind students that many well-known fairy tales contain similar, closely related animal characters in groups of three; for example, "The Three Billy Goats Gruff." Explain that these three characters sometimes illustrate teamwork as the characters help each other.

Reflect

Time: About 5 minutes

▶ Have students identify the focus of the activity (to show teamwork as characters) and discuss which groups kept this focus.

Apply

 ### Journal: Assessing

Have students write a few sentences in their journals explaining what happens when one person does not work with a team or group.

Characters Work Together

Look at the picture. Some of these ant characters are saying things to help others keep working. Think about other things the ant characters could say to help each other. Write them in the blank talk bubbles below.

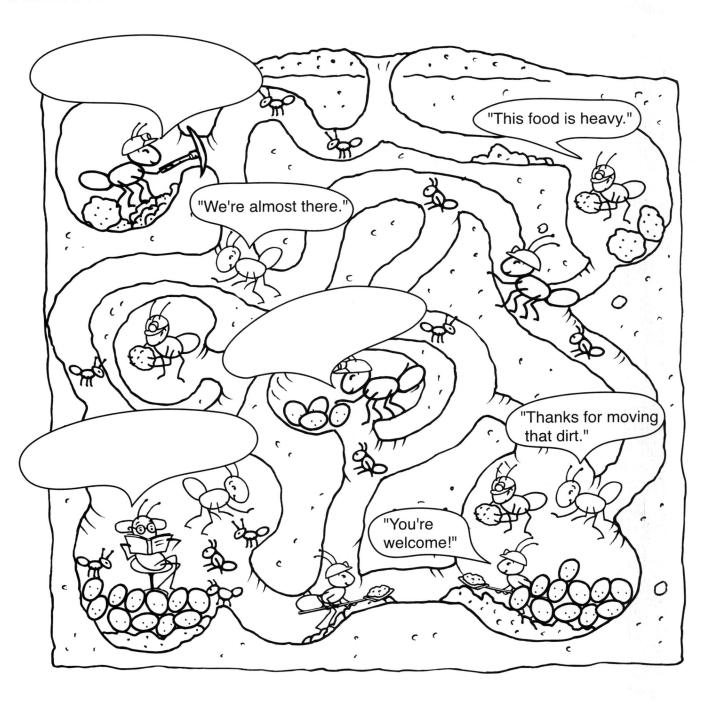

Unit Links Reading: City Wildlife

Objectives

Perception To review ways that actors reveal characters and to think about people's motivations in real life

Creative Expression To dramatize a character using appropriate movement, voice, and facial expressions

History and Culture To apply research about Ukrainian life to the character of the man in "The Mitten"

Evaluation To thoughtfully and honestly evaluate one's own participation using the four steps of criticism

Materials

📄 Copies of **"The Mitten,"** pp. 127–129

📄 Copies of the **Unit 2 Self-Criticism Questions,** p. 50

📄 Copies of the **Unit 2 Quick Quiz,** p. 51

○ *Artsource*® Performing Arts Resource Package (optional)

Standards

National Theatre Standard: The student uses research by finding information to support classroom dramatizations.

Lesson 6

Unit Activity: Dramatized Folktale

Focus

Time: About 10 minutes

Review Unit Concepts

"A character is a person in a dramatic activity. Characters' actions and speech help show who they are and what they think and feel. Characters act and react to each other. Characters work together to tell a story." "Un personaje es una persona en una actividad dramática. Las acciones y palabras de los personajes ayudan a demostrar quiénes son y cómo piensan y cómo se sienten. Los personajes se hablan y reaccionan a los demás personajes. Los personajes trabajan juntos para contar una historia."

► Review with students the ways in which they created characters in this unit.

► Review the unit vocabulary on page 34.

 History and Culture

Explain to students that "The Mitten" is a Ukrainian folktale. Bring in some nonfiction books about Ukraine and have students look for images and information about modern Ukrainian life. Have students share this information with each other and use three details from the research to write a paragraph about what the man's daily life might be like today. Discuss ways this information might affect their improvisation.

Classroom Management Tips

The following are tips for managing your classroom during the **Rehearsals** and **Activity:**

✔ **Set Ground Rules** Tell students that whenever you say "freeze" during this activity, they must stop whatever they are doing. Explain that if they cannot participate appropriately, they will have to sit at their desks. Seeing the other students having fun may help them choose to follow the ground rules next time.

✔ **Encourage Creativity** During the **First Rehearsal,** compliment creative elements in each tableau.

✔ **Take the First Risk** When you take on the roles of the reporter, the man, and the dog, model changes in movement and voice for students.

✔ **Accept Imitation** If students are sharing roles in "The Mitten," they may imitate each other. Encourage creativity, but do not discourage the imitators; imitation is a basic mode of learning.

Teach

First Rehearsal

▶ Distribute copies of **"The Mitten"** on pages 127–129. Have students simultaneously use narrative pantomime as you read the story aloud. Discuss students' scientific knowledge about each animal type.

▶ Divide students into groups. Have each group choose a scene from the story, discuss the characters' motivations, and create a tableau illustrating the scene. Allow students to look at and discuss each other's tableaux. Can they identify each character? Discuss the characters' relationships and feelings.

Second Rehearsal

▶ Have students select animal roles. (More than one student may choose the same animal.)

▶ Tell students, "Imagine the mitten has just burst open and all of you have run away. I am going to pretend to be a reporter, and I am going to interview each of you." Using an imaginary microphone, ask each character or group of characters questions such as, "What is your name?" "Tell me what just happened." "Why did you need to live in the mitten?" "Do you think everyone should have been allowed in the mitten?"

▶ Discuss the interviews as a class, asking students why they did or did not think everyone should have been allowed in the mitten. Discuss how the wants and needs of the fictional animals are similar to and different from the students' own in real life.

Character Activity

▶ Have students create space in the classroom for the activity. *(See page T3 for more about Pantomime.)*

▶ Explain that students will act and speak as the animal characters they chose in the **Second Rehearsal,** moving as a group if they share the same character. You will be the characters of the man and his dog.

▶ Explain to students that they are going to act out the story and then go past the story's ending. Say, "I wonder what happens to the animals after the mitten bursts? They are left in the cold. Where will they live? Keep acting as your characters after the mitten bursts and let's see what you decide to do."

▶ Work with students to improvise the story of "The Mitten," allowing them to solve the problem of what to do after the mitten bursts. Say "freeze" when you wish them to stop. Discuss whether the drama's message changed because of their extended story.

▶ Discuss the goals of the activity (to move and speak like their characters), and have students use them to develop evaluation criteria. Have them apply the criteria to their own performances.

Standards

National Theatre Standard: The student acts by assuming roles and interacting in improvisations. The student assumes roles that exhibit concentration and contribute to the action of classroom dramatizations based on personal experience and heritage, imagination, literature, and history.

Visual Arts: Form

Explain to students that artists sometimes create freestanding sculptures; some sculptures are groups of forms that show a certain feeling. Ask for four or five volunteers and, keeping it secret from the other students, assign them an emotion from "The Mitten" (such as the animals' fear of the man's dog). Ask the volunteers to create a living sculpture using their bodies to show this feeling. Have the class try to guess the feeling shown.

Theatrical Arts Connection

Television Show or describe part of a television commercial in which several characters interact. Discuss the ways in which these characters work together to sell a product. How do television commercials affect their audience differently than live theatre performances?

Electronic Media Have students view a Web site in which a group of characters interact, such as a site linked to **www.pbskids.org.** Discuss some ways in which these characters relate to each other.

Standards

National Theatre Standard: The student compares and connects art forms by describing theatre, dramatic media (such as film, television, and electronic media), and other art forms. The student describes visual, aural, oral, and kinetic elements in theatre, dramatic media, dance, music, and visual arts.

Close

Time: About 10 minutes

Assessment

► Have students evaluate their participation by completing the **Unit 2 Self-Criticism Questions** on page 50.

► Use the assessment rubric to evaluate the students' participation in the **Unit Activity** and to assess their understanding of character.

► Have students complete the **Unit 2 Quick Quiz** on page 51.

	3 Points	2 Points	1 Point
Perception	Gives full attention to review of unit concepts and vocabulary words. Masters the connection between motivation and real-life actions.	Gives partial attention to review of unit concepts and vocabulary words. Is developing an understanding of the connection between motivation and real-life actions.	Gives little or no attention to review of unit concepts and vocabulary words. Minimally understands the connection between motivation and real-life actions.
Creative Expression	Portrays a character using all of the following: appropriate movement, voice, and facial expressions.	Portrays a character using two of the following: movement, voice, or facial expressions.	Portrays a character using one of the following: movement, voice, or facial expressions.
History and Culture	Writes a paragraph about the man's daily life that uses three details from research about Ukraine.	Writes a paragraph about the man's daily life using two details from research about Ukraine.	Writes a paragraph about the man's daily life using one detail from research about Ukraine.
Evaluation	Thoughtfully and honestly evaluates own participation using the four steps of art criticism.	Attempts to evaluate own participation, but shows an incomplete understanding of evaluation criteria.	Makes a minimal attempt to evaluate own participation.

Apply

► Ask students, "Do people in real life have motivations, or reasons they speak or act, just like characters in stories?" *(yes)* "Think of something you did yesterday, such as playing a game or doing homework. What was your motivation?" *(I wanted to get a good grade on the test, I wanted to have fun with my family, and so on.)*

► Brainstorm with students some situations where understanding their real-life motivations could be helpful.

View a Performance

Plot in Theatre

►Discuss appropriate audience behavior, such as listening quietly, sitting still, and being respectful. Have students agree to apply this behavior during the performance.

► If you have the **Artsource®** videocassette or DVD, have students view *Voice of the Wood*, performed by Robert Faust and Eugene Friesen. Alternatively, have them view another recording of a theatre performance.

► Discuss the performance with students using the following questions:

Describe Who were the characters in the story? *(The luthier who makes instruments, the self-confident and unkind performer, and so on.)*

Analyze How do the two actors become different characters? *(They change their costumes; they change the way they speak and move.)* How do the luthier and cello player relate to each other? *(The luthier tries to help the performer, but he refuses; and so on.)* Do you think the luthier would describe the performer differently at the beginning and end of the story? *(Yes, because the performer finally listens to the luthier, and so on.)*

Interpret Compare and contrast these characters with the character you portrayed in the **Activity.** What can you learn from the way these actors spoke and moved onstage?

Decide Who was your favorite character? Why?

> "I regard the theatre as the greatest
> of all art forms, the most immediate
> way in which a human being can share
> with another the sense of what it is
> to be a human being."
>
> —Thornton Wilder
> (1897–1975), playwright

LEARN ABOUT CAREERS IN THEATRE

Say to students, "How does a makeup artist help an actor become a character?" *(He or she makes the actor look like the character.)* Explain to students that theatre actors often put on their own makeup, but that a makeup artist may help an actor in movies or television. If possible, show photographs of the characters from the musical *Cats*. Ask students to imagine they are makeup artists. What kind of design would they have used to create the animal characters in "The Mitten"? *(black stripes for the mouse's whiskers, and so on)* If you wish, provide face paints and mirrors and allow students to create their own.

Standards

National Theatre Standard: The student analyzes and explains personal preferences and constructs meanings from classroom dramatizations and from theatre, film, television, and electronic media productions.

Name _____ Date _____

Unit 2 Self-Criticism Questions

Think about how you acted as your character from "The Mitten." Then answer the questions below.

1. **Describe** How did you use your voice and body when you acted as your character?

   _____

   _____

   _____

2. **Analyze** How did your voice and body choices show who your character was and how your character felt?

   _____

   _____

   _____

3. **Interpret** How are you like and unlike your character?

   _____

   _____

   _____

4. **Decide** If you could do this activity again, would you change anything you did? Why or why not?

   _____

   _____

   _____

Unit 2 Quick Quiz

Completely fill in the bubble of the best answer for each question below.

1. A character is

- Ⓐ   a person who writes a story.
- Ⓑ   a place where a story is told.
- Ⓒ   a person in a story or play.
- Ⓓ   the story of a play.

2. The way a character acts can show

- Ⓕ   who the character is.
- Ⓖ   how the character feels.
- Ⓗ   what the character wants.
- Ⓙ   all of the above.

3. A character's motivation is

- Ⓐ   the reason a character says or does something.
- Ⓑ   the character's clothing.
- Ⓒ   another name for the plot of a play.
- Ⓓ   the character's job.

4. Which sentence is *not* true?

- Ⓕ   Animals cannot be characters in a story.
- Ⓖ   Characters work together to tell a story.
- Ⓗ   Characters react to each other.
- Ⓙ   Characters are the people and animals in a play.

Score _____ (Top Score 4)

UNIT 3
Visual Elements

Unit Overview

Lesson 1 • Visual Elements and the Five Ws Visual elements, such as costumes, makeup, props, and scenery, help to show the five Ws of a dramatic story. *Creative Movement*

Lesson 2 • Props The time period of a play, as well as characters' identities, can be revealed through props. *Props*

Lesson 3 • Costumes Clothing can show when and where a character lives and who a character is. *Costumes*

Lesson 4 • Makeup Character makeup or masks can communicate many things about a character. *Makeup and Masks*

Lesson 5 • Setting Creating an environment for a drama can help an audience understand when and where a drama is taking place. *Settings*

Lesson 6 • Unit Activity: Improvised Folktale This activity will give students the opportunity to create visual elements for an improvised performance.

See pages T3–T20 for more about **Theatre Technique Tips.**

Introduce Unit Concepts

"Visual elements are the things that an audience sees in a dramatic performance. Props, costumes, makeup, masks, setting, and character's movements are all visual elements." *"Los elementos visuales son las cosas que un público ve en una actuación dramática. Los props, el vestuario, el maquillaje, las máscaras, la escenografía y los movimientos de los personajes son todos elementos visuales."*

Visual Elements

▶ Ask students what parts of a play an audience sees. *(objects on a stage, backdrop, actors.)*

▶ Have students describe how they have used costumes, makeup, and personal props to transform themselves into characters for costume parties. *(I painted my face with white makeup to be a clown, and so on.)*

Vocabulary

Discuss the following vocabulary words.

properties propiedades—also called *props*; objects found onstage

personal props props personales—objects held and used by characters

setting marco escénico—the surroundings in which a play takes place

Unit Links

Visual Arts: Color and Value

▶ Tell students that *value* means "the degree of lightness or darkness of a color." Explain that different colors and values used in lighting and settings can emphasize objects or features and can give the audience a certain feeling. For example, bright lights draw attention to actors. A set with lots of grays can make the setting seem sad or boring.

▶ Show students the photograph of a brightly colored portrait, such as *Kneeling Child on Yellow Background* by Diego Rivera. Discuss the feeling created by the colors in the painting. Have students identify her costume and the setting.

Reading Theme: Imagination

▶ Ask students what the word *imagination* means. *(being able to think creatively, and so on)* Say, "Many books or plays seem very realistic; others have fantastic events, such as time traveling, or imaginative characters, such as elves." Have students share favorite stories and discuss imaginative elements.

▶ Choose an unusual setting, such as under the ocean or the surface of the moon. Have students suggest imaginary characters who could live there, and then have them use their imaginations to describe costumes and makeup an actor could wear when playing each character.

Teacher Background

Background on Visual Elements

Visual elements are all the visible aspects of a theatrical performance. They include the lighting, background, scenery, furniture, props, costumes, jewelry, makeup, masks, and wigs. Visual elements are an important part of any play; they communicate visually a play's time, place, theme, and mood.

Background on Makeup Design

In general, makeup for theatre is usually heavier than makeup used in daily life because it helps an audience to clearly see the actors' facial expressions from a distance. Makeup is not always used to transform actors' faces in realistic ways; often it is used to exaggerate certain features, to emphasize character traits, or to create fantastic characters. For example, dark, heavy eyebrows might suggest an aggressive personality.

Research in Theatre Education

"The study specifically examines fantasy play and finds that 'metaplay' [acts of directing by young players] . . . seems to have an especially strong and positive impact on children's story comprehension."

—James S. Catterall

on "You Can't Be Grandma; You're a Boy": Events Within the Thematic Fantasy Play Context that Contribute to Story Comprehension" in *Critical Links*

Differentiated Instruction

Reteach

Have students look at illustrations in a favorite book and explain what they can tell about the story based only on the illustrations.

Challenge

Have students choose a fairy tale, such as "Cinderella," and think of a new and imaginative setting for it, such as a kingdom on another planet. Have them plan the costumes, setting, and props needed to perform their idea as a drama.

Special Needs

Give all students an opportunity to fully experience each lesson activity. Some students with disabilities may excel in improvisation, set, or costume design. Be sensitive to their abilities and preferences, giving them opportunities to perfect their newfound talents.

Theatre's Effects Across the Curriculum

★ **Reading/Writing**
Reading Response Reading a story and identifying its visual elements helps build comprehension.

★ **Math**
Proportion As students create settings, they must consider size relationships and proportions.

★ **Science**
Observation Students use observations of different environments to create settings.

★ **Social Studies**
Culture Students explore other cultures as they imitate and compare makeup and costume traditions from other cultures.

★ **Music**
Multi-media Props, costumes, make-up, and setting can be important elements of both theatre productions and musical performances.

★ **Dance**
Props Props in theatre help reveal who a character is, as well as when and where he or she lives; students can use props to stimulate inventive movement possibilities for dances.

Objectives

 Perception To identify the five *W*s and visual elements in a poem

 Creative Expression
To use creative movement to create setting elements that show *when* and *where*

 History and Culture
To learn about scenery in Japanese theatre

 Evaluation To informally evaluate one's own work

Materials

📄 Copies of **"Visual Elements and the Five *W*s" Warm-Up,** p. 55

⭕ Journals or drawing paper

Vocabulary

visual elements

Standards

National Theatre Standard:
The student collaboratively plans and prepares improvisations. The student imagines and clearly describes characters, their relationships, and their environments.

Listening/Speaking Standard: The student interacts with peers in a variety of situations to develop and present familiar ideas.

Language Arts and Reading Standard:
The student identifies the importance of the setting to a story's meaning.

 Lesson 1

Visual Elements and the Five *W*s

Focus

Time: About 10 minutes

"In this lesson we will use creative movement to show when *and* where." *(See page T12 for more about Creative Movement.)*

Activate Prior Knowledge

▶ Hand out the **"Visual Elements and the Five *W*s" Warm-Up,** and read the poem aloud while students pantomime the fog's movements.

▶ Explain that this poet was comparing the movements of fog and a cat. Have students identify the poem's five *W*s. *(who: fog; where: harbor; what: the fog moves through the city, and so on)*

Teach

Time: About 10 minutes

Prepare Divide students into two groups. Clear a playing space.

Lead

▶ Secretly assign one of the following *when* and *where*s to each group: a mountain forest on a windy, winter day, a sunny shore by the ocean on a hot summer day. Have groups plan to show their locations using only their bodies as visual elements. Actors may portray anything, including plants or weather elements. Encourage them to use safe, expressive and rhythmic movements. Allow them to vocalize sounds.

▶ Have each group create their location. After a minute have the rest of the class guess the *when* and *where*.

▶ Have students discuss suggestions for improvement and replay the scene, implementing these suggestions.

Informal Assessment Did each student safely use creative movement to portray an element of a *when* and *where*?

 History and Culture

Explain that many cultures have theatre styles with few visual elements. For example, in Japanese *Kabuki*, scenery is very simple. Blue, white, and brown mats represent water, snow, and bare ground (respectively). Two-dimensional, painted scenes may stand behind actors. Have students suggest similar scenery they could have used.

Reflect

Time: About 5 minutes

▶ Have students discuss different movements that helped them to identify each *where* and *when*. How did they use each of their senses?

Apply

 Journal: Inventing
Have students draw a picture in their journals of the other group's *when* and *where* adding people or animals.

Visual Elements and the Five *W*s

Fog

by Carl Sandberg

The fog comes
on little cat feet.

It sits looking
over harbor and city
on silent haunches
and then moves on.

Unit Links   Reading: Imagination

Objectives

 Perception To identify ways in which props can show characters' identities

 Creative Expression To use personal props in an improvised scene

 History and Culture To consider imaginative uses of props in fantasy plays such as *Peter Pan*

Evaluation To informally evaluate one's own work

Materials

📄 Copies of **"Props" Warm-Up,** p. 57

○ Journals or writing paper

○ Paper bags each containing two different objects, such as a fan, pencils, watch, mirror, sunglasses, and so on, to be used as personal props (optional)

Vocabulary

props
personal props

Standards

National Theatre Standard: The student collaborates to establish playing spaces for classroom dramatizations and to select and safely organize available materials that suggest scenery, properties, lighting, sound, costume, and makeup.

Listening/Speaking Standard: The student uses eye contact and gestures that engage the audience.

Language Arts/Reading Standard: The student analyzes characters, including their traits, feelings, relationships, and changes. The student draws conclusions from information gathered.

 **Lesson 2 Props**

Focus

Time: About 10 minutes

"In this lesson we will use personal props in an improvised scene."
(See page T20 for more about Props.)

Activate Prior Knowledge

▶ Distribute the **"Props" Warm-Up,** and have students complete it.

▶ Have students explain why they chose their answers. *(Answers will vary.)* Say, "Props are objects onstage. A personal prop is a prop used by a certain character; it can show things about the character who owns or uses it."

Teach

Time: About 15 minutes

Prepare Divide students into pairs.

Lead Tell students they are going to improvise a scene in which two characters use props.

▶ If possible provide paper bags with objects or allow students to select objects from the classroom. Allow them to use the objects realistically or imaginatively (for example, a pen could become a microscope). For objects used imaginatively, have students use sense memories of the actual objects to help them better imagine these objects.

▶ Instruct each pair to decide on two realistic characters from a story or book who meet and use these objects. Have pairs improvise their short meeting scenes for the class.

Informal Assessment Did each student interact with the props as his or her character?

 History and Culture

Explain that actors and directors must consider the play when creating and using props. For example, in a realistic play a character might use a thimble when sewing, but in the play *Peter Pan*, Peter misunderstands the function of a thimble and thinks it is a gift called a "kiss." Have students use their imaginations to suggest stories or situations in which ordinary objects could have unusual functions.

Reflect

Time: About 5 minutes

▶ Have students discuss how they used their personal props in each scene. How are objects used similarly and differently in real life and in theatre? Have students evaluate their behavior as the audience.

Apply

📓 Journal: Explaining

Ask students to think of an object they use often, such as a pen or book bag. Is this object a favorite for some reason, and if so, why? Have students describe this object in their journals and explain why they use it often.

Name _____ Date _____

Props

Look at each pair of objects below. Who might use or wear each pair of objects? Choose one pair of objects, and describe a character who might use these objects on the lines below.

1.

4.

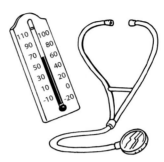

2.

5.

3.

6.

_____

_____

_____

_____

_____

Objectives

 Perception To identify ways in which costumes show who characters are

 Creative Expression To create and select costume pieces for invented characters

 History and Culture To learn how actors in several cultures used costumes to help audiences identify their characters

 Evaluation To informally evaluate one's own work

Materials

📄 Copies of **"Costumes" Warm-Up,** p. 59

○ Markers or crayons

○ Large sheets of construction paper, tape, and safety scissors

○ Journals or writing paper

Vocabulary

costume

Unit Links

Visual Arts: Color

A costume's color can communicate who a character is. As an example, tell students that some cultures consider purple to be a royal color, and therefore these cultures would clothe kings and queens in purple. Have students identify cultural colors for certain clothing, such as a white doctor's coat, and so on.

Standards

National Theatre Standard: The student collaborates to select and safely organize available materials that suggest scenery, properties, lighting, sound, costumes, and makeup.

Listening/Speaking Standard: The student makes a brief narrative presentation and includes well-chosen details to develop character, setting, and plot.

Social Studies Standard: The student creates written and visual material, such as stories, poems, pictures, maps, and graphic organizers to express ideas.

Lesson 3 — Costumes

Focus

Time: About 10 minutes

"In this lesson we will create costumes that show who a character is." *(See page T18 for more about Costumes.)*

Activate Prior Knowledge

▶ Hand out the **"Costumes" Warm-Up,** and have students use markers or crayons to design a costume for one character. Display student costume designs. Discuss how elements of each costume show who the character is.

Teach

Time: About 20 minutes

Prepare Divide students into groups of three. Distribute construction paper, tape, and safety scissors.

Lead

▶ Tell each group to decide on a *who, what,* and *where* to briefly improvise for the class using pantomime. Encourage students to select characters and places that represent various time periods in history in different cultures around the world, such as ancient Greeks or Native Americans.

▶ Have each group use the construction paper and tape to create costume pieces, such as hats, shirts, and vests.

▶ Have volunteers perform their brief pantomime.

Informal Assessment Did each group work together to create appropriate costumes and perform a pantomime?

History and Culture

Tell students that in both ancient Greece and Rome and in the English Renaissance theatre, performances included only a few actors, all of whom were men and boys. Each actor often played several different roles. The audience distinguished the roles that the actors were playing at a given time based on their costumes and masks. Have students compare and contrast images of costumes from each culture.

Reflect

Time: About 5 minutes

▶ Have students discuss the ways in which their various costumes helped to show who their characters were.

Apply

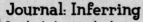 **Journal: Inferring**
In their journals, have students describe one person they have seen whose occupation is made clear by his or her clothing.

Costumes

Imagine you are a costume designer for the play *Peter Pan*. Choose one of the characters described below. Use a pencil and markers or crayons to design a costume for the actor playing this character.

Captain Hook (a mean pirate captain)

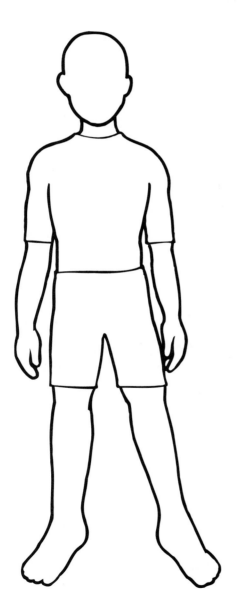

Tinker Bell (a tiny, flying fairy)

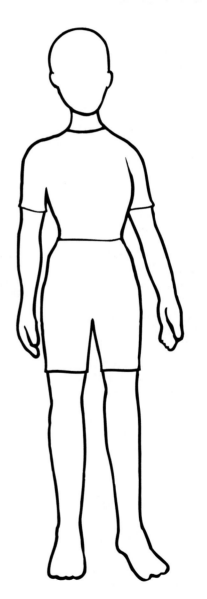

Objectives

 Perception To identify ways in which makeup shows who characters are

 Creative Expression To create masks for imaginary characters

 History and Culture To learn how actors in Chinese opera use elaborate makeup to show character traits

 Evaluation To informally evaluate one's own work

Materials

- 📄 Copies of "Makeup" Warm-Up, p. 61
- ○ Paper plates, safety scissors, and markers or crayons
- ○ Journals or writing paper

Vocabulary

makeup

Unit Links

Visual Arts: Color
Different values of colors are used in theatre makeup. Remind students that adding black to a color creates a shade, and adding white to a color creates a tint. Makeup artists use different values of flesh-colored makeup to create shadows and bright spots that make certain parts of an actor's face stand out.

Standards

National Theatre Standard: The student collaborates to establish playing spaces for classroom dramatizations and to select and safely organize available materials that suggest scenery, properties, lighting, sound, costumes, and makeup.

Listening/Speaking Standard: The student listens attentively and engages actively in a variety of oral language experiences.

Math Standard: The student uses logical reasoning to make sense of his or her world.

Lesson 4 — Makeup

Focus

Time: About 10 minutes

"In this lesson, we will create masks for imaginary characters."
(See page T19 for more about Makeup and Masks.)

Activate Prior Knowledge

▶ Distribute the **"Makeup" Warm-Up,** and have students create makeup designs. Discuss ways their designs might show information about the imaginary animals, such as gender or age.

Teach

Time: About 15 minutes

Prepare Give each student a paper plate. Make sure each student has access to safety scissors and markers or crayons.

Lead

▶ Have each student use the paper plate to create a mask for the imaginary animal character they created in the **Warm-Up.** Remind them that they can cut the edges of the paper plates to give their masks different shapes. They can draw on the plate using colors and shapes to indicate the type of animal and its personality. Assist them in cutting out eyeholes, if needed.

▶ When students are finished, have them hold their masks to their faces and safely move and interact as their characters while safely making animal sounds.

Informal Assessment Did each student create a mask for an imaginary animal character and incorporate safe movement while safely creating animal sounds?

 History and Culture

Tell students that the characters in Chinese operas use elaborate facial makeup. They paint thick lines and shapes around their facial features to emphasize traits, such as cowardice or fierceness. Discuss ways eyebrows could be painted to communicate anger or surprise, and have students draw them on their masks.

Reflect

Time: About 5 minutes

▶ Discuss some ways each mask communicated a character's personality traits. Compare and contrast the benefits of masks and makeup.

Apply

 **Journal: Designing**
Have students draw in their journals a makeup design in which they change only one facial feature on an actor to make him or her look like their animal from the mask activity.

Makeup

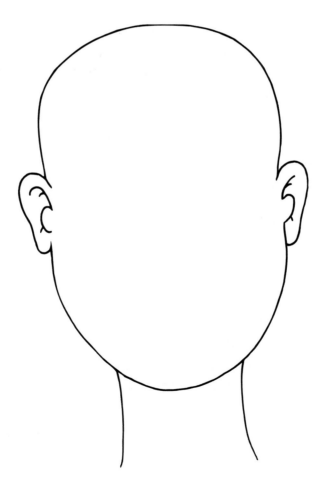

Read the poem. Imagine you are going to act
as an animal in a play. The animal could be
a purple cow or some other kind of imaginary
animal. Draw your animal makeup on
the face below.

The Purple Cow

by Gelett Burgess

I never saw a Purple Cow,

I never hope to see one;

But I can tell you, anyhow,

I'd rather see than be one.

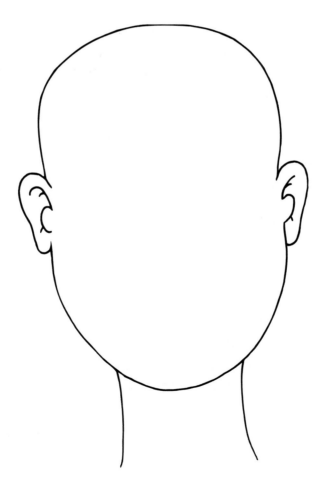

Unit Links Reading: Imagination

Objectives

Perception To identify physical aspects of various locations

Creative Expression To create a set that suggests a specific location

History and Culture To identify the setting of traditional dramatic performances in Africa

Evaluation To informally evaluate one's own work

Materials

- 📋 Copies of "Setting" Warm-Up, p. 63
- ◯ Blankets of various colors, chairs, a table, boxes, and any other simple objects that could be put to multiple uses
- ◯ Journals or writing paper

Vocabulary

setting
scenery
set

Standards

National Theatre Standard: The student collaborates to establish playing spaces for classroom dramatizations and to select and safely organize available materials that suggest scenery, properties, lighting, sound, costume, and makeup.

Listening/Speaking Standard: The student interacts with peers in a variety of situations to develop and present familiar ideas.

Language Arts/Reading Standard: The student identifies the importance of setting to a story's meaning.

Lesson 5 · Setting

Focus

Time: About 10 minutes

"In this lesson we will create settings to suggest specific places."
(See page T17 for more about Settings.)

Activate Prior Knowledge

▶ Distribute the **"Setting" Warm-Up,** and have students complete it. Discuss their answers. *(1. theatre; 2. bathroom; 3. park; 4. restaurant; 5. street; 6. classroom; 7. store; 8. ocean; 9. garage; 10. lab)*

▶ Explain that a play's setting is the place in which its story happens; onstage, this setting is suggested through the set, which includes scenery and props.

Teach

Time: About 15 minutes

Prepare Divide students into groups of five or six. Lay out the setting objects (see **Materials**).

Teach Say, "You only have these objects to create a set. It should *suggest* a place. For example, I could create an airplane by lining up rows of chairs and hanging a blanket over piled boxes for the cockpit door."

▶ Allow three minutes for the teams to look at the objects and plan sets they will create. All teams will take turns with the objects.

▶ When you say "set," a team will have two minutes to create its set. Have the class guess the place. When you say "strike," the team will have one minute to take its set apart before the next team begins. If you wish, have students share and implement suggestions for improving each set.

Informal Assessment Did each student help create a setting?

History and Culture

Tell students that in most areas of Africa, dramatic performances originated as festivals or dramatized storytelling. The "set" for many of these performances was the natural areas in which the people lived. Have students design the scenery for a play about African storytelling.

Reflect

Time: About 5 minutes

▶ Have students compare and contrast each set with the real-life place.

Apply

📓 Journal: Inferring

Have students think of times when they entered rooms in unfamiliar buildings. What aspects of the walls, furniture, and other setting details helped them figure out each room's purpose? Have students describe the room's details in their journals.

Name _____ Date _____

Setting

Each group of things below suggests a certain place.
Write the place in which you would find each group
of things on the lines below.

1. movie screen, dark walls, rows of seats

   _____

2. a window with white curtains, bathtub, sink

   _____

3. a view of a forest, picnic tables

   _____

4. dark red walls, tables, a menu board

   _____

5. several tall buildings, traffic lights, fire hydrant

   _____

6. a wall with a chalkboard and clock on it, rows of desks

   _____

7. tall white walls, shelves with food on them

   _____

8. a body of water, a blue sky, sand

   _____

9. dirty grey walls, rakes and shovels, a car

   _____

10. clean white walls, tables covered with microscopes and glass jars

    _____

Unit Links Reading: Imagination

Objectives

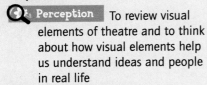 **Perception** To review visual elements of theatre and to think about how visual elements help us understand ideas and people in real life

Creative Expression To select, create, and use visual elements in an improvisation

History and Culture To learn about the role of spider stories in storytelling and theatre traditions of the Ashanti people of Ghana

Evaluation To thoughtfully and honestly evaluate one's own participation using the four steps of criticism

Materials

- Copies of **"The Rubber Man,"** pp. 130–131.

- Various objects such as blankets, chairs, baskets, and boxes to be used as parts of the setting and as props

- Articles of clothing to be used as costumes

- Paper plates, extra paper, nontoxic glue, safety scissors, and markers or crayons for mask creation

- Copies of the **Unit 3 Self-Criticism Questions**, p. 68

- Copies of the **Unit 3 Quick Quiz**, p. 69

- Tape or CD player and a recording of traditional Ghanian music (optional)

- *Artsource®* **Performing Arts Resource Package** (optional)

Standards

National Theatre Standard: The student identifies and describes the visual, aural, oral, and kinetic elements of classroom dramatizations and dramatic performances.

 Lesson 6

Unit Activity: Improvised Folktale

Focus

Time: About 10 minutes

Review Unit Concepts

"The visual elements of a dramatic activity are the things that the audience sees. The visual elements include props, costumes, makeup, and sets. All of these help to tell a play's story by defining some of the five Ws." *"Los elementos visuales de una actividad dramática son las cosas que un público ve. Los elementos visuales incluyen los props, el vestuario, maquillaje y la escenografía. Todo esto ayudar a contar la historia de un drama definiendo o contestando algunas de sus preguntas principales."*

► Review with students the ways in which they created visual elements in this unit.

► Review the unit vocabulary on page 52.

History and Culture

Tell students that spider stories involving Anansi are a major tradition of the Ashanti people of Ghana. In the first spider story, there are no stories to tell on Earth because the sky god keeps them all to himself. With advice from his wife, Anansi outwits the sky god and wins all of his stories, which Anansi brings back to Earth. In the other spider stories Anansi is a sly trickster who spends his time scheming to get what he wants. Bring in one or two illustrated children's books that portray an Ashanti spider story, such as Keleki's version, *How Stories Came to Earth*. Have students look at the illustrations in the books. Then have them each write a paragraph comparing at least three aspects of the illustrations with the visual elements that they created for the story.

Classroom Management Tips

The following are tips for managing your classroom during the **Rehearsals** and **Activity**:

✔ **Encourage Creativity** During the **First** and **Second Rehearsals,** compliment students on both their creativity and realism in planning settings and costumes and creating masks.

✔ **Emphasize Cooperation** Stress to students that they should all listen to the ideas of everyone in the group and in other groups and then decide together on the best way to portray the various visual elements.

✔ **Take an Active Role** Side coach the groups as they work on the visual elements in teams in a positive, constructive manner.

Teach

First Rehearsal

▶ Distribute copies of **"The Rubber Man"** on pages 130 and 131. Have students perform the story as narrative pantomime as you read the story aloud.

▶ Discuss possible elements of the story's setting. What might characters look like? How would each character move and speak?

▶ Divide students into groups of 12. Shine a bright light against a blank wall. Have each group briefly retell the story using shadow play.

▶ Assign tasks for the **Second Rehearsal** in the following way: four group members will work on planning the sets (Anansi's home, his favorite area in the forest, the village, and the chief's farm) using the objects you brought in, four will select or create costumes, and four will design the masks before all of them will become actors.

Second Rehearsal

▶ Re-create the groups from the **First Rehearsal.**

▶ Lay out the objects and costume pieces. Each set and costume group should make a list including the objects or costume pieces they will use and how they plan to use each of them in the improvisation.

▶ Distribute the paper plates, extra paper, nontoxic glue, safety scissors, and markers or crayons to the mask designers. Have each group of mask designers use these materials to create their masks.

▶ Encourage discussion between the mask designer group, set designer group, and costume designer group within each larger group of 12.

Visual Elements Activity

▶ Re-create the groups from the **First** and **Second Rehearsals.** Reread the story aloud.

▶ Have each group assign the following roles: Anansi, his wife, villagers, the Rubber Man, the chief's servant, and the chief. Give each group a few minutes to plan their improvisation. *(See page T4 for more about Improvisation.)* Have students agree to apply appropriate audience behavior.

▶ If you wish, play some rhythmic, traditional Ghanian music during the improvisations. Encourage students to use safe, expressive movement.

▶ Allow each group to briefly improvise the story of Anansi for the class. Give each group three to five minutes to set up and put on their costumes and masks. As scenes at each location end, have the group responsible for the settings rearrange the playing area.

▶ Have the class evaluate their behavior as an audience and the various visual elements; have them constructively suggest preferences and ways in which their own choices could be improved.

Standards

National Theatre Standard: The student collaborates to establish playing spaces for classroom dramatizations and to select and safely organize available materials that suggest scenery, properties, lighting, sound, costumes, and makeup.

Visual Arts: Color and Value

Explain to students that colors and values are used in painted scenery to create different feelings. For example, cool colors such as blue or green might be used in the scenery for a calm, peaceful scene. Have students use watercolors or oil pastels to plan (in miniature) a scenic, outdoor backdrop for one of the scenes from "The Rubber Man." Tell them to think about the way an audience should feel about this scene.

Theatrical Arts Connection

Electronic Media Have students view a Web site or an interactive computer game that tells a story (ideally an African folktale). Discuss the visual elements of the setting and characters' clothes.

Television Show without sound parts of several different kinds of unfamiliar television shows, such as an old western. Have students use the various visual elements to identify the setting and who the characters are.

Standards

National Theatre Standard: The student compares and connects art forms by describing theatre, dramatic media (such as film, television, and electronic media), and other art forms. The student articulates emotional responses to and explains personal preferences about the whole as well as the parts of dramatic performances.

Reflect

Time: About 10 minutes

Assessment

► Have students evaluate their participation by completing the **Unit 3 Self-Criticism Questions** on page 68.

► Use the assessment rubric to evaluate students' participation in the **Unit Activity** and to assess their understanding of visual elements.

► Have students complete the **Unit 3 Quick Quiz** on page 69.

	3 Points	2 Points	1 Point
Perception	Gives full attention to review of unit concepts and vocabulary words. Masters concepts related to visual elements and clearly connects them to aspects of real life.	Gives partial attention to review of unit concepts and vocabulary words. Developing an understanding of concepts related to visual elements and can connect some of them to aspects of real life.	Gives little attention to review of unit concepts and vocabulary words. Has a poor understanding of concepts related to visual elements and has difficulty connecting them to aspects of real life.
Creative Expression	Participates in creating/selecting sets, costumes, or masks for an improvised performance. Works with others to improvise this performance.	Partially participates in creating/selecting sets, costumes, or masks for an improvised performance. Somewhat works with others to improvise this performance.	Shows poor participation in creating/selecting sets, costumes, or masks for an improvised performance. Does not work well with others to improvise this performance.
History and Culture	Writes a paragraph that compares at least three aspects of illustrations of another spider story with the visual elements that students created for an improvisation of "The Rubber Man."	Writes a paragraph that compares two aspects of illustrations of another spider story with the visual elements that students created for an improvisation of "The Rubber Man."	Writes an incomplete paragraph that compares one aspect of illustrations of another spider story with the visual elements that students created for an improvisation of "The Rubber Man."
Evaluation	Thoughtfully and honestly evaluates own participation using the four steps of art criticism.	Attempts to evaluate own participation, but shows an incomplete understanding of evaluation criteria.	Makes a poor attempt to evaluate own participation.

Apply

► Discuss how visual elements in other subject areas can act as models to help them to understand concepts. If possible, share some examples from other subject areas, such as manipulatives used in math that illustrate fractions or models of the solar system.

► Ask, "How can a person's choice of clothing or objects he or she uses show his or her personality? Can ideas based on these things sometimes be wrong? Why?" *(a person's clothing or objects can show what he or she likes or how he or she wants to be seen; yes, these ideas can be wrong because the person could have to dress a certain way, and so on)*

View a Performance

Visual Elements in Dance

► Discuss appropriate audience behavior, such as listening quietly, sitting still, and being respectful. Have students agree to apply this behavior during the performance.

► If you have the *Artsource®* videocassette or DVD, have students view *Billy the Kid*, choreographed by Eugene Loring, composed by Aaron Copland, and performed by dancers from the Joffrey Ballet.

► Discuss the performance with students using the following questions:

Describe What visual elements were used in the ballet? *(costumes, scenery, lighting)*

Analyze How did actors use their bodies to show setting? *(They pretended to hold cards, and so on.)* How did scenery help show where the actors were? *(It looked like a desert.)* Would you have been able to guess the time period based on the costumes? Why or why not? *(I would have because the costumes looked like those from stories set in the old west, and so on.)*

Interpret Compare and contrast the ballet's visual elements with the visual elements you created in the **Activity.**

Decide What type of character would you like to play in this ballet? Describe the costume and makeup you would wear.

> "The heart of improvisation is transformation."
>
> —Viola Spolin (1906-1994), director/actress

LEARN ABOUT
CAREERS IN THEATRE

Ask students how costume designers help to transform actors into their characters. *(They assemble clothing that visually suggests who the characters are, as well as in what setting and time period the characters exist.)* Tell students that to transform human actors into animal characters, such as Anansi the spider, a costume designer's task can be very challenging. Show costume examples from the Broadway production of *The Lion King* or, if possible, have students view a video of a local community theatre production. Ask students to imagine that they had any materials that they wanted to design a costume for an actor portraying Anansi. How would they construct the costume? Have students compare and contrast the careers of an actor and a costume designer.

Standards

National Theatre Standard: The student compares and connects art forms by describing theatre, dramatic media (such as film, television, and electronic media), and other art forms. The student describes visual, aural, oral, and kinetic elements in theatre, dramatic media, dance, music, and visual arts.

Unit 3 Self-Criticism Questions

Think about how you created a visual element
for the performance of "The Rubber Man." Then
answer the questions below.

1. **Describe** What were your sets, costumes, or masks like?

   _____

   _____

   _____

2. **Analyze** How did the sets, costumes, or masks you
   created contribute to the performance of the story?
   How did they help show the five *W*s?

   _____

   _____

   _____

3. **Interpret** How is your own house or clothing similar
   to or different from the sets, costumes, or masks
   you created for the performance?

   _____

   _____

   _____

4. **Decide** If you could do this activity again, would you
   change anything you did? Why or why not?

   _____

   _____

Unit 3 Quick Quiz

Completely fill in the bubble of the best answer
for each question below.

1. A play's setting is

- (A) how characters feel.
- (B) the place in which a play happens.
- (C) how many characters there are.
- (D) a playwright's personality.

2. Props are

- (F) what the characters wear.
- (G) used to change an actor's face into a character.
- (H) objects that are found onstage.
- (J) none of the above.

3. An example of a visual element is

- (A) makeup.
- (B) what characters say.
- (C) characters' feelings about other characters.
- (D) all of the above.

4. Which sentence is *not* true?

- (F) Makeup can transform actors into animal characters.
- (G) Scenery can help show setting.
- (H) Costumes are visual elements.
- (J) Actors never hold props.

Score _____ (Top Score 4)

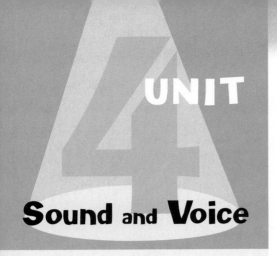

UNIT 4

Sound and Voice

Unit Overview

Lesson 1 • Sound and the Five Ws Voice helps convey character traits and emotions, and sound effects help convey the setting in a dramatic story. *Sound Effects*

Lesson 2 • Music in a Play Music helps to create mood in a dramatic story. *Creative Movement*

Lesson 3 • Voice Shows Character Voice conveys characters' traits in a drama. *Improvisation*

Lesson 4 • Sound Shows Setting Sound effects help to convey the settings in a dramatic story. *Sound Effects*

Lesson 5 • Tone and Inflection Varying vocal inflection and tone help to convey characters' emotions. *Improvisation*

Lesson 6 • Unit Activity: Reader's Theatre This activity will give students the opportunity to use their voices and create sound effects in Reader's Theatre.

See pages T3–T20 for more about **Theatre Technique Tips.**

Introduce Unit Concepts

"Sound effects help create the setting in a performance. Music helps to convey the mood, or the feelings that a performance creates. The way actors use their voices helps show what their characters are like and how they feel." *"Los efectos de sonido ayudan a crear el ambiente en una producción. La música ayuda a transmitir el talante o los sentimientos que una producción crea. La manera en que los actores usan sus voces ayuda a mostrar como son sus personajes y como se sienten."*

Sound and Voice

► Say the sentence, "I want to go home," using tone to express feelings, and then have students mimic you.

► Have students describe sounds that they hear in specific places.

Vocabulary

Discuss the following vocabulary words.

sound effects efectos de sonido—sounds that help convey setting and motivate action in a drama

inflection inflexión—change in pitch (highness or lowness) and volume of a voice

tone tono—the use of inflection to communicate feelings

Unit Links

Visual Arts: Texture and Balance

► Explain to students that the ways sound effects are blended together can create aural texture, or texture you can hear. Compare texture in blended sounds with textures artists use in sculptures.

► Show students an image of a painting, such as *Strawberry Tart Supreme* by Audrey Flack. Discuss balance in the painting. How does the painting make students feel? *(hungry, excited)* Have students make vocal sound effects that would show a person eating this tart.

Reading Theme: Money

► Have students describe various sounds related to money, such as the clinking of coins, the sound of cash register receipt printers, and so on. Have them vocally imitate these sounds.

► Discuss good and bad actions people take to get money. *(get jobs, steal, borrow)* Compare these actions with character actions from stories, such as the story of "Jack in the Beanstalk."

Teacher Background

Background on Sound and Voice

Sound effects, music, and character voices are all important to live theatre, as well as films, television shows, video games, and cartoons. Mechanical sound effects, such as doorbells, are used to motivate action; environmental sound effects help convey setting and environment. Some sound effects are used to create mood. Integral music used in theatrical performances helps motivate action and is written into the script, as with music played by a character onstage. Incidental music is background music used to create various moods. Actors use vocal tone and inflection, as in real life, to communicate emotional messages.

Background on Sound Effects

Theatrical sound effects most often used are either background noises, such as crickets chirping, or sounds which motivate action, such as a ringing telephone. They are often recorded and played over a theatre's amplification system, but they can also be live.

Research in Theatre Education

"Drama provides opportunities for children to use language for a wider variety of purposes than otherwise typically occurs in classrooms. Drama provides an opportunity to develop expressive language"

—James S. Catterall

on "Nadie Papers No. 1, Drama, Language and Learning. Reports of the Drama and Language Research Project, Speech and Drama Center, Education Department of Tasmania" in *Critical Links*

Differentiated Instruction

Reteach
Show students an active scene from an illustrated book. Ask them to identify the sounds that various objects or animals would make.

Challenge
Have students explore onomatopoeia and make a list of sound words, such as *hiss, buzz,* and *whoosh.* Have them identify various animals and objects that would make each sound.

Special Needs
Students with hearing impairments should always stand or sit where they can clearly see the face of the person who is speaking, whether it is you or other students in the class. Use visual gestures to indicate when you or another student are about to speak.

Theatre's Effects Across the Curriculum

★ **Reading/Writing**
Reading Text Exploring Reader's Theatre gives students a new way to explore the traits, feelings, and relationships of characters in a text.

★ **Math**
Number, Operation, and Quantitative Reasoning When students read and dramatize stories involving money, they consider values of different types of money.

★ **Science**
Scientific Processes When students identify environments based only on their sounds, they analyze and interpret information to construct reasonable explanations from direct and indirect evidence.

★ **Social Studies**
Economics When students read and dramatize stories involving money, they identify ways of earning, spending, and saving money.

★ **Music**
Elements Students can relate concepts of vocal pitch to the pitch and tempo of notes—a high pitch and fast tempo can signify excitement, while a low pitch and slow tempo can create a calm mood.

★ **Dance**
Body Awareness Learning to use voice to convey character makes students more aware of the corresponding degrees of tension in their body which can be used to create a dance for a character.

Objectives

 Perception To identify ways in which sounds convey the five Ws

 Creative Expression To show a scene's five Ws using pantomime and sound effects

 History and Culture To learn about the history of paper money

 Evaluation To informally evaluate one's own work

Materials

○ Various coins

○ Journals or writing paper

Vocabulary

sound effects

Standards

National Theatre Standard: The student collaborates to select interrelated characters, environments, and situations for classroom dramatizations. The student imagines and clearly describes characters, their relationships, and their environments.

Listening/Speaking Standard: The student reads prose and poetry aloud with fluency, rhythm, and pace, using appropriate intonation and vocal patterns to emphasize important passages of the text being read.

Math Standard: The student identifies mathematics in everyday situations.

 Lesson 1

Sound and the Five Ws

Focus

Time: About 10 minutes

"In this lesson we use pantomime and sound effects to show a scene's five Ws." *(See page T14 for more about Sound Effects.)*

Activate Prior Knowledge

► Put some coins in your pocket. Read aloud **"The Silver Penny,"** and jingle the coins whenever appropriate.

► Reread the story, stopping after each piece of dialogue to ask students which emotion it expresses. Have them expressively repeat some of these short phrases of dialogue.

► Have students discuss sound effects that could help convey the five Ws of "The Silver Penny."

Teach

Time: About 10 minutes

Prepare Divide students into groups of six or seven.

Lead Say, "One half of each group will pantomime a scene; the other half will hide and use their voices and hands safely to make sound effects for the pantomime."

► Allow time for groups to agree on conflict situations, such as a family packing their car to go on a vacation and finding that the car will not start, and plan their pantomimes.

► Give each group three minutes to perform their pantomime and sound effects for the class; have the class identify the five Ws. If time allows, have groups choose a new set of five Ws and switch roles.

Informal Evaluation Did each student safely create sound effects or use pantomime to convey the five Ws of a scene?

 History and Culture

Explain that when paper money was first created, it was backed by silver and gold held by a country's government; people were able to exchange paper money for this silver or gold. Discuss how sound effects for "The Silver Penny" would change if the coin had been a dollar bill.

Reflect

Time: About 5 minutes

► Discuss how sound effects helped students identify the five Ws of each scene. Would they change anything they did?

Apply

 ### Journal: Narrative Writing

Have students each write a story in their journals in which money plays a part, using as many sound words as possible.

The Silver Penny

by Hans Christian Anderson; translated by H. P. Paull (Adapted)

There was a penny that had come bright from the mint. "Hurrah!" it cried. "I'm off into the wide world!" And it was.

The penny was a silver one, and it had been a whole year in the world when, one day, it went on a journey. It was the last of the country's coins that were left with its traveling master. "Why, I've still got a penny from home!" he said. "It can travel along with me." And the penny clinked and skipped for joy as he put it back into his bag. But noticing one day that the purse wasn't shut, it crept to the opening in order to peep out. Now this it should never have done, but then it was curious, and you have to pay for that. It dropped straight onto the floor, and nobody heard it, nobody saw it.

In the morning the gentleman went away. And the penny didn't go with him, but was found, and went out with three other coins.

"Well, it's nice to see the world!" thought the penny.

"What sort of a penny's this?" somebody said all at once. "This isn't our money! It's false! No good!"

And here begins the penny's story, as it afterward told it.

"False! No good! It cut me," said the penny. And the penny would tremble in the fingers every time people would pretend it was a lawful coin.

"Miserable me!" said the penny, "Once I was passed to a poor penniless woman, and she was unable to get rid of me. But taking me back home the woman looked at me with great kindness. 'No,' she said, 'I'll punch a hole, thread a string through it, and then give the penny to the neighbor's little girl!'

"And so she punched a hole in me. I was hung round the little child's neck, and the child smiled at me.

"In the morning her mother looked at me. Getting out a pair of scissors she cut the thread. She put me in acid, and made me turn green; whereupon she sealed up the hole, rubbed me a little, and went off in the dark to use me. I was recognized as a bad penny the very next day.

"Year by year I thus passed from hand to hand and from house to house, always being abused and always looked down on.

"Then one day a traveler came and, of course, I was made to cheat him, and he was innocent enough to take me for good money; but he was just about to spend me when once more I heard the cries of 'No good! False!'

"'I took it for a good one,' said the man, taking a closer look at me. Then all at once his face lit up, as he said: 'Why, what's this? If it isn't one of our own coins; a good, honest penny from home with a hole punched in it, and they're calling it bad. Well, this is funny! I shall keep you and take you back home with me!'

"I was thrilled with joy: I had been called a good, honest penny and was going back home, where everybody would know me. My troubles were all over, and my joys were beginning, for I was of good silver. You have to hold out, for everything will come right in the end if you are really good and true! Well, that's my belief!" said the penny.

Objectives

Perception To identify ways in which music creates a feeling or mood

Creative Expression To express the feeling created by music using creative movement

History and Culture To learn about ballet

Evaluation To informally evaluate one's own work

Materials

- Copies of **"Music in a Play" Warm-Up,** p. 75

- Tape/CD player and a recording of jazz music (optional)

- Video/DVD player, and recording of *Beauty and the Beast;* have the movie cued up to its climax

- Journals or writing paper

Vocabulary

mood

Unit Links

Visual Arts: Texture

Both visual art and music create texture. Tell students that artists create paintings with visual texture. Visual texture looks bumpy or rough even though it cannot be felt. Discuss the way instruments in an orchestra create textured music by layering many sounds.

Standards

National Theatre Standard: The student selects movement, music, or visual elements to enhance the mood of a classroom dramatization.

Listening/Speaking Standard: The student knows personal listening preferences.

English Language Standard: The student establishes purposes for reading and listening such as to be informed, to follow directions, and to be entertained.

Lesson 2 — Music in a Play

Focus

Time: About 10 minutes

"In this lesson we will use creative movement to respond to music from a film's climax." *(See page T12 for more about Creative Movement.)*

Activate Prior Knowledge

▶ Distribute the **"Music in a Play" Warm-Up,** and have students complete it.

▶ Discuss student answers. Have students discuss favorite music styles and the way they make them feel. If possible, play a recording of jazz music and compare it with student answers on the **Warm-Up.**

Teach

Time: About 15 minutes

Prepare Set up and cue the movie.

Lead

▶ Have students watch the climax of a cartoon movie twice, once with the sound off and once with it on; in *Beauty and the Beast,* this is the Beast and Gaston's final battle.

▶ Discuss how the music made students feel. *(excited, nervous)* Did it make the scene more exciting? *(yes)*

▶ Choose one feeling the students described, such as excitement. Turn the television away and play the segment again so that only the music is heard. Have students stand beside their desks and respond to the music using safe, rhythmic movement and vocal sounds to show this emotion.

Informal Assessment Did each student attempt to use safe movement to show an emotion created by the music?

History and Culture

Tell students that ballet is a dance form in which stories are conveyed only through music and the motions of the dancers. The first ballet was performed in 1581 in the court of Catherine Medici who was then queen of France. This five-and-a-half-hour ballet told the story of the Greek goddess Circe who could turn men into animals. Have students compare and contrast the use of music and movement in the cartoon film and in ballet.

Reflect

Time: About 5 minutes

▶ Have students discuss how they felt as they listened and moved to various parts of the music.

Apply

Journal: Describing

Have students briefly describe in their journals music they would use in movies based on favorite books.

Name _____ Date _____

Music in a Play

Imagine the picture below is a scene from a play.
On the lines below, describe the type of music you
think these musicians are playing, and how it
might make the other people in this picture feel.

_____

_____

_____

_____

_____

_____

_____

Objectives

 Perception To identify ways in which actors can use voice to convey character

 Creative Expression To use voice and puppets to improvise a story's extended ending

 History and Culture To learn how opera singers use voice to convey character traits

Evaluation To informally evaluate one's own work

Materials

📄 Copies of **"Voice Shows Character" Warm-Up,** p. 77

○ Socks or other puppets

○ Tape or CD player and recording of an opera, such as *The Magic Flute* (optional)

○ Journals or drawing paper

Vocabulary

dialogue

Standards

National Theatre Standard: The student uses variations of locomotor and nonlocomotor movement and vocal pitch, tempo, and tone for different characters.

Listening/Speaking Standard: The student listens and responds to a variety of oral presentations, such as stories, poems, skits, songs, personal accounts, or informational speeches.

English/Language Arts Standard: The student analyzes characters, including their traits, feelings, relationships, and changes.

 Lesson 3

Voice Shows Character

Focus

Time: About 10 minutes

"In this lesson we will use our voices to show character personalities in an improvisation." *(See page T4 for more about Improvisation.)*

Activate Prior Knowledge

► Distribute the **"Voice Shows Character" Warm-Up.** Have students read the story and underline examples of speech.

► Say, "Actors sometimes change the sound of their voices or the ways they speak when they act as characters." Read the following line twice, once using a gruff, low voice and once using a warm, middle-range voice: "Now I feel rich." Have students choose the appropriate reading and explain their reasons. *(the second, because a woman would not have such a low voice)*

Teach

Time: About 15 minutes

Prepare Divide students into pairs, and provide them with puppets.

Lead Say, "The Hedley Kow [pronounced "koo"] was probably surprised that the woman was not afraid. What if the woman had invited the Hedley Kow to dinner? Could they have become friends?"

► Tell students that each pair will answer these questions by using puppets to dramatize the story and improvise an extended ending.

► Have each pair divide the roles, plan their extension, and decide how each character's voice should sound.

► Have each pair perform its dramatization and extended ending.

Informal Assessment Did each student safely use his or her voice to convey a character?

 History and Culture

Tell students that opera is a performing art in which dramatic plays, either tragic or comic, are set to music and all the lines are sung. Explain that the actors in opera have highly trained voices, which they use to convey character traits and emotions. If possible, play students an excerpt from *The Magic Flute* by Mozart.

Reflect

Time: About 5 minutes

► Have students compare and contrast the ways in which they used their voices and puppets to create different versions of the characters.

Apply

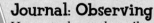 **Journal: Observing**

Have students describe in their journals one wordless sound, such as "hmm" or "ahh," that they have heard someone use and explain what it meant in a particular situation.

Name _____ Date _____

Voice Shows Character

The Hedley Kow*

a folktale from England; retold in *More English Fairy Tales*,
edited by Joseph Jacob (Adapted)

One warm evening a poor woman was coming home. Near the road she saw a big black pot.

"My goodness," she said. "What's in it?" She looked under the lid and gasped—the pot was full of gold coins!

The woman looked at the coins and said, "Now I feel rich!" She tied her scarf to the heavy pot and dragged it down the road.

After awhile she stopped to rest. But now the pot was full of silver!

"Silver!" she said. "Well, silver is better. People like to steal gold." And she went down the road, dragging the pot behind her.

"I need to rest again," she said after awhile. As she stopped, she peeked into the pot. But now there was a lump of iron in her pot, not silver!

"Well, how lucky I am," the woman said. "I will sell this iron for much money. Iron is much better than silver."

The woman went back to dragging the pot behind her, but when she stopped to rest again, she saw a great stone in the pot!

"What luck!" said the woman, "but a stone is just what I need to hold my door!"

The woman hurried home with the pot. But when the woman went to untie her scarf, the pot made a loud noise! It jumped and rolled and turned into a horse! The horse kicked and laughed a mean laugh.

"I am a hobgoblin called the Hedley Kow!" the horse said.

The woman stared at it for a minute.

"Well," she said. "I really do have good luck. I got to see the Hedley Kow with my own two eyes."

And she went into her house to think about her good luck.

*kow is pronounced "koo"

Objectives

 Perception To identify the sounds in a setting

 Creative Expression To use voice and objects to create the sounds of a setting

 History and Culture To learn about radio dramas

Evaluation To informally evaluate one's own work

Materials

- Copies of **"Sound Shows Setting" Warm-Up,** p. 79
- Various items that can be used to create sounds, such as cellophane or paper, glasses of water and straws, or wooden bowls
- Microphone, tape recorder, and blank cassette tape (optional)
- Journals or writing paper

Vocabulary

setting

Unit Links

Visual Arts: Balance

Remind students that artists arrange the elements of their artwork so that the finished product has a sense of balance. Discuss ways sound effects in a play need to be balanced; for example, what if a doorbell sound was too loud? *(It would be distracting.)*

Standards

National Theatre Standard: The student visualizes environments and constructs design to communicate locale and mood using aural aspects using a variety of sound sources.

Listening/Speaking Standard: The student makes descriptive presentations that use concrete sensory details to set forth and support unified impressions of people, places, things, or experiences.

Social Studies Standard: The student understands how individuals have created or invented new technology and affected life in communities around the world, past and present.

 Lesson 4

Sound Shows Setting

Focus

Time: About 10 minutes

"In this lesson we will use sounds to create a setting." *(See page T14 for more about Sound Effects.)*

Activate Prior Knowledge

▶ Hand out the **"Sound Shows Setting" Warm-Up,** and have students complete it. Discuss student answers. Have students use their voices to imitate some of the identified sounds.

Teach

Time: About 10 minutes

Prepare Gather the various sound effects items and, if possible, a microphone and tape recorder. Provide a table or door behind which students can hide. Divide students into four groups.

Lead Tell students that they will use their voices and certain objects to portray a setting, such as a jungle, a beach, an airport, and so on.

▶ Distribute sound effect objects to each group.

▶ Have each group decide on a setting to portray using sound effects. Have the group choose any objects that they wish to use and decide what sounds each student will make to create the setting.

▶ One at a time, have each group go into the hidden area and create their setting using sound effects that last one minute while recording, if possible. Have the class guess the setting.

Informal Assessment Did each student participate in creating sound effects that portrayed a particular setting?

 History and Culture

Explain that before television was invented, many Americans listened to radio dramas. These dramas relied on sound effects to evoke settings. Sound effects artists were very creative, opening and shutting small doors for large door sounds and crinkling cellophane to mimic fire. If possible play part of a recorded radio drama, such as *The Mercury Theatre on the Air,* on the Internet; have students compare these sound effects with the ones they created.

Reflect

Time: About 5 minutes

▶ Replay the different sound effects. Discuss how the sound effects illustrated similarities and differences between life and theatre.

Apply

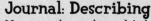 **Journal: Describing**

Have each student think about all the sounds that characterize a favorite place and write a paragraph describing these sounds in his or her journal.

Sound Shows Setting

Look at the setting in the picture below. What types of sounds would you hear in this setting? On the lines below write the names of the things that would make sounds and describe how they would sound. Use creative words, such as *whir, beep, click,* and so on.

_____

_____

_____

_____

_____

_____

Objectives

 Perception To identify ways tone and inflection communicate feelings or meaning

 Creative Expression To improvise character lines using tone and inflection

 History and Culture To learn about the inflection of English-language speakers in different parts of the world

 Evaluation To informally evaluate one's own work

Materials

- 📋 Copies of **"Tone and Inflection" Warm-Up,** p. 81
- ❍ Age-appropriate short story dealing with issues of wealth and poverty, such as "The Hundred Dresses" by Eleanor Estes (optional)
- ❍ Tape recorder, blank tape, and microphone
- ❍ Journals or drawing paper

Vocabulary

tone
inflection

Standards

National Theatre Standard: The student improvises dialogue to tell stories and formalizes improvisations by writing or recording the dialogue.

Listening/Speaking Standard: The student plans and presents dramatic interpretations of experiences, stories, poems, or plays with clear diction, pitch, tempo, and tone.

English/Language Arts Standard: The student connects life experiences with the life experiences, language, customs, and culture of others.

 Lesson 5

Tone and Inflection

Focus

Time: About 5 minutes

"In this lesson we will improvise dialogue using inflection and tone to communicate emotions." *(See page T4 for more about Improvisation.)*

Activate Prior Knowledge

► Say, "Actors use inflection—high or low and loud or soft voice sounds—to create tone. Tone communicates feelings or meaning. Actors may also communicate by emphasizing certain words."

► Distribute the **"Tone and Inflection" Warm-Up.** Model different uses of tone and emphasis. Have students form pairs and do the exercise.

Teach

Time: About 15 minutes

Prepare Divide students into small groups. Read aloud a short story focused on issues of wealth and poverty, such as "The Hundred Dresses" by Eleanor Estes, and have students act it out using narrative pantomime.

Lead

► Allow two minutes for each group to divide roles and choose a scene from the story. Students should each portray at least two roles, safely altering their tone for each character.

► Have each group improvise dialogue for the class. Record their dialogue.

► Play the recorded dialogue. If time allows, have volunteers discuss and revise their improvisations.

Informal Assessment Did each student safely use tone?

 History and Culture

Point out that people in many countries, including Great Britain, Australia, and the United States, speak the English language. Explain that people in each country use different pronunciation and inflection, so English can sound very different. If possible, locate audio clips on the Internet of people from different regions of America, Ireland, or Australia. Discuss ways an actor might work to portray a character from one region.

Reflect

Time: About 5 minutes

► Have students discuss why it was or was not challenging to focus on using tone to communicate emotion.

Apply

 Journal: Explaining
Discuss sounds in real life that are used to attract people's attention. Have students explain one such example in their journals.

Unit 4 • **Sound and Voice**

Name _____ Date _____

Tone and Inflection

Read the following sentences. Notice that they do not have end marks. Think about how you could say the sentences in different ways to ask a question, make a command, or express excitement. Say each of these sentences in different ways to a partner.

1. You are going to come with me
2. Please be quiet
3. What could be inside this cave
4. Let's stop and rest for a minute
5. Are you finished yet

Read the following sentences. Say each sentence to your partner four times. Each time you say it, say one word more loudly than the rest.

6. I know he escaped.
7. Do not say that.
8. Please leave me alone.

Describe how you said the sentences above to communicate different things.

_____

_____

_____

_____

_____

Objectives

Perception To review the use of sound and voice in dramatic performances and identify how sound and voice convey meaning in the real world

Creative Expression To use voice and sound effects to perform a script as Reader's Theatre

History and Culture To learn about three wishes in fairy tales as teaching a lesson or moral

Evaluation To thoughtfully and honestly evaluate one's own participation using the four steps of criticism

Materials

📄 Copies of "Wishing for Gold," pp. 132–138

📄 Copies of the **Unit 4 Self-Criticism Questions,** p. 86

📄 Copies of the **Unit 4 Quick Quiz,** p. 87

○ *Artsource®* **Performing Arts Resource Package** (optional)

Standards

National Theatre Standard: The student explains how the wants and needs of characters are similar to and different from their own.

Lesson 6 · Unit Activity: Reader's Theatre

Focus

Time: About 10 minutes

Review Unit Concepts

"Sound effects are used in dramatic performances to help convey the setting and actions of characters. Music is used to help create the mood of a performance. Actors use inflection and tone to convey characters' traits and emotions." **"Se usan efectos de sonido en producciones dramáticas para ayudar a transmitir el ambiente y acciones de personajes. Se usa música para crear el ambiente o talante de una producción. Actores usan inflexión y tono para transmitir las características y emociones de los personajes."**

► Review with students the ways they used sound and voice in this unit.

► Review the unit vocabulary on page 70.

History and Culture

Point out to students that many fairy tales and folktales from around the world involve an imaginary creature granting a person a limited number of wishes. Often the person uses the first wishes unwisely and has to use the last wish to return to his or her former condition. Have students recall or read another story involving three wishes, such as "The Fisherman and His Wife" by the Brothers Grimm. Have them each write several sentences describing the story's moral, comparing the story to "Wishing for Gold," and explaining how they would use wishes in a similar situation.

Classroom Management Tips

The following are tips for managing your classroom during the **Rehearsals** and **Activity:**

✔ **Encourage Creativity** During the **Second Rehearsal,** compliment students on inflection and tone that communicates appropriate emotional messages and on their ideas for creating sound effects.

✔ **Encourage Subtlety** Tell students that just because the emphasis is on sound does not mean they have to speak in overly loud voices or make noisy sound effects. Discuss safe use of voice, such as supporting the voice with the stomach muscles (diaphragm) and not yelling or screaming. Explain that the sound effects in this story are meant to complement the voices, not overpower them.

Teach

First Rehearsal

▶ Distribute copies of **"Wishing for Gold"** on pages 132 through 138. Have students follow along as you read the script aloud.

▶ Have students volunteer to play different characters; evenly assign different character roles, following student preferences as much as possible.

▶ Tell students that you are going to act as a reporter and interview them. Using an imaginary microphone, ask students questions relating to the value they place on money, such as, "Why did you wish for gold?" "Do you wish that you had asked the sand fairy for a different wish?" or "Mr. Peasemarsh, why did you call the police?"

▶ Compare and contrast different answers from students portraying the same roles. Have students identify and discuss character motivations. Compliment use of inflection and tone.

Second Rehearsal

▶ Have students volunteer to perform as characters or create sound effects. Divide these volunteers into two groups: one composed of at least ten actors (or more if there will be several narrators) and the other composed of all remaining students.

▶ Have the ten or more actors divide the roles in the story and practice safely using various inflections and tones to create the voices of their characters. Have the other students discuss how they could create sound effects to help dramatize the script, choose any objects that they will use to create them, and practice making their sound effects.

Sound and Voice Activity

▶ Have students re-form their groups from the **Second Rehearsal;** have students acting in character roles sit next to each other on a row of chairs, and have students who are making sound effects gather nearby.

▶ Explain that they are going to perform a Reader's Theatre version of the script, so the actors will only use their voices. *(See page T9 for more about Reader's Theatre.)*

▶ Tell students who have reading parts that the most important thing is to safely use inflection and tone to convey the characters' feelings and personalities. Tell students responsible for sound effects that the most important thing for them to do is to make sure their timing is right and that their sound effects do not overpower the voices.

▶ Have students perform the script as Readers' Theatre.

▶ Discuss the performance. If time allows, have student readers and volunteers from the sound effects group switch roles and perform the story again.

Standards

National Theatre Standard: The student uses variations of locomotor and nonlocomotor movement and vocal pitch, tempo, and tone for different characters.

Unit Links

Visual Arts: Balance
Remind students that sound, voice, and music must all work together to create a balanced performance, just as art elements such as color, value, and shape work together to create balanced artwork. Discuss how the sound effects and readers' voices complemented each other in the **Sound and Voice Activity.** Play a piece of music for students and have them describe the different sounds that blend together. Have students create safe movements and vocal sounds in response to the music and compare and contrast the use of balance in visual arts, live theatre, and music.

Theatrical Arts Connection

Film/Video Show students a segment from a cartoon film with no sound other than music, such as "Rhapsody in Blue" in *Fantasia* or *Fantasia 2000*. Have them discuss the various moods created by the music and the characters' movements. Also have them share their emotional responses to various parts of the segment as well as the segment as a whole.

Television Have students view a cartoon and discuss the various sound effects that are used. Have students explain how the sound effects complement the actions of the characters and the setting.

Standards

National Theatre Standard: The student articulates emotional responses to and explains personal preferences about the whole as well as parts of dramatic performances. The student compares and connects art forms by describing theatre, dramatic media (such as film, television, and electronic media) and other art forms.

Reflect

Time: About 10 minutes

Assessment

► Have students evaluate their participation by completing the **Unit 4 Self-Criticism Questions** on page 86.

► Use the assessment rubric to evaluate students' participation in the **Unit Activity** and to assess their understanding of sound effects and voice.

► Have students complete the **Unit 4 Quick Quiz** on page 87.

	3 Points	2 Points	1 Point
Perception	Gives full attention to review of unit concepts and vocabulary words. Masters an understanding of how tone conveys emotion and how sound evokes emotion.	Gives partial attention to review of unit concepts and vocabulary words. Is developing an understanding of how tone conveys emotion and how sound evokes emotion.	Gives minimal attention to review of unit concepts and vocabulary words. Has a poor understanding of how tone conveys emotion and how sound evokes emotion.
Creative Expression	Fully participates in creating sound effects or in creating a character's vocal tone and inflection for Reader's Theatre.	Participates somewhat in creating sound effects or in creating a character's vocal tone and inflection for Reader's Theatre.	Shows minimal participation in creating sound effects or in creating a character's vocal tone and inflection.
History and Culture	Writes sentences that do all of the following: explain a story's moral, compare and contrast the story with "Wishing for Gold," and describe own actions in a similar situation.	Writes sentences that do two of the following: explain a story's moral, compare and contrast the story with "Wishing for Gold," or describe own actions in a similar situation.	Writes sentences that do one of the following: explain a story's moral, compare and contrast the story with "Wishing for Gold," or describe own actions in a similar situation.
Evaluation	Thoughtfully and honestly evaluates own participation using the four steps of art criticism.	Attempts to evaluate own participation, but shows an incomplete understanding of evaluation criteria.	Makes a minimal attempt to evaluate own participation.

Apply

► Discuss with students some ways that sound, inflection, and tone in real life help them to understand various aspects of people and places. *(People's voices convey emotion and can also indicate what country or region they are from; sounds convey aspects of place that may not be visible, such as fire alarms going off.)*

► Have students identify examples of sounds that make them feel a certain way no matter when they hear them, such as birds chirping or the roar of a motorcycle.

View a Performance

Sound and Voice in Music

► Discuss appropriate audience behaviors, such as listening quietly, sitting still, and being respectful. Have students agree to apply this behavior during the musical performance.

► If you have the **Artsource®** audiocassette and videocassette or DVD, have students listen to the audio first and then watch the video for *Every Picture Tells a Story*, with music composed by Paul Tracey and storyboards created by John Ramirez. Alternatively, show part of an animated feature film.

► Discuss the performance with students using the following questions:

Describe What did you hear in each musical piece on the audio? *(cries of gulls, horn, rattle, flute, and so on)*

Analyze How did the music help tell the story of the documentary and of the final storyboard? *(One song made the documentary and storyboard seem fun, and so on.)*

Interpret Think about the story told by the storyboard. How do you think each character's voice would sound?

Decide What other stories could be told using the music from the audio?

"In a good play every speech should be as fully flavored as a nut or apple."

—J.M. Synge
(1871–1909), playwright

LEARN ABOUT CAREERS IN THEATRE

Explain to students that, in the production of plays, sound designers use a wide array of objects to create the sounds. For example, for a scene with a horse pulling a carriage, a sound designer might use sticks attached to padded blocks being pounded in a box of dirt or gravel to make the sound of footsteps and use springs to make the sound of the carriage creaking. Sound designers usually read the play first. They may begin planning immediately, or they may view the first rehearsals for a production and then decide how they will add sound to complement various actions and settings. Have students compare the careers of sound and costume designers.

Standards

National Theatre Standard: The student compares and connects art forms by describing theatre, dramatic media (such as film, television, and electronic media), and other art forms.

Name _____ Date _____

Unit 4 Self-Criticism Questions

Think about how you created a sound effect or a character's voice for the performance of "Wishing for Gold." Then answer the questions below.

1. **Describe** How did you use your voice to convey the traits and emotions of your character, or how did you create sound effects?

   _____

   _____

2. **Analyze** How did the character voice or sound effect that you created contribute to the performance of the story?

   _____

   _____

3. **Interpret** In what ways is your own way of speech like and unlike that of your characters, or in what ways are the sound effects you created like or unlike sounds in real life?

   _____

   _____

4. **Decide** If you could do this activity again, would you change anything you did? Why or why not?

   _____

   _____

Unit 4 Quick Quiz

Completely fill in the bubble of the best answer
for each question below.

1. Sound effects
- Ⓐ   can help show some of the five *W*s.
- Ⓑ   are used in movies.
- Ⓒ   can help show setting.
- Ⓓ   all of the above

2. Inflection is
- Ⓕ   a type of sickness.
- Ⓖ   high or low and loud or soft sounds made
  with the voice.
- Ⓗ   very exciting music.
- Ⓙ   a feeling a character has.

3. Tone of voice
- Ⓐ   can show how a character feels.
- Ⓑ   does not show any of the five *W*s.
- Ⓒ   can never sound happy or excited.
- Ⓓ   all of the above

4. Which sentence is true?
- Ⓕ   Sound effects are always really loud.
- Ⓖ   Music is only used in a play when characters dance.
- Ⓗ   Sound and voice are not important in a
  television show.
- Ⓙ   Music, sound, and voice help to tell a play's story.

Score _____ (Top Score 4)

UNIT 5

Movement

Unit Overview

Lesson 1 • Movement and the Five Ws Movement can help to show the five Ws of a play. *Pantomime*

Lesson 2 • Action and Inaction Characters in a play choose whether or not to take physical action. *Theatre Game*

Lesson 3 • Moving Shadow Puppets The movement of shadow puppets can mimic animal movement. *Shadow Puppets*

Lesson 4 • Rhythm and Repetition Actors may use patterns of repeated movement. *Creative Movement*

Lesson 5 • Action and Reaction Characters physically react to each other's actions. *Improvisation*

Lesson 6 • Unit Activity: Pantomime This activity will give students the opportunity to use pantomime to dramatize a literary selection.

See pages T3–T20 for more about **Theatre Technique Tips.**

Introduce Unit Concepts

"When actors portray characters, they use different types of movement. They use movements that help move the plot forward, movements that form patterns, and movements to show actions and reactions." "Cuando actores representan personajes, usan tipos diferentes de movimiento. Usan movimientos que ayudan a avanzar la trama, movimientos que forman modelos y movimientos que muestran acciones y reacciones."

Movement

► Have students stand and move as characters for different ages and actions, such as a baby crawling or a teenager mowing the grass.

► Describe scenarios, such as receiving an unexpected present, and have students describe the ways in which they might move in these situations. Discuss how emotion affects movement.

Vocabulary

Discuss the following vocabulary words.

movement movimiento—in theatre, changes in an actor's physical position onstage

repetition repetición—in terms of movement, actions that are performed over and over

rhythm ritmo—in terms of movement, a pattern of movements that are performed over and over

Unit Links

Visual Arts: Pattern, Rhythm, and Movement

► Explain that rhythm in artwork involves repeating elements such as color or line to create visual movement; pattern refers to repeated motifs or shapes on two-dimensional surfaces. Discuss and compare rhythm in artwork with the ways actors, musicians, and dancers can use rhythm. *(Actors and dancers can use repeated movement, and so on.)*

► Show students an image of an artwork, such as *Great Blue Heron* by John James Audubon. Discuss how the colors move students' eyes across the painting. Tap a pencil, and have them use movement to act like the heron, adjusting their movements to the pencil's rhythm.

Reading Theme: Storytelling

► Discuss students' favorite stories. What types of stories do students like to share with their friends? *(funny stories, stories about my day)*

► Explain that storytelling is important in cultures around the world. Share picture books of folktales with rhythmic language, such as *A Story, A Story* by Gail E. Haley, and identify examples of repetition. How could students tell this story through movement? *(We could act like the characters, and so on.)*

Teacher Background

Background on Movement

Along with visual elements, actors' movements help create the visual story of a theatrical production. Actors choose movements based on a character's motivations, personality, culture, and other factors. Many actors study special movement techniques to help them to overcome physical habits and better use their bodies when they are acting as characters.

Background on Directing

Traveling movement onstage is known as blocking. Actors, directors, and stage managers work together to create blocking in a play. A director may plan a play's blocking in advance, or he or she may allow actors to improvise movements before formalizing blocking. Movement onstage must always balance the motivations of the characters, details of the setting, and the needs of the actors against the needs of the audience.

Research in Theatre Education

"...dramatic play is a vehicle whereby children can both practice and learn about literacy skills and begin to develop 'storying' skills which might be used in story writing."

—Jennifer Ross Goodman,

"A Naturalistic Study of the Relationship between Literacy Development and Dramatic Play in Five-Year-Old Children."

Differentiated Instruction

Reteach
Have students pantomime everyday actions, such as brushing their teeth, eating, doing their homework, and so on.

Challenge
Have students choose one or two characters from a book. Have them make a list of details about this character, such as the character's motivation, feelings, personality, age, and so on. Then have them convey the character's movement in a particular scene using their entire bodies.

Special Needs
Students with physical disabilities may be restricted in their movements. For these students, focus on facial expressions and on moving the parts of their bodies that they are able to use. Also, encourage students who use wheelchairs or walkers to incorporate these items into theatre games and performances.

Theatre's Effects Across the Curriculum

★ **Reading/Writing**
Reading Text Physically dramatizing characters from a literary work gives students a new way to unlock and explore a text's meaning.

★ **Math**
Patterns, Relationships, and Algebraic Thinking When students use rhythm and repetition in movement, they are using patterns to make predictions about the next movement.

★ **Science**
Biology When students consider the way animal characters are physically portrayed, they must think about the way each animal looks and moves.

★ **Social Studies**
Culture When students learn about traditional rites of Native Americans and traditions in African theatre, they have the opportunity to learn about cultural heritage.

★ **Music**
Repetition Exploring physical repetition may help students understand aural repetition; in many songs the music of each verse remains the same despite changing lyrics.

★ **Dance**
Rhythmic Repetition As students identify rhythm and repetition, they are learning about key principles of choreography.

Objectives

 Perception To identify ways in which movement can help tell a story

 Creative Expression To use narrative pantomime to show some of the five *W*s of a story

 History and Culture To learn about how animals are portrayed in the Sun Dance shared by several Native American tribes

 Evaluation To informally evaluate one's own work

Materials

📄 Copies of **"Movement and the Five *W*s" Warm-Up**, p. 91

◯ Journals or writing paper

Vocabulary

sound effects

Unit Links _____

Visual Arts: Movement

Movement helps tell stories in art and in theatre. Show an artwork in which rhythm creates visual movement that communicates an idea, such as *Looner Eclipse* by John Hoover. Have students identify how their eyes move up the bird's necks in the artwork. Compare and contrast this use of movement with the students' own use of movement to show the five *W*s of a scene.

Standards

National Theatre Standard: The student collaborates to select interrelated characters, environments, and situations for classroom dramatizations.

Listening/Speaking Standard: The student makes descriptive presentations that use concrete sensory details to set forth and support unified impressions of people, places, things, or experiences.

Social Studies Standard: The student understands ethnic and/or cultural celebrations of the United States and other nations.

 Lesson 1

Movement and the Five Ws

Focus

Time: About 10 minutes

"In this lesson we will use narrative pantomime to show some of the five *W*s of a scene." *(See page T3 for more about Pantomime.)*

Activate Prior Knowledge

► Hand out the **"Movement and the Five *W*s" Warm-Up** to students, and have them answer the questions. Discuss students' answers. What can students tell from the characters' body positions? Have students describe how the picture shows different types of movement.

Teach

Time: About 15 minutes

Prepare Divide students into groups of three.

Lead Have each group think of a story from real life that they like to retell. It could be something interesting that happened to one of them, such as making a new friend or learning to ride a bike.

► Have each group come forward. Have one student tell the story while the other two safely use pantomime to convey some or all of the five *W*s. After a minute, have the class guess the five *W*s. Compare their answers with the details each group intended to show.

► Have narrators and actors switch roles; allow all groups to replay simultaneously.

Informal Assessment Did each student safely use narrative pantomime to portray the five *W*s?

 History and Culture

Discuss personalities the animals on the **Warm-Up** seem to have. Tell students that many cultures imagine that animals have human traits. Share with students the way dancers portray animals in the Sun Dance. Many Native American tribes, including the Arapaho, Cheyenne, and Blackfoot, perform the Sun Dance in early summer. Dancers portray various animals, and express *who* the animals are thought to be rather than *what* they do as animals. For example, an eagle dancer uses movements expressing bravery and strength. Show pictures of such dancers, if possible. Compare and contrast the way dancers show *who* with the way the students showed *who* in the lesson.

Reflect

Time: About 5 minutes

► Have students compare and contrast the way they showed the five *W*s through movement.

Apply

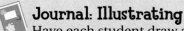 **Journal: Illustrating**
Have each student draw a self-portrait in his or her journal that shows body language used to convey a message.

Name _____ Date _____

Movement and the Five *W*s

Look at the picture below. How does movement in this picture show *who, what, when, where,* and *why?* Answer the questions at the bottom of the page.

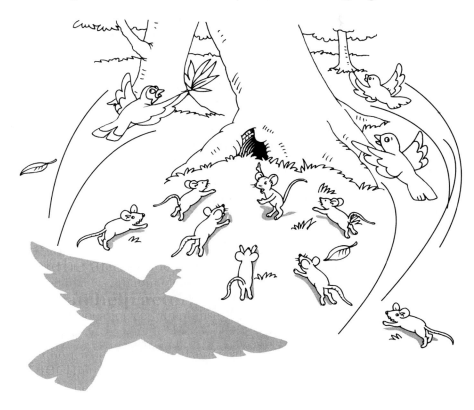

Who are the characters? **What** are they doing?

_____

_____

Where and **when** is this happening?

_____

_____

Why do you think each character is moving?

_____

_____

Objectives

Perception To identify examples and consequences of character action and inaction

Creative Expression To play a theatre game that uses action and inaction

History and Culture To learn about the African storytelling tradition of the *griot*

Evaluation To informally evaluate one's own work

Materials

▤ Copies of **"Action and Inaction" Warm-Up,** p. 93

○ Journals or writing paper

Vocabulary

action
inaction

Standards

National Theatre Standard: The student identifies and describes the visual, aural, oral, and kinetic elements of classroom dramatizations and dramatic performances.

Listening/Speaking Standard: The student actively participates in class discussions (for example, asking and responding to questions, explaining information, listening to discussions).

English/Language Arts Standard: The student connects life experiences with the life experiences, languages, customs, and cultures of others.

Lesson 2 · Action and Inaction

Focus

Time: About 10 minutes

"In this lesson we will play a theatre game that explores action and inaction." *(See page T5 for more about Theatre Games.)*

Activate Prior Knowledge

► Hand out the **"Action and Inaction" Warm-Up,** and have students complete it.

► Say, "Characters decide whether to take physical action in a story. Their inaction affects other characters. What might have happened if Anansi had chosen inaction?" *(People might not have gotten stories.)*

► Discuss students' action predictions. Choose one prediction, and have students pantomime this action in unison.

Teach

Time: About 15 minutes

Prepare Clear a large but restricted playing area.

Lead Say, "We are going to play a game of 'Freeze Tag' in slow motion."

► Choose one student to be "It." Explain that students must run and dodge in slow motion, and that when the student who is "It" tags another person, the student who is "It" must freeze while the student who is tagged becomes the new "It." Students who have not been "It" will continue to move in slow motion until all students are frozen.

► Play the game, reminding students to move in slow motion.

Informal Assessment Did each student move in slow motion and freeze when he or she tagged another student?

 History and Culture

If possible, show a video of an amateur storyteller or have one visit the class. Compare and contrast this performance with the African storytelling tradition of a *griot*. Explain that a griot tells myths, legends, laws, and stories from history. Drums and rattles set the story's beat, and the audience joins in by chanting and singing. Lead students in clapping a beat, and allow volunteers to respond to the beat by telling short sections of real-life stories while acting them out.

Reflect

Time: About 5 minutes

► Have students identify action and inaction in the game.

Apply

📓 Journal: Explaining

Have students write journal entries describing a time when they chose inaction over physical action, why they chose this, and what the consequences were.

Action and Inaction

Look at the picture below. A storyteller is telling a story. Read the beginning of his story in the talk bubble below. Do you think Anansi will do something to get the stories? What will he do? Draw what you think Anansi will do next in the talk bubble.

Long ago the Sky King had all the stories. Anansi, the spider man, wanted to get the stories for the people on Earth.

Unit Links Reading: Storytelling

Objectives

 Perception To identify ways in which animals move

 Creative Expression To use shadow puppets to dramatize a story

 History and Culture To learn about shadow puppets in ancient India

Evaluation To informally evaluate one's own work

Materials

- Copies of **"Moving Shadow Puppets" Warm-Up,** p. 95

- Safety scissors, stiff paper or thin cardboard, tape, plastic drinking straws, thumb tacks

- An overhead projector or a shadow screen (a stretched sheet with a light shining at it from behind)

- Journals or writing paper

Standards

National Theatre Standard: The student identifies and describes the visual, aural, oral, and kinetic elements of classroom dramatizations and dramatic performances.

Listening/Speaking Standard: The student listens and responds to a variety of oral presentations, such as stories, poems, skits, songs, personal accounts, or informational speeches.

Science Standard: The student observes and identifies characteristics among species that allow each to survive and reproduce.

Lesson 3

Moving Shadow Puppets

Focus

Time: About 10 minutes

"In this lesson we will use movement with shadow puppets." *(See page T8 for more about Puppetry.)*

Activate Prior Knowledge

▶ Remind students about the butterfly's life cycle. Distribute the **"Moving Shadow Puppets" Warm-Up,** and have students stand and use narrative pantomime as you read the story aloud.

▶ Discuss different ways in which an ant, caterpillar, and butterfly move.

Teach

Time: About 15 minutes

Prepare Divide students into groups of three. Set up the projector or shadow screen, and distribute the puppet materials.

Lead Explain that the students in each group will make shadow puppets of the ant, the chrysalis, and the butterfly. Students may cut out legs or wings separately, and you will help them use thumb tacks to create moveable limbs. They will attach their puppets to drinking straws to create shadow puppets. Tell students to keep in mind how they will look when they are projected.

▶ Have each group make its puppets and then use their shadow puppets to tell the story as you reread the story aloud.

Informal Assessment Did each student create a shadow puppet and use a shadow puppet to convey movement?

History and Culture

Tell students that shadow puppetry has been used in many countries throughout the world. In India, traditional puppets were four to five feet tall and made of stiff leather. They had articulated joints, which meant that they had hinged arms and legs that could bend. They were moved behind a hanging sheet of fabric, and coconut husks filled with burning oil lined the ground behind the fabric. Have students experiment with their puppets' moveable joints; discuss ways they could use sticks to move these joints behind a screen.

Reflect

Time: About 5 minutes

▶ Have students discuss ways they moved their shadow puppets. How might they use their bodies to convey these characters?

Apply

Journal: Designing

Discuss movements various wild animals use to survive. In their journals, have each student choose an animal and draw the design of a shadow puppet for this animal, describing how the puppet could be jointed for movement.

Name _____ Date _____

Moving Shadow Puppets

The Ant and the Chrysalis

from *Aesop's Fables* (Adapted)

An Ant was running around in the sunshine looking for food. Suddenly he came upon a Chrysalis. Something inside the Chrysalis was moving around, and the Chrysalis swayed in front of the Ant.

"Poor animal!" said the Ant. "What a bad life you have! While I can run around freely, you are trapped inside this shell," and the Ant shook his head and walked away.

The Chrysalis did not say anything.

A few days later the Ant walked by and saw the Chrysalis was empty— nothing but a shell was left. A wind blew across the Ant, and when he looked up, he saw a beautiful Butterfly flying above him.

"Are you sorry for me now?" the Butterfly said. "You can tell me about your power to run around—if you can catch me!" The Butterfly flew up high in the air. The Ant never saw her again.

This story shows that some things look different than what they are.

Unit Links Reading: Storytelling

Rhythm and Repetition

Objectives

 Perception To identify repetition in a story

 Creative Expression To use repetition and rhythm in creative movement

History and Culture To learn about repetition in storytelling traditions

Evaluation To informally evaluate one's own work

Materials

○ Journals or writing paper

Vocabulary

rhythm
repetition

Focus

Time: About 10 minutes

"In this lesson we will use rhythm and repetition in creative movement." *(See page T12 for more about Creative Movement.)*

Activate Prior Knowledge

▶ Read aloud **"The Endless Story."** Ask students to identify the repetitive element in the story. *(the locusts carrying away grains of corn)* Have them describe the movements of the locusts and relate this to why the king becomes so irritated by the story.

Teach

Time: About 15 minutes

Prepare Have students stand beside their seats.

Lead Say, "Imagine that you were the storyteller and you wanted to tell a different, endless story." Have students suggest examples of repetitive movement from nature, such as the knock of a woodpecker on a tree.

▶ Choose one idea. Work with the class to think of a story in which this action could occur endlessly.

▶ Retell the beginning of the students' story, and at the appropriate moment, have students safely use rhythmic, repetitive movements to show the movement of the force or animal. Continue to describe their actions, as in "and then another wave rose and crashed on the shore, and then another wave rose and crashed on the shore," and so on.

▶ Say, "Stop! You will drive me mad. I can listen to this story no longer," when you want students to stop.

Informal Assessment Did each student safely use repetitive and rhythmic movement?

History and Culture

Tell students that repetition has been an important part of oral storytelling traditions in nearly all cultures for thousands of years. Repetition helps listeners to remember and relate previous parts of a story to later parts. The repetition in many stories also helps to build suspense in a plot. Have students identify examples of repetition in "The Three Little Pigs" and "The Three Billy Goats Gruff."

Reflect

Time: About 5 minutes

▶ Discuss similarities and differences between movements.

Apply

 Journal: Describing
Have students describe in their journals the rhythmic movements of various common objects, such as washing machines and garden sprinklers, using colorful language.

Standards

National Theatre Standard: The student assumes roles that exhibit concentration and contribute to the action of classroom dramatizations based on personal experience and heritage, imagination, literature, and history.

Listening/Speaking Standard: The student listens and responds to a variety of oral presentations, such as stories, poems, skits, songs, personal accounts, or informational speeches.

Mathematics Standard: The student identifies and extends whole-number and geometric patterns to make predictions and solve problems.

The Endless Story

from *Fifty Famous Stories Retold* by James Baldwin

In the Far East there was a great king who had no work to do. Every day, and all day long, he sat on soft cushions and listened to stories. And no matter what the story was about, he never grew tired of hearing it, even though it was very long.

"There is only one fault that I find with your story," he often said. "It is too short."

All the storytellers in the world were invited to his palace; and some of them told tales that were very long indeed. But the king was always sad when a story was ended.

At last he sent word into every city and town and country place, offering a prize to any one who should tell him an endless tale. He said,—

"To the man that will tell me a story which shall last forever, I will give my fairest daughter for his wife, and he shall be king after me."

But this was not all. He added a very hard condition. "If any man shall try to tell such a story, and then fail, he shall have his head cut off."

One young man invented a story that lasted three months; but at the end of that time, he could think of nothing more. His fate was a warning to others, and it was a long time before another storyteller was so rash as to try the king's patience.

But one day a stranger from the south came into the palace.

"Great king," he said, "is it true that you offer a prize to the man who can tell a story that has no end?"

"It is true," said the king.

"Very well, then," said the stranger. "I have a pleasant story about locusts that I would like to relate."

"Tell it," said the king. "I will listen to you."

The storyteller began his tale.

"Once upon a time a certain king seized upon all the corn in his country, and stored it away in a strong granary. But a swarm of locusts came over the land and saw where the grain had been put. After searching for many days they found on the east side of the granary a crevice that was just large enough for one locust to pass through at a time. So one locust went in and carried away a grain of corn; then another locust went in and carried away a grain of corn; then another locust went in and carried away a grain of corn."

Day after day, week after week, the man kept on saying, "Then another locust went in and carried away a grain of corn."

A month passed; a year passed. At the end of two years, the king said,—

"How much longer will the locusts be going in and carrying away corn?"

"O king!" said the storyteller, "they have as yet cleared only one cubit; and there are many thousand cubits in the granary."

"Man, man!" cried the king, "you will drive me mad. I can listen to it no longer. Take my daughter; be my heir; rule my kingdom. But do not let me hear another word about those horrible locusts!"

And so the strange storyteller married the king's daughter. And he lived happily in the land for many years. But his father-in-law, the king, did not care to listen to any more stories.

Action and Reaction

Objectives

 Perception To explore how movement conveys action and reaction

Creative Expression To improvise scenarios involving actions and reactions using movement and facial expression

 History and Culture To learn about the origin of slapstick comedy

 Evaluation To informally evaluate one's own work

Materials

📄 Copies of **"Action and Reaction" Warm-Up,** p. 99

○ Journals or drawing paper

Vocabulary

action
reaction

Standards

National Theatre Standard: The student selects interrelated characters, environments, and situations for classroom dramatizations.

Listening/Speaking Standard: The student connects experiences and ideas with those of others through speaking and listening.

Science Standard: The student analyzes and interprets information to construct reasonable explanations from direct and indirect evidence.

Focus

Time: About 10 minutes

"In this lesson we will use improvisation to show actions and reactions of characters." *(See page T4 for more about Improvisation.)*

Activate Prior Knowledge

► Explain to students that an action is something that a character does, and a reaction is what another character does in response to an action. Relate action and reaction to cause and effect.

► Distribute the **"Action and Reaction" Warm-Up,** and have students complete it. Have students share their answers. How could they tell what the actions and reactions were with no words to help them? *(body position and facial expressions)*

Teach

Time: About 15 minutes

Prepare Divide students into pairs.

Lead Have each pair think of a scenario in which the action of one character might cause another character to react in a certain way, such as one character taking a blanket away from another who is sleeping.

► Give students one minute to plan an initial action, but tell them they will improvise their subsequent reactions.

► Have each pair perform its improvisation for the class. Have the class identify the actions and reactions that the pair portrayed.

Informal Assessment Did each student use body movement and facial expression to convey an action or reaction of a character?

History and Culture

Explain to students that the slapstick comedy that they see in many cartoons relies mainly on exaggerated body movement and facial expression for humor and very little on dialogue. The term *slapstick* comes from the *commedia dell'arte,* an improvised comedic theatre of the sixteenth to eighteenth centuries in Italy. In this theatre, a character called Harlequin would use a harmless paddle made of two pieces of wood that slapped together when the paddle seemed to hit another character. Harlequin's actions produced funny reactions in the other characters.

Reflect

Time: About 5 minutes

► Discuss how students' movements were similar to or different from real-life reactions.

Apply

Journal: Illustrating

Have each student think of a time when he or she had a very strong positive or negative reaction to the action of another person. Have students draw their reaction in their journals.

Action and Reaction

The pictures below tell a short story. Below each picture, write the action performed by one character and the reaction of the other character.

_____

_____

_____

_____

_____

_____

_____

_____

_____

_____

_____

_____

_____

_____

Objectives

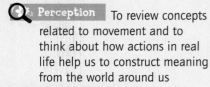

Perception To review concepts related to movement and to think about how actions in real life help us to construct meaning from the world around us

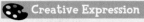
Creative Expression

To dramatize a literary selection using pantomime

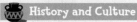
History and Culture

To explore reasons why people enjoy experiencing dramatizations

Evaluation To thoughtfully and honestly evaluate one's own participation using the four steps of criticism

Materials

○ Curtain or sheet to be used as a shadow screen

○ A bright, adjustable light to shine against the shadow screen

○ Craft paper, markers, tape, safety scissors

○ Costume pieces, such as hats, coats, or shirts (optional)

▤ Copies of the **Unit 5 Self-Criticism Questions,** p. 104

▤ Copies of the **Unit 5 Quick Quiz,** p. 105

○ *Artsource®* Performing Arts Resource Package (optional)

Standards

National Theatre Standard: The student identifies and compares the various settings and reasons for creating dramas and attending theatre, film, television, and electronic media productions.

Lesson 6 — Unit Activity: Pantomime

Focus

Time: About 10 minutes

Review Unit Concepts

"Actions are the things that characters do, and reactions are other characters' responses to those actions. Inaction is the state of not moving. Repetition and rhythm are created by repeated movements. Characters use movements and facial expressions to show their actions and reactions." **"Acciones son las cosas que los personajes hacen, y reacciones son las respuestas de otros personajes a esas acciones. La inacción es el estado de no mover. Se crean la repetición y el ritmo con movimientos repetidos. Los personajes usan movimientos y expresiones faciales para mostrar sus acciones y reacciones."**

▶ Review the different ways in which they used movement in this unit.

▶ Review the unit vocabulary on page 88.

History and Culture

Explain to students that people throughout the world have used theatre to present stories and literary works and to discuss social issues. Discuss reasons people might prefer to either attend a theatrical performance or read a story. Have students compare and contrast the reasons people like to watch live theatre, movies, and television shows and to interact with electronic media, such as computer games. Then have each student choose a favorite story they have read and write a paragraph explaining why they would like to see a dramatization of the story, sharing three specific details of how they would like it to be dramatized.

Classroom Management Tips

The following are tips for managing your classroom during the **Rehearsals** and **Activity.**

✔ **Set Ground Rules** Explain to students that when they dramatize the three robbers getting out of and into the box, they should think of ways to position their bodies other than simply squashing one another. Make sure that students portray these scenes safely.

✔ **Encourage Creativity** During the **First Rehearsal,** compliment students on expressive use of body positioning to create their tableaux. During the **Second Rehearsal** and the **Movement Activity,** compliment students on expressive movement and facial expression.

✔ **Take an Active Role** Assume the role of director and help the student director in each group. While you do this, model ways to work together in a positive, constructive manner rather than in an aggressive, critical manner.

Teach

Time: Two 15-minute rehearsal periods
One 15-minute activity period

First Rehearsal

► Set up a curtain or sheet as a shadow screen. It can be draped across two tall objects or hung from the ceiling. It should be tall enough that students can stand behind it and remain unseen. Set up a light to shine against it, but do not turn it on yet.

► Read aloud **"The Box of Robbers"** on pages 139 through 142. Have students share personal reactions and describe the characters, their relationships, and environment. Would they have acted as Martha did?

► Divide students into groups of four. Have each group choose a scene from the story and act it out behind the shadow screen. Tell them to focus on their body positions. When you say, "Freeze," have them create a tableau. Switch on the light.

► Have other groups explain how the actors' body positions convey what is happening.

Second Rehearsal

► Divide students into groups of six. *(See page T3 for more about Pantomime.)*

► Assign half of the groups the following questions: "How do you think the three bandits ended up in the box? Why did Martha's uncle send the box?" Assign the other half of the groups the questions, "What if Martha had not put the bandits back in the box? Could she have helped the bandits? What might happen next?"

► Have the groups decide on answers to their assigned questions. Tell them to discuss how they could make, find, and use scenery, props, and costume pieces to complement their pantomimes.

► Have students use paper, markers, tape, and safety scissors to create props, scenery, and costume pieces. If you wish, allow them to use clothing pieces you provide for costumes.

Movement Activity

► Re-form the groups from the **Second Rehearsal.** Have students clear a space for the pantomimes.

► Explain that, for the narrative pantomime, one student in each group will narrate and direct the action, using expressive facial expressions and body language to communicate feelings, while the others safely pantomime character actions as the story is told. Remind them that even though one student will direct the storytelling, they should make decisions together.

► Have each group divide character roles and choose a narrator. Give students time to plan. Remind them to concentrate on physically showing actions, reactions, and any choices of inaction. Have students agree to apply appropriate audience behavior.

► Allow groups to share their narrative pantomimes with the class. Have students compare and contrast the different ideas and how they were shown through movement.

Standards

National Theatre Standard: The student assumes roles that exhibit concentration and contribute to the action of classroom dramatizations based on personal experience and heritage, imagination, literature, and history.

Lesson 6 • Unit Activity

101

Unit Links

Visual Arts: Pattern

Tell students that visual pattern is created by repetition of a motif on a two-dimensional surface. Compare and contrast this with body movement that can form a pattern. Have students choose one character action from their pantomimes and repeat this action to form a rhythmic pattern of movement. If possible, allow students to choose music or sing a song to create a beat for the movement.

Theatrical Arts Connection

Electronic Media Have students view and interact with an interactive computer program or CD-Rom that visually portrays science concepts, such as the movement of the planets around the sun. Discuss how the movement helped them to better understand the science concept being explained. Why do people use such interactive programs? *(to more easily learn about science, to really see things they cannot otherwise see)*

Television Have students discuss the ways in which various cartoons animate objects to make them characters in a story and give them human qualities, such as a train whistle appearing to expand its lungs with air and turning red before screaming out a warning.

Standards

National Theatre Standard: The student analyzes classroom dramatizations and, using appropriate terminology, constructively suggests alternative ideas for dramatizing roles, arranging environments, and developing situations along with means of improving the collaborative process of planning, playing, responding, and evaluating.

Reflect

Time: About 10 minutes

Assessment

▶ Have students evaluate their participation by completing the **Unit 5 Self-Criticism Questions** on page 104.

▶ Use the assessment rubric to evaluate students' participation in the **Unit Activity** and to assess their understanding of movement.

▶ Have students complete the **Unit 5 Quick Quiz** on page 105.

	3 Points	2 Points	1 Point
Perception	Gives full attention to review of unit concepts and vocabulary words. Masters the way people and animal movements convey meaning in real life.	Gives partial attention to review of unit concepts and vocabulary words. Is developing an understanding of the way people and animal movements convey meaning in real life.	Gives minimal attention to review of unit concepts and vocabulary words. Has a minimal understanding of the way people and animal movements convey meaning in real life.
Creative Expression	Participates using varied and distinct facial expressions and movement when pantomiming or narrating a literary selection.	Participates using a few facial expressions and movement when pantomiming or narrating a literary selection.	Shows poor participation when pantomiming a literary selection.
History and Culture	Writes a paragraph that explains why he or she would like to see a theatrical performance of a favorite story, giving three specific details regarding how he or she would like it to be dramatized.	Writes a paragraph that somewhat explains why he or she would like to see a theatrical performance of a favorite story, giving two specific details regarding how he or she would like it to be dramatized.	Writes a paragraph that gives a minimal explanation as to why he or she would like to see a theatrical performance of a favorite story, giving one specific detail regarding its dramatization.
Evaluation	Thoughtfully and honestly evaluates own participation using the four steps of art criticism.	Attempts to evaluate own participation, but shows an incomplete understanding of evaluation criteria.	Makes a minimal attempt to evaluate own participation.

Apply

▶ Children are often very good at reading nonverbal signals. Discuss the various ways in which students use the movements of other people, animals, and objects to interpret various situations and environments; for example, how would they interpret the meaning of a dog wagging its tail with its ears pricked up versus a dog baring its teeth with its tail motionless? *(A dog wagging its tail is probably happy, but a dog that is baring its teeth and not wagging its tail may be angry.)*

▶ Have students identify nonverbal communication from the **Activity.** Discuss situations in which it might be wiser to rely on the actions of people rather than their words to interpret those people's thoughts and feelings.

View a Performance

Movement in Dance

► Discuss appropriate audience behaviors, such as listening quietly, sitting still, and being respectful even if a performance includes things with which students are not familiar. Have students agree to apply this behavior during the performance.

► If you have the *Artsource®* videocassette or DVD, have students view the American Indian Dance Theatre's performances of *Eagle Dance* and *Hoop Dance.* Alternatively, you may share another Native American dance tradition. Explain that many Native American tribes perform eagle dances. The *Hoop Dance* is based on a story about a dying man who uses hoops to teach and tell stories about creatures in the natural world.

► Discuss the performances with students using the following questions:

Describe What types of movement did the dancers use in each dance? *(Some flapped their arms like eagles; the hoop dancer turned while moving the hoops around his body.)*

Analyze What feeling did the *Eagle Dance* create? *(serious, mysterious feeling)* How did the dancers respond to the rhythmic music and chanting? *(They moved in time with it.)* Describe any shapes in the *Hoop Dance* that made you think of creatures in the natural world.

Interpret Compare these dancers' rhythmic movements with character movements you used in the **Activity.**

Decide Would you like to perform this kind of dance? Why or why not?

> "You can throw away the privilege of acting, but that would be such a shame. The tribe has elected you to tell its story. You are the shaman/healer, that's what the storyteller is, and I think it's important for actors to appreciate that."
>
> —Ben Kingsley
> (1943–), actor

LEARN ABOUT
CAREERS IN THEATRE

Explain to students that in the production of both amateur and professional plays, lighting designers use a variety of techniques and colors of light to support and enhance performances. Light can be used in various ways to put emphasis on an actor's movement. Discuss with students where they would use lighting effects in their pantomimes. Would they ever shine a light on one character and not on another? Why or why not? Have students view a taped or live amateur performance, such as a community theatre performance. Discuss the unique challenges amateur lighting designers might face when designing lighting for such a performance.

Standards

National Theatre Standard: The student articulates emotional responses to and explains personal preferences about the whole as well as parts of dramatic performances.

Name _____ Date _____

Unit 5 Self-Criticism Questions

Think about how you participated in the pantomime of "The Box of Robbers." Then answer the questions below.

1. **Describe** What types of movement and facial expressions did you use? If you were the narrator, how did your words lead to movement?

_____

_____

2. **Analyze** How did your group's movements and facial expressions help tell the story and show the characters?

_____

_____

3. **Interpret** How do you use your body and face in real life to show reactions and feelings?

_____

_____

4. **Decide** If you could do this activity again, would you change anything you did? Why or why not?

_____

_____

_____

Unit 5 Quick Quiz

Completely fill in the bubble of the best answer
for each question below.

1. An example of inaction is

   Ⓐ   a character repeating an action.

   Ⓑ   a character using a rhythmic action.

   Ⓒ   a character not moving.

   Ⓓ   a character using dance.

2. Rhythm is

   Ⓕ   any movement onstage.

   Ⓖ   a regular pattern of movements done over
and over.

   Ⓗ   only movement that does not show character.

   Ⓙ   all of the above.

3. A reaction is

   Ⓐ   any action that is done over and over.

   Ⓑ   any movement that has rhythm.

   Ⓒ   always inaction.

   Ⓓ   a response to another character's action.

4. Which sentence is *not* true?

   Ⓕ   Movements can show a character's feelings.

   Ⓖ   Movements sometimes show a character's
actions and reactions.

   Ⓗ   Movements can be done over and over.

   Ⓙ   Movements do not help tell a play's story.

Score _____ (Top Score 4)

UNIT 6

Subject, Mood, and Theme

Unit Overview

Lesson 1 • Subject and the Five Ws The five Ws of a drama help a director determine subject. *Dramatization*

Lesson 2 • Mood and the Five Ws Thinking about the five Ws can help directors understand the mood of a play. *Dramatic Movement*

Lesson 3 • Directors Help Show Theme A director makes sure all elements of a play support its theme. *Dramatization*

Lesson 4 • Characters Show Theme The actions of characters in a plot help communicate theme. *Pantomime*

Lesson 5 • Finding Theme Setting can help support a drama's theme. *Setting*

Lesson 6 • Unit Activity: Scripted Play This activity will give students the opportunity to write and dramatize scripts.

See pages T3–T20 for more about **Theatre Technique Tips.**

Introduce Unit Concepts

"All of the parts of a play help to tell what the play is about. They also show how the playwright wants the reader or audience to feel about this subject." "Todos los componentes de un drama ayudan a decir de que se trata. También muestran como el dramaturgo quiere que el lector o audiencia se sienta sobre este sujeto."

Subject, Mood, and Theme

▶ Explain that a play's subject is usually an abstract idea; for example, the subject of a play version of "Beauty and the Beast" could be "beauty on the inside versus beauty on the outside." Say, "Theme is what a play's story communicates about a subject. What does 'Beauty and the Beast' say about this subject?" *(Inner beauty is most important.)*

▶ Discuss possible moods created by a play about the end of summer. *(sadness because summer is ending; excitement because a new school year is starting)*

Vocabulary

Discuss the following vocabulary words.

subject sujeto—usually an abstract concept, such as *fear* or *truth;* it answers the question, "What is this play about?"

theme tema—an attitude toward a play's subject shown through its action; the basic idea of a play

mood talante—the emotional feeling created by a play

Unit Links

Visual Arts: Harmony, Variety, and Emphasis

▶ Explain to students that artists create harmony by repeating elements such as shape or color and create variety by changing the use of these elements. Discuss how elements in a drama, such as lighting or music, can work together to produce a single, harmonious mood or a variety of moods.

▶ Show students an image of a sculpture, such as *Mountain Man* by Frederic Remington. Have students identify examples of emphasis, or the way the sculpture's shapes to focus their attention.

Reading Theme: Country Life

▶ Discuss books or movies set in the country. What are some possible aspects of country life? *(farms, animals, less pollution, and so on)*

▶ Depending upon where each student lives, have him or her imagine moving from the city to the country or vice versa. Have students improvise a scene about such a move, conveying possible resulting moods, such as excitement or sadness, through tone and movement.

Teacher Background

Background on Subject, Mood, and Theme

The terms *subject* and *theme* are used differently in theatre than in literature. In theatre a play's subject is usually an abstract concept, such as *right versus wrong* or *courage*. Many plays have several subjects that could arguably be correct. In theatre, theme refers to the play's attitude toward the subject. If a play's subject were *power* its theme might be *absolute power corrupts people*. Subject and theme dictate a play's mood, or emotional atmosphere.

Teacher Background on Directing

The director is usually responsible for making the final decision regarding a production's subject, theme, and mood. A director must make a decision about a play's spine, otherwise known as the argument. The spine combines subject and theme and is informed by things such as the Major Dramatic Question and a playwright's other works.

Research in Theatre Education

"Acting out a story produces better understanding than either just talking about it or drawing a picture of what was learned. This meaning-making, through hands-on learning opportunities, is a significant piece of the knowledge-base puzzle on literacy."

—Bruce Wilson

on "The Effect of Dramatic Play on Children's Generation of Cohesive Text" in *Critical Links*

Differentiated Instruction

Reteach
Have students choose a picture book and identify its mood based upon the story and pictures. Have them dramatize this book, using movement and voice to portray this mood.

Challenge
Have students choose a subject, such as kindness, and choose a theme based upon how they feel about this subject, such as, "Being kind is more important than being right." Have students improvise a story based upon this subject and theme.

Special Needs
If students have trouble understanding this unit's concepts, use fables to introduce these concepts. Although a theme and a moral are not synonymous, morals provide practice in thinking about what a story is "saying." Discuss the basic facts of the story and explain how they communicate an idea about life.

Theatre's Effects Across the Curriculum

★ **Reading/Writing**
Writing Process Writing a script gives students the opportunity to follow the steps of the writing process in a theatrical activity.

★ **Math**
Patterns and Relationships When students analyze the themes of stories and dramatizations, they make generalizations from concrete plot and character details.

★ **Science**
Science Concepts When students dramatize stories by acting as animal characters, they consider the physical characteristics of different species when creating movement and speech styles.

★ **Social Studies**
Citizenship When students interpret themes of certain stories, they identify characteristics of good citizenship, such as a belief in justice, truth, and equality.

★ **Music**
Leads and Ensemble As students experience the usefulness of both ensemble and central roles in a drama, they can relate this to opera, in which many people sing in the chorus but some sing the lead.

★ **Dance**
Mood As students explore the effect of mood on a character's posture, movement, and voice, they can relate it to dance movements, which will be altered by a character's intentions and mood.

Objectives

 Perception To connect a story's five *W*s with its subject

 Creative Expression To dramatize and extend a story in a way that shows its five *W*s and its subject

 History and Culture To identify common subjects used by *El Teatro Campesino*

Evaluation To informally evaluate one's own work

Materials

📄 Copies of **"Subject and the Five *W*s"** Warm-Up, p. 109

⭕ Journals or writing paper

Vocabulary

subject

Unit Links

Visual Arts: Harmony
In both art and theatre, harmony is created when related or similar elements give the entire work a feeling of unity. Have students discuss real-life examples of repeated elements or patterns that create harmony, such as patterns on clothing. Compare this to the way actors, visual elements, sound effects, and music must work together to show a play's subject.

Standards

National Theatre Standard: The student collaborates to select interrelated characters, environments, and situations for classroom dramatizations.

Listening/Speaking Standard: The student listens and responds to a variety of oral presentations such as stories, poems, skits, songs, personal accounts, or informational speeches.

Reading Standard: The student retells or acts out the order of important events in stories.

Lesson 1

Subject and the Five *W*s

Focus

Time: About 10 minutes

"In this lesson we will use dramatization to show a story's five *W*s and its subject." *(See page T6 for more about Dramatization.)*

Activate Prior Knowledge

▶ Hand out the **"Subject and the Five *W*s"** Warm-Up. Read the excerpt aloud, and then reread it while students perform a narrative pantomime.

▶ Have students complete the **Warm-Up.** Discuss students' answers, having them support their answers using information from the text. Say, "A play's five *W*s help a director figure out its subject. Subject answers the question, 'What is this play about?' A play about Elnora's problem could be about 'escape.'"

Teach

Time: About 15 minutes

Prepare Divide students into groups of four or five.

Lead Say, "Each group will dramatize the selection from the **Warm-Up,** and then ask 'What if?' to show what happens when Elnora goes to school. The subject of both scenes should still be 'escape.' Decide on the five *W*s of the new scene; how do they relate to the subject? For example, will Elnora's experience of a city school show that she is escaping to a better life or that she is not escaping at all?"

▶ Allow time for planning, giving suggestions as needed.

▶ Have each group perform its dramatization and new scene.

Informal Assessment Did each student participate in a dramatization and help to show its five *W*s and its subject?

History and Culture

Explain that one of the most famous Hispanic American theatre companies was *El Teatro Campesino,* founded in California in 1965 by Luis Valdez. This theatre company originally performed for farm workers. Its plays' subjects related to problems they experienced, such as unfair pay or discrimination. Discuss why people enjoy seeing plays with subjects related to their lives. *(They can learn to deal with similar problems, and so on.)*

Reflect

Time: About 5 minutes

▶ Compare and contrast the way each extension showed the same subject.

Apply

Journal: Inferring

Have students write journal entries describing a possible subject of a favorite movie, using information from the movie's five *W*s to support their idea of subject.

Subject and the Five *W*s

Titles of stories give us clues about the subject.
Read the story beginning, and then write your own
title for this story beginning on the line below.

_____

from *A Girl of the Limberlost* by Gene Stratton Porter (Adapted)

Elnora walked by instinct, for her eyes were blinded with tears. She left the road where it turned south at the corner of the Limberlost, climbed a snake fence, and entered a path worn by her own feet. She followed it around the north end of the swamp and then entered a footpath leading to the city. Again she climbed a fence and was on the open road.

For an instant she leaned against the fence staring before her, then turned and looked back. Behind her lay the land on which she had been born to hard work; before her lay the city through whose schools she hoped to find means of escape and the way to reach the things for which she cared.

Objectives

 Perception To identify ways in which the five *W*s can help one identify mood

 Creative Expression To use dramatic movement to create mood while showing the five *W*s of a scene

 History and Culture To learn about moods often associated with country life and city life in literature and theatre

Evaluation To informally evaluate one's own work

Materials

📄 Copies of "Mood and the Five *W*s" Warm-Up, p. 111

⭕ Journals or writing paper

Vocabulary

mood

Standards

National Theatre Standard: The student collaborates to select interrelated characters, environments, and situations for classroom dramatizations. The student articulates emotional responses to and explains personal preferences about the whole as well as the parts of dramatic performances.

Listening/Speaking Standard: The student makes descriptive presentations that use concrete sensory details to set forth and support unified impressions of people, places, things, or experiences.

Science Standard: The student understands how humans adapt to variations in the physical environment.

Lesson 2 — Mood and the Five *W*s

Focus

Time: About 10 minutes

"In this lesson we will use dramatic movement to show mood and the five *W*s of a scene." (*See page T13 for more about Dramatic Movement.*)

Activate Prior Knowledge

▶ Hand out the **"Mood and the Five *W*s" Warm-Up,** and have students complete it.

▶ Discuss students' answers. Say, "Mood is a feeling shown through a story or image. What mood does each image show? How did the five *W*s help you identify these moods?" (*The images show fear, peace, and anger; the mood was fear because the cat was hiding, and so on.*)

Teach

Time: About 15 minutes

Prepare Divide students into pairs.

Lead

▶ Tell each pair to use dramatic movement to create the five *W*s for a scene that communicates a particular mood, such as fear or sympathy. For example, one pair might show fear by being shipwrecked people struggling ashore in a storm.

▶ Have all pairs simultaneously perform their dramatic movements.

▶ Allow volunteers to share their movements with the class.

Informal Assessment Did each student use dramatic movement to show the mood and five *W*s of a scenario?

🏺 History and Culture

Tell students that the contrast between the stress of city life and the peace of country life has been explored in literature and theatre for hundreds of years. Explain that plays that explore this theme have created country scenes in which the mood is peaceful and happy. Playwrights sometimes use such traditions by ironically creating plays that do not have the traditional mood associated with a setting. Discuss whether students would create a mood of peace in a play set in the country. Why or why not?

Reflect

Time: About 5 minutes

▶ Discuss how their movement created various moods.

Apply

🎮 Journal: Explaining

Have each student write a journal entry explaining whether he or she would prefer to live in the city or the country and why, based on the feeling he or she has about each place.

Unit 6 • **Subject, Mood, and Theme**

Mood and the Five *W*s

Look at each picture below. Write sentences
explaining the *who, what, where, when,* and *why*
for each picture.

_____

_____

_____

_____

_____

_____

Objectives

 Perception To identify the theme of a story

 Creative Expression To act as a director or actor in a dramatization that shows theme

History and Culture To learn about the traditionally negative portrayal of fox characters and identify one such character as an antihero

Evaluation To informally evaluate one's own work

Materials
○ Journals or drawing paper

Vocabulary
theme

Visual Arts: Emphasis
Artwork and plays convey themes. Discuss the ways an artwork can communicate a theme by using emphasis to communicate what an artwork's focus is. Have students compare the ways artists communicate theme with the way they communicated theme in the lesson dramatization.

Standards

National Theatre Standard: The student directs by planning classroom dramatizations.

Listening/Speaking Standard: The student plans and presents dramatic interpretations of experiences, stories, poems, or plays with clear diction, pitch, tempo, and tone.

Social Studies Standard: The student uses problem-solving and decision-making skills, working independently and with others, in a variety of settings.

Lesson 3 Directors Help Show Theme

Focus
Time: About 10 minutes

"In this lesson we will explore how a director helps the actors show theme in a dramatization." *(See page T6 for more about Dramatization.)*

Activate Prior Knowledge
► Read aloud **"Reddy Fox Learns a Trick."** Say, "Imagine this story was performed as a play. One possible subject of this play might be 'survival.' What does the story say about this subject?" *(Older, wiser people can help you learn how to survive.)* Explain that this would be the play's theme, because theme is what the play communicates about its subject. Directors decide on a theme and help actors and designers show it.

Teach
Time: About 25 minutes

Prepare Divide students into groups of four.

Lead
► Have each group divide the roles of Reddy Fox, his grandmother, the dog, and the director. The director in each group should explain to the actors how he or she envisions the setting and movement; the actors should discuss these ideas and work with the director. Allow a few minutes for planning and practice. Each director should make changes to any movements or speech that do not help show theme.

► Have each group member take a turn as director as time allows.

Informal Assessment Did each student show theme by directing and/or acting in dramatizations?

 History and Culture

Point out that unlike this lesson's story, the fox has traditionally been portrayed as a villainous character in European stories. For example, beginning in the twelfth century, French stories were created about Reynard the Fox. Reynard was a treacherous, greedy, and sly character who traveled around causing trouble, but he was portrayed so audiences like him. Explain that this type of character is known as an antihero. Have students identify some modern antiheroes.

Reflect
Time: About 5 minutes

► Discuss whether working with a director helped students show one theme. Why or why not?

Apply

Journal: Explaining
Discuss a movie that students are familiar with. Have students imagine they are directing a new version of that movie; have them explain whether they would change the movie's theme and why.

Reddy Fox Learns a Trick

from *The Adventures of Reddy Fox* by Thornton W. Burgess

Reddy Fox lived with Granny Fox. Granny Fox was the wisest, slyest, smartest fox in all the country round, and now that Reddy had grown so big, she thought it about time that he began to learn the things that every fox should know. So every day she took him hunting with her and taught him all the things that she had learned.

Every day Granny Fox led Reddy Fox over to the long railroad bridge and made him run back and forth across it until he had no fear of it whatever. At first it had made him dizzy, but now he could run across at the top of his speed and not mind it in the least. "I don't see what good it does to be able to run across a bridge; anyone can do that!" exclaimed Reddy one day.

Suddenly Granny Fox lifted her head. "Hark!" she exclaimed.

Reddy pricked up his sharp, pointed ears. Way off back, in the direction from which they had come, they heard the baying of a dog. The voice of the dog grew louder as it drew nearer.

"He certainly is following our track," said Granny Fox. "Now, Reddy, you run across the bridge and watch from the top of the little hill over there. Perhaps I can show you a trick that will teach you why I have made you learn to run across the bridge."

Reddy trotted across the long bridge and up to the top of the hill, as Granny had told him to. Then he sat down to watch. Granny trotted out in the middle of a field and sat down. Pretty soon a young hound broke out of the bushes, his nose in Granny's track.

Then he looked up and saw her, and his voice grew still more savage and eager. Granny Fox started to run as soon as she was sure that the hound had seen her, but she did not run very fast. Reddy did not know what to make of it, for Granny seemed simply to be playing with the hound and not really trying to get away from him at all. Pretty soon Reddy heard another sound. It was a long, low rumble. Then there was a distant whistle. It was a train.

Granny heard it too. As she ran, she began to work back toward the long bridge. The train was in sight now. Suddenly Granny Fox started across the bridge so fast that she looked like a little red streak. The dog was close at her heels when she started and he was so eager to catch her that he didn't see either the bridge or the train. But he couldn't begin to run as fast as Granny Fox. Oh, my, no! When she had reached the other side, he wasn't halfway across, and right behind him, whistling for him to get out of the way, was the train.

The hound gave one frightened yelp, and then he did the only thing he could do; he leaped down, down into the swift water below, and the last Reddy saw of him he was frantically trying to swim ashore.

"Now you know why I wanted you to learn to cross a bridge; it's a very nice way of getting rid of dogs," said Granny Fox, as she climbed up beside Reddy.

Objectives

 Perception To identify how characters help portray the theme of a story

 Creative Expression To use narrative pantomime to portray characters that show theme

 History and Culture To learn that some animals have been traditionally portrayed in stories as good or evil

 Evaluation To informally evaluate one's own work

Materials

📄 Copies of **"Characters Show Theme" Warm-Up,** p. 115

○ Journals or writing paper

Standards

National Theatre Standard: The student assumes roles that exhibit concentration and contribute to the action of classroom dramatizations based on personal experience and heritage, imagination, literature, and history.

Listening/Speaking Standard: The student makes descriptive presentations that use concrete sensory details to set forth and support unified impressions of people, places, things, or experiences.

Science Standard: The student identifies some inherited traits of animals.

Lesson 4

Characters Show Theme

Focus

Time: About 5 minutes

"In this lesson we will use narrative pantomime to explore how characters help show a story's theme." *(See page T3 for more about Pantomime.)*

Activate Prior Knowledge

► Distribute the **"Characters Show Theme" Warm-Up,** and have students complete it. Discuss students' answers. *(Answers should express the wisdom of planning ahead.)*

Teach

Time: About 20 minutes

Prepare Divide students into groups of three.

Lead

► Have each group briefly rewrite "The Ant and the Grasshopper." They may add dialogue, but they should not change the story's theme.

► Have all groups simultaneously perform narrative pantomimes. One student in each group should read the story while the other two perform the narrative pantomime. After each pantomime, the group should discuss how they could emphasize the theme even more, and incorporate these changes while switching roles.

► Have volunteer groups share their pantomimes with the class.

Informal Assessment Did each student read the story and use pantomime to express character actions that helped show theme?

 History and Culture

Tell students that many cultures use animals in folktales that portray morals. Explain that a moral is not the same as a theme; a theme may not necessarily point to a lesson in the way a moral does. Discuss the way animals are given human traits in stories like "The Ant and the Grasshopper." Point out that no variety of animal is inherently good or evil; animals act according to their instincts. Have students discuss reasons why some animals are traditionally portrayed as good or evil, using examples of their natural traits to support their answers.

Reflect

Time: About 5 minutes

► Discuss how each pantomime helped students develop the theme.

Apply

📱 Journal: Modifying

Have students rewrite the story of the "The Ant and the Grasshopper," changing the animals' behavior to match a new theme.

Characters Show Theme

The pictures below tell the fable of the ant and the grasshopper. Look at the subject below. Write this story's theme.

Subject: thinking ahead

Theme: _____

_____

Objectives

 Perception To practice interpreting the theme of a play

 Creative Expression To interpret a play's theme and use scenery to show this theme

 History and Culture To learn about the basis of the Nez Perce legend and consider ways this legend's theme teaches a lesson

 Evaluation To informally evaluate one's own work

Materials

📄 Copies of **"Finding Theme" Warm-Up,** p. 117

○ Two large (at least 4' × 4') sheets of paper, non-toxic markers, and tape

○ Journals or drawing paper

Standards

National Theatre Standard: The student imagines and clearly describes characters, their relationships, and their environments.

Listening/Speaking Standard: The student makes descriptive presentations that use concrete sensory details to set forth and support unified impressions of people, places, things, or experiences.

Social Studies Standard: The student explains the significance of selected individual writers and artists and their stories, poems, statues, paintings, and other examples of cultural heritage to communities around the world.

 Lesson 5 # Finding Theme

Focus

Time: About 5 minutes

"In this lesson we will create scenery to show the theme of a play." *(See page T17 for more about Settings.)*

Activate Prior Knowledge

▶ Hand out copies of the **"Finding Theme" Warm-Up,** and have students follow along as you read it. Have students describe the characters, their relationships, and their setting.

▶ Discuss the story's subject. *(greed or selfishness)* Discuss possible themes. *(Greed will only lead to trouble; selfishness hurts everyone.)*

Teach

Time: About 15 minutes

Prepare Divide students into two groups. Distribute the scenery materials.

Lead Tell students that they are going to create scenery that, rather than being realistic, will show an image that conveys a theme of the script. For example, the scenery could show the Yellow Jacket and Ant rock formation (see **History and Culture**) surrounded by sad faces.

▶ Have each group collaboratively agree on a theme for their dramatization, and create a scenic image that shows this theme.

▶ Have each group tape its scenery to the front of the classroom and perform their dramatization, working to show theme. Have students safely pantomime fighting.

Informal Assessment Did each student help find and illustrate a theme through scenery?

 History and Culture

Explain that this lesson's story is a Nez Perce tribal legend concerning a rock formation in Idaho. Explain that the Nez Perce are a Native American tribe from areas of Idaho and Oregon. Show students images on the Internet of the Ant and Yellow Jacket formation in the Nez Perce National Historical Park. Discuss how this story's theme could be used to teach people how to behave. *(It would remind people not to be selfish.)* Have students think of ways they could incorporate images of this rock formation into their scenery.

Reflect

Time: About 5 minutes

▶ Have students discuss the process of identifying and showing theme.

Apply

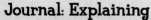 **Journal: Explaining**
Have students write journal entries explaining why they agree or disagree with their group's theme of "Yellow Jacket and Ant."

Finding Theme

Warm-Up

Yellow Jacket and Ant

a Nez Perce folktale

Characters

NARRATORS	**ANT—CHIEF OF ALL ANTS**
YELLOW JACKET—CHIEF OF ALL YELLOW JACKETS	**COYOTE—KING OF ALL ANIMALS**

NARRATOR(S): Long ago yellow jackets and ants did not get along. One day Chief Ant saw Chief Yellow Jacket sitting on a rock eating dried salmon.

YELLOW JACKET: Mmm, mmm.

ANT: Hey! You can't eat there without asking me!

YELLOW JACKET: I have always eaten my dinner here.

ANT: That doesn't matter. Why didn't you ask me?

YELLOW JACKET: None of your business!

ANT: Now you're going to get it!

NARRATOR(S): Yellow Jacket and Ant began to fight. They locked arms and bit and poked and kicked each other. But along came Coyote . . .

COYOTE: Hey! There is plenty of room for everyone. Stop fighting!

NARRATOR(S): Ant and Yellow Jacket heard him, but they kept on fighting.

COYOTE: I'm warning you. Stop fighting now or I will turn you both to stone.

NARRATOR(S): But Ant and Yellow Jacket would not listen. Coyote waved his paws and turned them into stone. You can still see them to this day, frozen because of their greed.

Objectives

 Perception To review concepts related to subject, theme, and mood and relate mood and subject to friendship

 Creative Expression To incorporate subject, theme, and mood in the creation and dramatization of a scripted fable

 History and Culture To learn common themes in African fables and folktales and to learn about African dilemma tales

 Evaluation To thoughtfully and honestly evaluate one's own participation using the four steps of criticism

Materials

○ Pencils and paper, clothing to be used as costumes, face paint, and objects to be used as props

🗐 Copies of the **Unit 6 Self-Criticism Questions**, p. 122

🗐 Copies of the **Unit 6 Quick Quiz**, p. 123

○ *Artsource®* Performing Arts Resource Package (optional)

Standards

National Theatre Standard: The student analyzes classroom dramatizations and, using appropriate terminology, constructively suggests alternative ideas for dramatizing roles, arranging environments, and developing situations along with means of improving the collaborative process of planning, playing, responding, and evaluating.

Unit Activity:
Scripted Play

Focus

Time: About 10 minutes

Review Unit Concepts

"Directors identify a play's subject, its theme, and the moods they wish to create. All aspects of a production must work together to communicate subject, theme, and mood." "Directores identifican el sujeto de un drama, su tema, y los talantes que esperan crear. Todos los aspectos de una producción tienen que trabajar juntos para comunicar sujeto, tema, y talante."

► Review with students the different ways in which they identified and conveyed subject, theme, and mood in this unit.

► Review the unit vocabulary on page 106.

 History and Culture

Tell students that many African fables and folktales associate certain animals with certain themes. For example, in one common tale the lion, the king of beasts, allows his victims to go free out of kindness, and then he is rewarded in some way by his good deed. Another type of tale told in many parts of Africa is the dilemma tale, which is deliberately told without an ending. The audience discusses and decides what the ending should be based on their interpretation of the theme of the unfinished story. Dilemma tales therefore have different endings according to different interpretations of the theme. After students have completed the **Activity,** have volunteers share their scripts with the class, leaving out the stories' endings. Have the rest of the class decide another way each story might end based on its theme.

Classroom Management Tips

The following are tips for managing your classroom during the **Rehearsals** and **Activity:**

✔ **Writing Process Reminders** If students become discouraged or distracted while working on their scripts, remind them of what is involved with the steps of prewriting, drafting, and revising. Use this activity as an opportunity to reinforce proper writing habits. Use the opportunity to compare the creative drama process with the creative writing process.

✔ **Take an Active Role** Participate in brainstorming sessions if students are having trouble thinking of original ideas.

✔ **Encourage Creativity** Tell students to think about how each animal in their fable is traditionally portrayed in stories and to make choices that do not follow these traditions. Instead, encourage them to give their animal characters unique personalities.

Teach

First Rehearsal

► Divide students into groups of three or four.

► Tell students that each group is going to work together to make up a fable to be dramatized. Review with students the elements of fables: they are short stories that often have animal characters and their themes convey a moral or lesson in life. Tell students that they will all use the subject "friendship," and that each fable should be set in the country, but that each group may decide its fable's theme and mood. *(See page T10 for more about Script Writing.)*

► Have each group complete prewriting and drafting activities by choosing a moral (or theme), thinking of animal characters, and then improvising situations in which their characters explore the subject of friendship while interacting with movement and dialogue.

► Have students choose one of their improvised ideas. Discuss aspects of blocking, or planned movement, that students can include in their scripts. Show students an example of a simple script, such as the script on page 117, and have each group write a quick draft of their short script, using the example as a model. Have students turn in their drafts; review them for aspects of theme and mood before the **Second Rehearsal.**

Second Rehearsal

► Have students re-form their groups from the **First Rehearsal.** Distribute each group's scripts with your comments, and have students make changes based upon these comments.

► Have each group decide which characters they will play and discuss the ways in which they will dramatize their script, including characters' positioning and movement, vocal expression, and simple costumes and props. One member of each group should act as the director and, if needed, the narrator.

► Have the groups rehearse their plays, and then make any content changes that they think are necessary. Have them check their scripts for spelling and grammar mistakes.

Subject, Mood, and Theme Activity

► Have students make room in the classroom for their performances.

► Allow a few minutes for students to prepare any costumes and props.

► Have each group come forward and perform their play while other students apply appropriate audience behavior.

► Have the class identify each scripts' theme and the mood the performance created, and then have them share what they liked best about each script and constructively suggest ways in which the script could be improved.

Standards

National Theatre Standard: The student improvises dialogue to tell stories, and formalizes improvisations by writing or recording the dialogue.

Visual Arts: Variety

Different elements of theatre and visual art work together to communicate a feeling or mood. Have students identify the moods of each script from the **Activity,** and then have them discuss the ways in which the different elements in each of their scripted performances worked together. Compare this use of variety with the use of variety in art, such as different textures pasted into a collage or the use of complimentary colors to create visual interest.

Theatrical Arts Connection

Electronic Media Have students view an appropriate interactive Web site with many visual elements. Have students identify the mood these elements create. How does this mood relate to the focus of the Web site? What is the role of such electronic media in modern America? *(to inform while entertaining)*

Film Have students view the climax or high point of an appropriate film with which they are not familiar. Discuss the mood at this point of the movie; does a film's high point usually create an excited or tense mood? Have students guess one of the film's subjects and themes based on this excerpt.

Standards

National Theatre Standard: The student compares and connects art forms by describing theatre, dramatic media (such as film, television, and electronic media), and other art forms.

Reflect

Time: About 10 minutes

Assessment

▶ Have students evaluate their participation by completing the **Unit 6 Self-Criticism Questions** on page 122.

▶ Use the assessment rubric to evaluate students' participation in the **Unit Activity** and to assess their understanding of subject, mood, and theme.

▶ Have students complete the **Unit 6 Quick Quiz** on page 123.

	3 Points	2 Points	1 Point
Perception	Gives full attention to review. Has mastered an understanding of the way mood and subject are used with respect to friendship.	Gives partial attention to review. Is developing an understanding of the way mood and subject are used with respect to friendship.	Gives minimal attention to review. Has a minimal understanding of the way mood and subject are used with respect to friendship.
Creative Expression	Fully participates in all of the following: prewriting, drafting, rehearsing, revising, and performing a script.	Participates in four of the following: prewriting, drafting, rehearsing, revising, and performing a script.	Participates in three of the following: prewriting, drafting, rehearsing, revising, and performing a script.
History and Culture	Masters the ability to infer a new ending for a script based on its theme.	Is developing the ability to infer a new ending for a script based on its theme.	Minimally infers a new ending for a script based on its theme.
Evaluation	Thoughtfully and honestly evaluates own participation using the four steps of art criticism.	Attempts to evaluate own participation, but shows an incomplete understanding of evaluation criteria.	Makes a minimal attempt to evaluate own participation.

Apply

▶ Discuss the mood created by different types of music and sounds in real life, and the way advertisers use these moods to their advantage. For example, discuss the types of music played in different stores. How do they affect people who are shopping there? *(They make people feel happy; they make people want to stay; and so on.)*

▶ Have students discuss the subjects of national holidays, such as Thanksgiving or the Fourth of July. What symbols are used to represent these holidays and their subjects? *(Thanksgiving's subject is thankfulness; the Fourth of July has a subject of patriotism; Thanksgiving symbols include turkeys and harvest baskets; Fourth of July symbols include flags and fireworks.)*

View a Performance

Subject, Mood, and Theme in Dance

▶ Discuss appropriate audience behaviors, such as listening quietly, sitting still, and being respectful. Have students agree to apply this behavior during the performance.

▶ If you have the **Artsource®** videocassette or DVD, have students view "Isicathulo (Gum Boot Dance)" performed by the African American Dance Ensemble in South Africa.

▶ Discuss the performance with students using the following questions:

Describe What movements did the performers use? *(clapping, jumping and turning, and so on.)* Describe the music. *(drumbeats, fast)* How did the performers use their voices? *(They called out and chanted.)*

Analyze How did the music create mood? *(It made the dance seem exciting and energetic.)* Describe the dancers' characters. *(One dancer acted as though she didn't know how to dance, and the others pretended to teach it to her.)* What subjects or themes could the dance be communicating, based on the dancers' character interaction? *(learning; it is fun to learn a new dance, and so on.)*

Interpret Have you seen other dances that are similar to this dance? Describe and compare them with this dance.

Decide What was your favorite part of the dance? How could the dancers have shown another theme by changing their movements?

"No one makes you write plays: the world could sort of get along without me turning out a play every year, so I do this because I enjoy it enormously."

—Terrance McNally
(1939–), playwright

LEARN ABOUT
CAREERS IN THEATRE

Tell students that a person who writes plays is called a playwright. Explain that playwrights are different from other types of writers because they write stories for the purpose of being performed in a theatre. As they write, playwrights envision their works being performed onstage. Although other types of written works are successfully performed onstage, they were written for the purpose of being read by individual readers. Many playwrights first write their plays, and then see if anyone is willing to produce them, although theatres sometimes ask playwrights to write plays.

Standards

National Theatre Standard: The student compares and connects art forms by describing theatre, dramatic media (such as film, television, and electronic media), and other art forms.

Unit 6 Self-Criticism Questions

Think about how you created and performed a
script for a play. Then answer the questions below.

1. **Describe** What was the plot of your script? Describe
   the characters and their relationships.

   _____

   _____

2. **Analyze** How did your script show a theme and mood?

   _____

   _____

3. **Interpret** Do you think this script's theme could help
   someone live a better life? How could it do this?

   _____

   _____

4. **Decide** If you could rewrite your script, would
   you change anything? Why or why not?

   _____

   _____

   _____

Unit 6 • **Subject, Mood, and Theme**

Name _____ Date _____

Unit 6 Quick Quiz

Completely fill in the bubble of the best answer
for each question below.

1. The subject of a play is
- Ⓐ its main character.
- Ⓑ where the characters are.
- Ⓒ a type of scenery.
- Ⓓ what the play is about.

2. The theme of a play is
- Ⓕ all of the actions of the characters.
- Ⓖ the basic or main idea of a play.
- Ⓗ a feeling created through music.
- Ⓙ all of the above.

3. A director can help actors show
- Ⓐ theme.
- Ⓑ mood.
- Ⓒ subject.
- Ⓓ all of the above.

4. Which sentence is *not* true?
- Ⓕ Characters' actions and words help show
       a play's theme.
- Ⓖ Theme can be shown through scenery.
- Ⓗ Mood is a feeling created by a play.
- Ⓙ A story or dramatic activity has either
       a subject or a theme.

Score _____ (Top Score 4)

Kotick Saves the Seals

from "The White Seal" in *The Jungle Book*

by Rudyard Kipling

Activity Story

When Kotick the white seal sees his friends being hunted and killed by men, he knows he must do something to stop it. His father, Sea Catch, tells him that the only way to save the seals is to find the island where no men ever come. Kotick is told by a walrus to go and ask the Sea Cow about this island. By following the Sea Cow, Kotick finds the island and rushes back to tell the other seals.

Sea Catch, his father, and all the other seals laughed at Kotick when he told them what he had discovered, and a young seal about his own age said, "This is all very well, Kotick, but you can't come from no one knows where and order us off like this. Remember we've been fighting for our nurseries, and that's a thing you never did. You preferred prowling about in the sea."

The other seals laughed at this, and the young seal began twisting his head from side to side. He had just married that year, and was making a great fuss about it.

"I've no nursery to fight for," said Kotick. "I only want to show you all a place where you will be safe. What's the use of fighting?"

"Oh, if you're trying to back out, of course I've no more to say," said the young seal with an ugly chuckle.

"Will you come with me if I win?" said Kotick. And a green light came into his eye, for he was very angry at having to fight at all.

"Very good," said the young seal carelessly. "If you win, I'll come."

He had no time to change his mind, for Kotick's head was out and his teeth sunk in the blubber of the young seal's neck. Then he threw himself back on his haunches and hauled his enemy down the beach, shook

Unit Links Reading: Friendship

Copyright © SRA/McGraw-Hill. Permission is granted to reproduce this page for classroom use.

him, and knocked him over. Then Kotick roared to the seals: "I've done my best for you these five seasons past. I've found you the island where you'll be safe, but unless your heads are dragged off your silly necks you won't believe. I'm going to teach you now. Look out for yourselves!"

Kotick flung himself at the biggest sea catch he could find, caught him by the throat, choked him and bumped him and banged him till he grunted for mercy, and then threw him aside and attacked the next. His curly white mane stood up with rage, and his eyes flamed, and his big dog teeth glistened, and he was splendid to look at. Old Sea Catch, his father, saw him tearing past, and Sea Catch gave a roar and shouted: "He may be a fool, but he is the best fighter on the beaches! Don't tackle your father, my son! He's with you!"

Kotick roared in answer, and old Sea Catch waddled in with his mustache on end. It was a gorgeous fight, for the two fought as long as there was a seal that dared lift up his head,

and when there were none they paraded grandly up and down the beach side by side, bellowing.

At night, just as the Northern Lights were winking and flashing through the fog, Kotick climbed a bare rock and looked down on the scattered nurseries and seals.

"Now," he said, "I've taught you your lesson."

"My wig!" said old Sea Catch, boosting himself up stiffly. "The Killer Whale himself could not have cut them up worse. Son, I'm proud of you, and what's more, I'll come with you to your island—if there is such a place."

"Who comes with me to the Sea Cow's tunnel? Answer, or I shall teach you again," roared Kotick.

There was a murmur like the ripple of the tide all up and down the beaches. "We will come," said thousands of tired voices. "We will follow Kotick, the White Seal."

Then Kotick dropped his head between his shoulders and shut his eyes proudly.

A week later he and his army (nearly ten thousand seals) went away north to the Sea Cow's tunnel, Kotick leading them, and the seals that stayed at Novastoshnah called them idiots. But next spring, when they all met off the fishing banks of the Pacific, Kotick's seals told such tales of the new beaches beyond Sea Cow's tunnel that more and more seals left Novastoshnah. Year after year more seals went away from Novastoshnah, and Lukannon, and the other nurseries, to the quiet, sheltered beaches where Kotick sits all the summer through, getting bigger and fatter and stronger each year in that sea where no man comes.

Unit Links Reading: Friendship

The Mitten

a Ukrainian folktale

Activity Story

A man was walking through the city park one snowy, winter day with his dog. His mittens hung out of his pockets, and as he walked along, one mitten fell out of his pocket onto the snow.

A mouse came scuttling up and when it saw the mitten it stopped, climbed right in, and said:

"Hmm, this mitten is nice and warm. I will live here."

After a while a Frog came hopping up and when he saw the mitten he stopped and called out:

"Croak! Croak! Who is living in this mitten?"

"I am Crunch-Munch the Mouse. And who are you?"

"I'm Hop-Stop the Frog and I'm freezing cold. Please can I come in?"

"Alright," the Mouse said, "Jump on in!"

So the Frog jumped in and the Mouse moved over and the two of them made their home in the mitten.

After a while a Rabbit came scurrying up and when he saw the mitten he stopped and called out:

"Hello there! Who is living in this mitten?"

"We are Crunch-Munch the Mouse and Hop-Stop the Frog. And who are you?"

"I'm Fleet-Feet the Rabbit. May I join you?"

"Alright," the Mouse and Frog said, "Jump in!"

So the Rabbit jumped in and the Mouse and the Frog moved over and the three of them made their home in the mitten.

After a while a Fox came scampering up. "You-hoo! Who is living in this mitten?"

"We are Crunch-Munch the Mouse, Hop-Stop the Frog, and Fleet-Feet the Rabbit. And who are you?"

"I'm Smily-Wily the Fox. Won't you make room for me?"

So the Mouse and the Frog and the Rabbit moved over and the Fox climbed in and the four of them made their home in the mitten.

After a while a wolf came stalking up and when he saw the mitten he stopped and called out:

"Hello, friends! Who is living in this mitten?"

"We are," said Crunch-Munch the Mouse, Hop-Stop the Frog, Fleet-Feet the Rabbit, and Smily-Wily the Fox. "And who are you?"

"I'm Howly-Prowly the Wolf, and I mean to get in!"

"Very well. Go ahead!"

So the Wolf climbed in and the Mouse and the Frog and the Rabbit and the Fox moved over and the five of them made their home in the mitten.

After a while a wild Boar came sauntering up.

"Grunt! Grunt! Who is living in this mitten?"

"We are," said Crunch-Munch the Mouse, Hop-Stop the Frog, Fleet-Feet the Rabbit, Smily-Wily the Fox and Howly-Prowly the Wolf. "And who are you?"

"I'm Snout-Rout the Boar. And I'm sure you want me too."

"Dear, dear!" they said. "Everybody wants to get into this mitten. You won't find it easy to get in, Snout-Rout!"

"Never mind! I'll manage!"

"In you go, then! But don't say we didn't warn you!"

So the Boar squeezed in and then there were six of them in the mitten and they were so cramped that they could not move!

By and by with a crackling of twigs a bear came lumbering up and when he saw the mitten he stopped and bellowed:

"Hello, good people! Who is living in this mitten?"

"We are," said Crunch-Munch the Mouse, Hop-Stop the Frog, Fleet-Feet the Rabbit, Smily-Wily the Fox, Howly-Prowly the Wolf, and Snout-Rout the Boar. "And who are you?"

"Ho, ho, ho! I'm Grumbly-Rumbly the Bear. And though you're quite a crowd, I know you'll make room for me!"

"How can we? We're cramped as it is!"

"Where there's a will, there's a way!"

"Oh, all right, edge in, but don't forget that you're not the only one."

So the Bear squeezed in, too, and now there were seven of them inside and they were so cramped that the mitten was fit to burst.

It was just about then that the Old Man missed his mitten and decided to go back in search of it. He walked and he walked and his Dog ran and ran until at last he saw the mitten lying in the snow and moving!

"Bow-wow-wow!" went the Dog.

And the seven friends inside the mitten were so frightened that they all tried to jump out at once. The mitten burst apart, and away they ran as fast as their legs could carry them!

Then the Old Man came up and he picked up the pieces of his mitten and that was the end of that.

Unit Links Reading: City Wildlife

The Rubber Man

a Ghanian folktale

Anansi the spider was very lazy and he loved to trick people. Every morning he told his wife, "Today I am going to work my farm." But he did not go to the farm. He did not even have a farm! Instead, he went to the forest and slept all day in the cool, cool shade of an *iroko* tree.

"Do you need help with your farming?" his wife asked.

"No, no!" said Anansi. "I do not need help."

"Do you need help with your planting?" his neighbors asked.

"No, no!" Anansi said. "My farm is not yet ready."

One day Anansi said to his wife, "Go to the village and buy me some nuts to plant on my farm. I need a bag of nuts for my planting."

Full of joy, his wife rushed to the village and bought Anansi a big bag of nuts. The next day Anansi took the bag of nuts into the forest. He settled himself in the cool, cool shade of an *iroko* tree, ate some nuts, and slept. "This is the life!" he thought to himself as he went home.

For many days, Anansi left early in the morning, and ate nuts and slept all day. He would go home to his wife in the evening, saying, "Ahh, how hard I have worked today! You are lucky you have such an easy life—staying in the cool house all day long. What I need now is a nice, big meal."

Soon Anansi's neighbors began to harvest their nut crops, and they brought home big baskets of nuts from their farms. "When will you harvest our nut crop?" his wife asked him. "Do you want me to help you?"

"No, no!" Anansi said quickly, "I will bring them home myself in a few days," and he hurried out the door. But Anansi was worried. How could he bring home a crop of nuts? He did not have any nuts! He did not even have a farm!

Anansi thought and thought all day in the cool, cool shade of an *iroko* tree, until suddenly he had an idea. "I will steal some nuts!" he said to himself. "I will steal some nuts from the chief's farm!"

That night, while his wife was sleeping, Anansi snuck out and went to the chief's farm. Now the chief's farm was very large and full of all kinds of crops, but largest and best

Unit Links   Reading: Imagination

Copyright © SRA/McGraw-Hill. Permission is granted to reproduce this page for classroom use.

of all was his nut crop. Anansi filled a big bag full of nuts from the nut trees, hid it in the forest, and snuck back home.

"Today I shall bring home some nuts," he told his wife. She was very happy, of course, and made Anansi a large and tasty breakfast. Anansi ate breakfast, went out to the forest, and sat all day in the cool, cool shade of an *iroko* tree. That night he brought some of the nuts home, moaning, "How tired I am from all that work!"

This went on for many days, but soon Anansi was out of nuts again, so once more he snuck out in the night and went to the chief's farm. This time, while Anansi was filling his bag full of nuts from the nut trees, one of the chief's servants saw him.

"I must find a way to catch this thief," the servant thought, and he had an idea. The servant went to the forest to find some *gutts-percha* trees. He made a sticky brown rubber man out of *gutts-percha* sap and set the rubber man out near the nut trees on the chief's farm.

Soon Anansi was out of nuts again, so he snuck out in the middle of the night and went to the chief's farm. Near the nut trees, he saw the shape of a man in the darkness.

"Who are you?" Anansi whispered.

The rubber man said nothing.

"Come now, do not be rude. Tell me what you are doing here!" Anansi whispered again, growing angry.

The rubber man said nothing.

"Why will you not answer me?" Anansi cried out, and he hit the rubber man on the head. His hand was stuck!

"Let go of my hand!" he cried, and he pushed the rubber man's arm, but now his other hand was stuck! Anansi kept pushing and kicking the rubber man until he could not move anymore.

"Now everyone will know I was the thief," Anansi thought miserably, but there was nothing he could do about it.

Poor Anansi! The next morning, the servant brought Anansi before the chief, and the chief told the whole village about Anansi's lies.

Anansi the spider was so embarrassed that he went and hid in a dark place and did not speak to anybody, and this is why spider's children and his children's children and his children's children's children always hide in dark places.

Unit Links Reading: Imagination

Wishing for Gold

Activity Story

from *Five Children and It*
by E. Nesbit; adapted and retold as Reader's Theatre

Characters

NARRATOR(S)

THE PSAMMEAD—
a sand fairy. Sand fairies
have eyes like snail's
eyes, ears like bat's ears,
and a lot of brown fur.

CYRIL—the oldest
boy; 12

ANTHEA—the oldest
girl; 11

ROBERT—the middle
boy; 10

JANE—the youngest
girl; 9

MARTHA—their
nursemaid or nanny

THE BABY—their baby
brother; nicknamed
"The Lamb" (does
not speak)

MR. PEASEMARSH—
a man who sells
horses in the town
of Rochester

WILLIAM—works for
Mr. Peasemarsh

A POLICEMAN

Cyril, Anthea, Robert, and Jane are brothers and sisters who go to spend a summer in the country. One day, while they are playing in a sand pit, they find a strange looking creature called a Psammead (pronounced "Sam-ee-ad")—or sand fairy—who gives them a new wish every day. Each wish, however, only lasts until the sun sets.

The children are very happy, and they begin to make wishes. But no matter what they wish for, something always seems to go wrong . . .

NARRATOR(S):	Cyril, Anthea, Robert, and Jane woke up and were very happy. They could not wait to make a new wish!
MARTHA:	Now I'm going to take the baby with me to town. Please be good for the other servants while I'm gone.
NARRATOR(S):	The four children ran to the sand pit. They dug in the sand until they found the sand fairy. He seemed cranky.
PSAMMEAD:	*(yawning)* Well, all right. What's today's wish going to be?
ROBERT:	Can we ask for a little wish first?
PSAMMEAD:	What is it?
ROBERT:	We don't want the servants to be able to see the gifts you give us.
NARRATOR(S):	The Psammead swelled himself out, and then said—
PSAMMEAD:	That was easy. What's the next wish?
ROBERT:	We want to be rich.
PSAMMEAD:	It won't do you much good, you know. How much do you want? Do you want it in gold or paper money?

Unit Links Reading: Money

ROBERT:	Gold, please—and millions of it.
PSAMMEAD:	Well, get out of the sand-pit, or you will be buried alive.
NARRATOR(S):	The children ran out to the road. When they looked back, they had to shut their eyes because the gold was as bright as the sun! The sand-pit was full of gold coins. Jane picked up one.
JANE:	It's not like our money.
CYRIL:	Well, it's still gold. Let's fill our pockets. We need to use the money before sunset. I'll tell you what, there's a pony and cart in the village. We'll pay for a ride to the town of Rochester. Then we'll buy lots of things.
NARRATOR(S):	They all filled their pockets with gold and set off. The gold was very heavy. When they came to an inn, they said Cyril should go in and buy them ginger-ale to drink. The others sat in the sun and waited.
ROBERT:	Oh, drat! How hot it is!
ANTHEA:	There's Cyril with the ginger-ale!

CYRIL:	They wouldn't take the gold. I had to buy the ginger-ale with my own money.
ANTHEA:	It's my turn now to try to buy something with the money. I'm next oldest. Where is the pony-cart kept?
NARRATOR(S):	Anthea went to find the man who kept the pony-cart. She was back soon.
ANTHEA:	I only showed the driver one gold coin. I told him it was mine, and asked if he would drive us to Rochester for it. And he said, "Right-oh."
NARRATOR(S):	It was very nice to be driven in a pony-cart. When they got to town, they found out that getting the fairy money was easy, but using it was hard.
ANTHEA:	I tried to buy a new hat. The lady told me my gold coins were no good. She seemed to think I'd stolen them.
JANE:	I tried to buy cotton gloves and a purse, but the woman in the shop would not take the gold.
ROBERT:	I tried to buy toys and books, but no one wanted my gold.

NARRATOR(S):	Finally, Anthea said they should go buy a horse and cart.
ROBERT:	I hear you have horses and carts for sale.
MR. PEASEMARSH:	That is true.
ROBERT:	We would like to buy some, please.
MR. PEASEMARSH:	*(laughs)* Oh you would, would you?
ROBERT:	Show us a few horses, please.
NARRATOR(S):	The children did not like the way Mr. Peasemarsh laughed at this. He called to his partner—
MR. PEASEMARSH:	Oh William!
WILLIAM:	Yes, Mr. Peasemarsh?
MR. PEASEMARSH:	Look at this young duke. Want's to buy all our horses and hasn't a penny.
NARRATOR(S):	Anthea and Jane wanted to leave, but Robert was mad.
ROBERT:	I'm not a young duke, and as for a penny, what do you call this?
NARRATOR(S):	And he pulled out two fat handfuls of gold coins. Mr. Peasemarsh grabbed one coin and looked at it.

Unit Links Reading: Money

MR. PEASEMARSH: Shut the door, William. Go and get the police.

NARRATOR(S): William went. The children were very scared.

MR. PEASEMARSH: Now then—where did you get the gold?

JANE: It's ours. A fairy gave it to us.

MR. PEASEMARSH: A fairy? Go on, now.

ROBERT: No, it's true.

NARRATOR(S): William came back with a policeman.

POLICEMAN: Well, come along, children. Don't make a fuss.

NARRATOR(S): The four children were taken along the streets of Rochester. Tears of anger filled their eyes. Suddenly, they heard someone they knew—

MARTHA: Well, if ever I did! Oh Robert, whatever have you done?

NARRATOR: It was Martha and the baby! Martha, of course, could not see the gold coins. The children had wished that the servants would not see any of the sand fairy's gifts.

MARTHA: I don't see nothing. There's no gold there—only the poor child's hands.

Unit Links Reading: Money

NARRATOR:	Just then the sun set, and all of the coins disappeared.
POLICEMAN:	What! Turn out your pockets!
NARRATOR:	They did but their pockets were empty.
MARTHA:	It's time I took these poor children home. I told you they did not have any gold!
NARRATOR:	Martha got a cart and they rode back home together. She was angry with them for going to Rochester alone, and told them they could not go out the next day. And so after one day of being rich, the children were left with nothing.

The Box of Robbers

from *American Fairy Tales* by L. Frank Baum (Adapted)

Martha is left with a maid one afternoon. When the maid goes out for a moment, Martha goes into the attic to find a doll's playhouse and finds a mysterious chest belonging to her uncle. She finds an old key and unlocks the chest.

With a cry of joy Martha turned the key with both hands; then she heard a sharp "click," and the next moment the heavy lid flew up of its own accord!

The little girl leaned over the edge of the chest an instant, and the sight that met her eyes caused her to start back in amazement.

Slowly and carefully a man unpacked himself from the chest, stepped out upon the floor, stretched his limbs and then took off his hat and bowed politely to the astonished child. He was tall and thin and his face seemed badly tanned or sunburnt.

Then another man emerged from the chest, yawning and rubbing his eyes like a sleepy schoolboy. He was of middle size and his skin seemed as badly tanned as that of the first.

While Martha stared open-mouthed at the remarkable sight a third man crawled from the chest. He had the same complexion as his fellows, but was short and wide.

All three were dressed in a curious manner. They wore short jackets of red velvet braided with gold, and knee breeches of sky-blue satin with silver buttons. Over their stockings were laced wide ribbons of red and yellow and blue, while their hats had broad brims with high, peaked crowns, from which fluttered yards of bright-colored ribbons.

They had big gold rings in their ears and rows of knives and pistols in their belts. Their eyes were black and glittering and they wore long, fierce mustaches, curling at the ends like a pig's tail.

"My! but you were heavy," exclaimed the short one, when he had pulled down his velvet jacket and brushed the dust from his sky-blue breeches. "And you squeezed me all out of shape."

"It was unavoidable, Lugui," responded the thin man, lightly; "the lid of the chest pressed me down upon you. Yet I tender you my regrets."

"As for me," said the middle-sized man, "you must agree I have been your nearest friend for years; so do not be disagreeable."

"Who are you?" asked Martha, who until now had been too astonished to be frightened.

"Permit us to introduce ourselves," said the thin man, flourishing his hat gracefully. "This is Lugui," the short man nodded; "and this is Beni," the middle-sized man bowed; "and I am Victor. We are three bandits."

"Bandits!" cried Martha, with a look of horror.

"Exactly. Perhaps in all the world there are not three other bandits so terrible and fierce as ourselves," said Victor, proudly.

"'Tis so," said the short man, nodding gravely.

"But it's wicked!" exclaimed Martha.

"Yes, indeed," replied Victor. "We are extremely and tremendously wicked. Perhaps in all the world you could not find three men more wicked than those who now stand before you."

"'Tis so," said the short man, approvingly.

"But you shouldn't be so wicked," said the girl; "it's—it's—naughty!"

Victor cast down his eyes and blushed.

"Naughty!" gasped Beni, with a horrified look.

"'Tis a hard word," said Lugui, sadly, and buried his face in his hands.

"I little thought," murmured Victor, in a voice broken by emotion, "ever to be so reviled—and by a lady! Yet, perhaps you spoke thoughtlessly. You must consider, miss, that our wickedness has an excuse. For how are we to be bandits, let me ask, unless we are wicked?"

Martha was puzzled and shook her head, thoughtfully. Then she remembered something.

"You can't remain bandits any longer," said she, "because you are now in America."

"America!" cried the three, together.

"Certainly. You are on Prairie avenue, in Chicago. Uncle Walter sent you here in this chest."

The bandits seemed greatly confused by this. Lugui sat down on an old chair with a broken rocker and wiped his forehead with a yellow silk handkerchief. Beni and Victor fell back upon the chest and looked at her with pale faces and staring eyes.

When he had somewhat recovered himself Victor spoke.

"Your Uncle Walter has greatly wronged us," he said, reproachfully. "He has brought us to a strange country where we shall not know whom to rob or how much to ask for a ransom."

"'Tis so!" said the short man, slapping his leg sharply.

"Perhaps Uncle Walter wanted to reform you," suggested Martha.

"Are there, then, no bandits in Chicago?" asked Victor.

"Well," replied the girl, blushing in her turn, "we do not call them bandits."

"Then what shall we do for a living?" inquired Beni, despairingly.

"A great deal can be done in a big American city," said the child. "My father is a lawyer and my mother's cousin is a police inspector."

"Ah," said Victor, "that is a good employment. The police need to be inspected."

"Then you could do other things," continued Martha, encouragingly. "You could be motor men on trolley cars, or clerks in a department store. Some people even become aldermen to earn a living."

The bandits shook their heads sadly.

"We are not fitted for such work," said Victor. "Our business is to rob."

Martha tried to think.

"It is rather hard to get positions in the gas office," she said, "but you might become politicians."

"No!" cried Beni, with sudden fierceness; "we must not abandon our high calling. Bandits we have always been, and bandits we must remain!"

"'Tis so!" agreed the short man.

"Even in Chicago there must be people to rob," remarked Victor, with cheerfulness.

Martha was distressed.

"I think they have all been robbed," she objected.

"Then we can rob the robbers, for we have experience and talent beyond the ordinary," said Beni.

"Oh, dear; oh, dear!" moaned the girl; "why did Uncle Walter ever send you here in this chest?"

The bandits became interested.

"That is what we should like to know," declared Victor, eagerly.

"But no one will ever know, for Uncle Walter was lost in Africa," she continued, with conviction.

"Then we must accept our fate and rob to the best of our ability," said Victor. "So long as we are faithful to our beloved profession we need not be ashamed."

"'Tis so!" cried the short man. "Brothers! We will begin now. Let us rob the house we are in."

"Good!" shouted the others and sprang to their feet.

Beni turned threatingly upon the child.

"Remain here!" he commanded. "If you stir one step your blood will be on your own head!" Then he added, in a gentler voice: "Don't be afraid; that's the way all bandits talk to their captives. But of course we wouldn't hurt a young lady under any circumstances."

"Of course not," said Victor. "S'blood!" he cried fiercely.

"S'bananas!" cried Beni, in a terrible voice.

"Confusion to our foes!" hissed Victor.

And then the three bent themselves nearly double and crept stealthily down the stairway with cocked pistols in their hands and glittering knives between their teeth, leaving Martha trembling with fear and too horrified to even cry for help.

How long she remained alone in the attic she never knew, but finally she heard the catlike tread of the returning bandits and saw them coming up the stairs in single file.

All bore heavy loads of plunder in their arms, and Lugui was balancing a mince pie on the top of a pile of her mother's best evening dresses. Victor came next with an armful of bric-a-brac, a brass candelabra, and the parlor clock. Beni had the basket of silverware from the sideboard, a copper kettle, and papa's fur overcoat.

"We have much wealth," said Victor, holding the mince pie while Lugui added his spoils to the heap; "and all from one house! This America must be a rich place."

He then cut himself a piece of the pie and handed the remainder to his comrades. Whereupon all three sat upon the floor and consumed the pie while Martha looked on sadly.

"We should have a cave," remarked Beni; "for we must store our plunder in a safe place. Can you tell us of a secret cave?" he asked Martha.

"There's a Mammoth cave," she answered, "but it's in Kentucky. You would have to ride on a train a long time to get there."

The three bandits looked thoughtful and munched their pie silently, but the next moment they were startled by the ringing of the electric doorbell, which was heard plainly even in the remote attic.

"What's that?" demanded Victor, in a hoarse voice, as the three scrambled to their feet.

Martha ran to the window and saw it was only the postman, who had dropped a letter in the box and gone away again. But she had an idea of how to get rid of her troublesome bandits, so she cried out:

"It's the police!"

The robbers looked at one another with genuine alarm, and Lugui asked, tremblingly, "Are there many of them?"

"A hundred and twelve!" exclaimed Martha, after pretending to count them.

"Then we are lost!" declared Beni; "for we could never fight so many and live."

The three wicked ones groaned aloud.

Suddenly Martha turned from the window.

"You are my friends, are you not?" she asked.

"We are devoted!" answered Victor.

"We adore you!" cried Beni.

"We would die for you!" added Lugui, thinking he was about to die anyway.

"Then I will save you," said the girl.

"How?" asked the three, with one voice.

"Get back into the chest," she said. 'I will then close the lid, so they will be unable to find you."

They looked around the room in a dazed and irresolute way, but she exclaimed:

"You must be quick! They will soon be here to arrest you."

Then Lugui sprang into the chest and lay flat upon the bottom. Beni tumbled in next and packed himself in the back side. Victor followed after pausing to kiss her hand to the girl in a graceful manner.

Then Martha ran up to press down the lid, but could not make it catch.

"You must squeeze down," she said to them.

Lugui groaned.

"I am doing my best, miss," said Victor, who was nearest the top; "but although we fitted in very nicely before, the chest now seems rather small for us."

"'Tis so!" came the muffled voice of the short man from the bottom.

"I know what takes up the room," said Beni.

"What?" inquired Victor, anxiously.

"The pie," returned Beni.

"'Tis so!" came from the bottom, in faint accents.

Then Martha sat upon the lid and pressed it down with all her weight. To her great delight the lock caught, and, springing down, she exerted all her strength and turned the key.

Answer Key

UNIT 1	UNIT 2	UNIT 3	UNIT 4	UNIT 5	UNIT 6
Quick Quiz	Quick Quiz	Quick Quiz	Quick Quiz	Quick Quiz	Quick Quiz
1. B	**1.** C	**1.** B	**1.** D	**1.** C	**1.** D
2. G	**2.** J	**2.** H	**2.** G	**2.** G	**2.** G
3. B	**3.** A	**3.** A	**3.** A	**3.** D	**3.** D
4. H	**4.** F	**4.** J	**4.** J	**4.** J	**4.** J

Spanish Vocabulary List

UNIT 1

plot trama—los eventos que ocurren en una historia

complications complicaciones—nuevos eventos o personajes que complican el problema o conflicto de la trama, haciéndolo más difícil de resolver

UNIT 2

character personaje—una persona o un animal en un libro, poema, obra teatral o historia

motivation motivación—los motivos o razones que un personaje tiene para hablar o actuar

UNIT 3

properties propiedades—también se llaman props; los objetos que se encuentran en el escenario

personal props props personales—objetos en manos de los personajes que éstos también usan

setting marco escénico—el lugar en que un drama tiene lugar

UNIT 4

sound effects efectos de sonido—sonidos que ayudan a comunicar el ambiente y motivar la acción en un drama

inflection inflexión—cambio en tono (lo que tiene de alto o bajo) y volumen de una voz

tone tono—el uso de la inflexión para comunicar sentimientos

UNIT 5

movement movimiento—en teatro, cambios en donde está un actor sobre el escenario

repetition repetición—en términos de movimiento, acciones que se repiten una y otra vez

rhythm ritmo—en términos de movimiento, un modelo de movimientos que se repiten una y otra vez

UNIT 6

subject sujeto—usualmente un concepto abstracto, como el "miedo" o la "verdad"; contesta la pregunta, "¿De qué se trata la obra dramática?"

theme tema—una actitud hacia el sujeto de un drama demostrada por su acción; la idea básica de un drama

mood talante—el sentimiento emocional creado por el drama

Teacher's Handbook

Table of Contents

Introduction to the Teacher's Handbook

The purpose of the Teacher's Handbook is to prepare you, as the teacher, to explore and use drama in the classroom. Theatre arts, as a component of fine arts, satisfy the human need for personal expression, celebration, and communication. As students have the opportunity to tell and retell stories, create characters, and explore production elements, they will learn more about themselves and the world in which they live.

Preparing a Lesson

Creating Journals

Before you begin using the theatre lessons in this book, have each student select a notebook to be used as a journal. A journal feature in each lesson provides students with an opportunity to draw or write in response to the lesson and to apply the lesson concepts to real life.

Selecting Lessons

Although all 36 lessons teach important theatre concepts, some teachers may not have the time to explore all of these lessons. Eighteen core lessons have been selected and marked with an icon in the table of contents. By using the **Unit Openers,** the core lessons, and the **Theatre Technique Tips,** it is possible to meet all of the theatre standards in the National Standards for Arts Education.

Gathering Materials

► In the left column of each lesson is a materials list. Before class, gather any materials needed for the lesson. These often include photocopies of a lesson **Warm-Up** page. **Read Alouds** do not need to be copied, as you will read these pages aloud to the class.

► The last lesson in each unit is a **Unit Activity.** The stories for these lessons are in the back of the book beginning on page 124. Sometimes these stories will need to be photocopied and distributed to students; they will not need to be copied when they are a **Read Aloud.**

Using the Theatre Technique Tips

The first section in the Teacher's Handbook is the **Theatre Technique Tips.** These tips are referenced in the lessons at point of use. Each Technique Tip covers a style of Creative Expression used in the lessons, such as pantomime or script writing. Use these tips to introduce students to the techniques the first time they are used in a lesson or for review.

Exploring the Professional Development Articles

These articles provide valuable information about the use and benefits of drama in the classroom. By covering topics such as classroom management, definitions of terms, and inclusion of students with disabilities, these articles offer the support a classroom teacher needs to implement drama in the classroom.

Using the Scope and Sequence, Glossary, and Index

The **Scope and Sequence, Glossary,** and **Index** will help you find what a concept or term means and where they are covered within this and other grade levels in *Theatre Arts Connections.*

Theatre Technique Tips
Pantomime

Focus

General Definition

Pantomime is acting without words. When actors pantomime a story they use facial expressions and expressive movements to communicate. Although there are other uses of this term, in this program *pantomime* is defined as "movement that uses silent action to tell a story."

Related Concepts

► Narrative pantomime, a more specific type of pantomime, involves many actors pantomiming in unison while a story or poem is read aloud. In this type of pantomime, the actors do not interact with one another; instead, all students portray characters at the same time.

► *Pantomime* and *mime* are not synonymous. Mime is a special art form that is closely related to pantomime; however, a mime uses a specific, stylized form of pantomime to communicate an idea and theme. Mimes often paint their faces in such a way to make their facial expressions more easily seen from a distance. Miming is an intensely disciplined art, and most mimes study specialized techniques for years.

Teach

Introduce students to skills related to pantomime in one or more of the following ways:

► Relaxation allows actors to use their bodies safely and expressively. Have students relax their bodies in preparation for pantomime by closing their eyes and consciously tensing and relaxing each muscle in their bodies, beginning with their toes and working their way up to their neck muscles.

► Discuss student observations of people's nonverbal signals in real life, such as the way slumped shoulders might communicate depression or weariness. Have students imitate some nonverbal signals, working to imagine and identify each character's specific situation, thoughts, feelings, and motivation.

► Discuss the importance of interacting with invisible objects in a realistic way. Have students hold two different objects, such as a pencil and a glass, noting each object's shape and weight. Have them pantomime holding one of these objects, focusing on retaining the object's exact dimensions, weight, texture, and firmness.

► Placement is very important in pantomime. Invisible objects such as a shelf or a door handle must remain the same throughout a pantomime. For example, if an actor pantomimes setting a glass down on a table and then returns to pick it up, the glass must appear to be in the same location in space. Have students practice this by each in turn pantomiming an interaction with an object, such as opening a door, so that the object's location does not seem to change.

Reflect

Have students consider any of the following questions that apply to their exploration of pantomime:

► Did your pantomime have a distinct beginning, middle, and end?

► Describe your character's feelings and desires. How did you use your body to communicate them?

► Did you use distinct body movements?

► How could you improve next time?

Theatre Technique Tips
Improvisation

Focus

General Definition

Improvisation is spontaneous. When students work together on improvisations, they are developing skills in creativity, imagination, and listening to others. In this program *improvisation* is defined as "acting without a script or rehearsal."

Related Concepts

► Scene improvisation is situation-focused. Actors may quickly choose the characters, setting, and situation (including conflict) for a scene and then act the scene out. Although it is spontaneous an improvisation of a scene should still have a beginning, a middle, and an end through which characters solve a problem.

► Character improvisations can allow actors to further explore characters from stories or plays. They can improvise characters interacting in situations different from those in stories, such as two actors improvising a meeting between characters from different books. Actors should focus on character details and work to infer new actions and speech based on previous characterization.

Teach

Introduce students to skills related to improvisation in one or more of the following ways:

► Tell students that they should usually not "deny" by contradicting other actors during an improvisation. Say, "If another actor improvises the statement, 'I love your blue hair,' do not automatically say, 'My hair isn't blue.' Accept the believability of the situation and other actors' creativity. Use your imagination to respond."

Have the class improvise characters who wake up on a spaceship and must figure out how to get back to Earth.

► Explain that during an improvisation, actors avoid asking questions, especially questions that are answered with *yes* or *no*. These shut down the action of an improvisation. Have student pairs improvise the following: one student chooses the basic identities of two characters and their situation but keeps them secret from the other student. As they improvise the scene the student who does not know the secret facts may not ask direct questions about the facts, but must instead follow the other character's lead.

► Say, "Actors must focus on their characters' motivation and the conflict in the improvisation." Create an improvisation at a bus stop. Have each student decide on the facts of a certain character, including his or her motivation for being at the bus stop. Begin the improvisation, allowing students to go and wait at the bus stop as their characters and to interact with each other.

Reflect

Have students consider any of the following questions that apply to their exploration of improvisation:

► What were some challenges of "thinking on your feet"?

► Did you keep your focus on the facts of your situation and characterization? Did you work toward your character's goal?

► Did you accept others' ideas onstage?

Theatre Technique Tips
Theatre Games

Focus

General Definition

Theatre games are closely related to improvisation. In this program *theatre game* is defined as "an active game that helps students focus on some aspect of performance skills or story development."

Related Concepts

▶ Many theatre games focus on problem-solving skills by asking students to accomplish a goal, or focus, while observing certain rules. A student is successful during a theatre game when he or she keeps the focus and accomplishes the goal. A theatre game might involve organizing actions into a sequence of events, showing emotion through arm or leg movement alone, showing feeling using a made-up language, or group creation of a movement machine through use of repeated movements.

▶ It is often helpful to use a technique known as sidecoaching, or calling out phrases or words, to help students keep their focus on solving a problem. If students play a theatre game that is a slow-motion version of freeze tag, you might say things like, "Remember to move in slow motion! Control your bodies."

Teach

Introduce students to skills related to theatre games in one or more of the following ways:

▶ Remind students that being funny or clever is not the focus of theatre games. One type of theatre game involves creating an emotion machine. Choose an emotion, such as joy, and have one student begin repeating an action and a word or sound to illustrate joy, such as throwing his or her arms up and saying,

"Hooray!" Other students should add their own repetitive actions and speech or sound to the machine, but their actions must be reactions to another student's action.

▶ Tell students that theatre games help them focus on listening to and watching each other carefully when they work together. Another theatre game is called the mirror game. Have student pairs sit across from each other. One student should act as the leader, while the other must mirror the leader's actions. They should focus on making it impossible to tell which student is the leader.

Reflect

Have students consider either of the following questions that apply to their exploration of theatre games:

▶ What was the focus of the theatre game you played? Did you keep that focus?

▶ How do you think theatre games help actors become better at playing characters?

Theatre Technique Tips

Dramatization

Focus

General Definition

Story dramatization is an important aspect of drama in the classroom. It allows students to better understand and interpret written texts by enacting the events from stories. In this program *dramatization* is defined as "using movements and dialogue to act out a scene from a story, book, play, or other text."

Related Concepts

► Dramatization is related to improvisation in that students are not required to memorize lines; however, dramatization differs from improvisation in that the characters, situations, and storylines are predetermined and fixed.

► Some story dramatizations might not involve speech; such dramatizations would be defined as pantomimes in our program, as the focus would be on physicalizing stories. Dramatizations involving dialogue without action are not categorized separately unless students are presenting a certain type of script dramatization known as Reader's Theatre.

Teach

Introduce students to skills related to dramatization in one or more of the following ways:

► Choose a book students have recently read as a class and a specific scene. Have students identify when and where the scene takes place, the weather, actions performed by the characters, the characters' attitudes and feelings, and any other relevant information. Have groups of students assign roles and discuss how to use speech and movement to act out this scene as the characters. For younger students, you may find it helpful to read the scene aloud, pausing at certain places to allow student groups to act out what you have just read. Discuss any choices they had to make about details that were not described in the book.

► Read aloud a narrative poem, such as "A Remarkable Adventure" by Jack Prelutsky. Have students listen carefully and then write or describe the events from the poem in order. Divide students into groups that contain the appropriate number of actors. Have student groups assign roles and decide how they are going to act out the characters' actions. Reread the poem, and then have student groups share their speech and actions with the class. Discuss how dramatizing the poem changed the students' understanding of the events.

Reflect

Have students consider either of the following questions that apply to their exploration of dramatization:

► Compare and contrast your dramatization with the book or story you dramatized. Did you change anything?

► How did your dramatization help you better understand the original story?

Theatre Technique Tips
Tableau

Focus

General Definition

A tableau is often used as an acting exercise, but it may also be used to begin or end a scene in a play. In this program *tableau* is defined as "a living snapshot or sculpture formed with actors' bodies that shows a moment of action in a story or illustrates the theme of a story."

Related Concepts

▶ Tableau is closely related to pantomime, as in tableaux actors must use their body positions and facial expressions to communicate characters and situations. Unlike pantomime, actors cannot use movement to further communicate. In a tableau, actors may use stylized body positions and exaggerated facial expressions.

▶ A tableau may be based on imaginary or historical characters and situations, or may illustrate character relationships from a book, play, or other existing text.

Teach

Introduce students to skills related to tableaux in one or more of the following ways:

▶ If students have not created tableaux before, you may wish to begin by having them improvise a situation or dramatize a story. Tell them to freeze, and have other students examine their body positions, describing what they know about the characters and their situations through the tableau alone. Allow student groups to plan their tableaux the second time through, choosing body positions and facial expressions that might better show their feelings and relationships.

▶ Show students the image of an appropriate photo, painting, or sculpture, and have student groups create tableaux based on this work.

▶ Have older student groups create tableaux illustrating the theme of a story or the moral of a fable. For example, students might illustrate the moral, "A friend in need is a friend indeed" by creating a tableau in which one character is helping another character study for a test. Discuss different interpretations of each theme or moral.

▶ Tell students that when creating a tableau, especially one based on a made-up situation, they need to make concrete decisions about their characters and relationships. If students do not seem to be doing this in their tableaux, hold an imaginary microphone in front of different students within a tableau, and have them speak their characters' thoughts. Take suggestions from the class as to how the bodies of the students in a tableau could show their thoughts and feelings.

Reflect

Have students consider any of the following questions that apply to their exploration of tableau:

▶ How would you compare and contrast tableaux and photographs or paintings?

▶ How did your tableau show who each character was and what his or her relationships were to the other characters?

▶ What was challenging about creating your tableau?

Theatre Technique Tips
Puppetry

Focus

Puppetry involves giving life to and creating characters from objects. In this program *puppetry* is defined as "bringing an object to life in front of an audience."

Related Concepts

▶ Shadow puppets are figures, usually two-dimensional, which are manipulated behind a screen, or stretched cloth. When a light shines on the puppets from behind the screen, they cast shadows on the screen. Sometimes actors use their hands or bodies as shadow puppets; actors may also use their bodies to create a montage, or shadow tableau.

▶ Stick puppets are cut-out shapes attached to items such as craft sticks.

▶ Hand puppets are puppets that fit over actors' hands like gloves. Sometimes they have moveable mouths; other times they may only have movable arms and heads.

▶ There are many types of puppet theatres or stages. For use in the classroom, students may create a simple stage by covering a table with a large blanket, kneeling behind it, and moving their puppets as if the top of the table is the puppets' "floor." A more complex, traditional European stage involves a three-paneled or enclosed structure. The front panel of this theatre has an opening or hole and may have curtains that open and close. Puppeteers sit within the structure and use the opening as a proscenium puppet stage. This type of puppet theatre could be simulated by cutting an opening in a trifold presentation board.

Teach

Introduce students to skills related to puppetry in one or more of the following ways:

▶ Creating puppets may involve a few simple steps or may become very complicated. To introduce students to hand puppet creation, bring in socks or mittens and allow students to glue or sew on facial features using jiggly eyes, sequins, yarn, or beads. Tell students to make a list of their characters' traits before beginning. Appropriately tailor the complexity of the materials and methods involved to the age of the students.

▶ Explain that when a hand puppet talks, its entire body should move. Other puppets onstage should freeze to indicate they are "listening." When using a moveable mouth puppet the student's fingers should move the puppet's head while his or her thumb should move the mouths. The thumb only should be moved when a puppet is speaking. Puppeteers must work to match their puppets' mouth movements to their speech. Puppets appearing from below a table stage should gradually enter while bobbing up and down as if climbing a flight of stairs; when they exit, puppets should seem to go back down a flight of stairs.

▶ Have older students create puppets with jointed arms and legs attached to rods; show examples of similar puppets from Jim Henson's Muppets or Indonesian shadow theatre.

Reflect

Have students consider either of the following questions that apply to their exploration of puppetry:

▶ What can you do as a puppeteer that you cannot do as an actor and vice versa?

▶ How could you better match your puppet's mouth movements to the words you speak?

Theatre Technique Tips
Reader's Theatre

Focus

Reader's Theatre allows students to focus on vocal characterization and sound effects. In this program *Reader's Theatre* is defined as "a style of theatre in which performers read from a script, creating characterizations through their voices, facial expressions, and upper-body posture."

Related Concepts

▶ Choral readings, in which groups or individual actors speak or chant lines, were popular in speech and drama competitions of the 1930s and 1940s. They are thought by some to be the predecessor of modern Reader's Theatre.

▶ Reader's Theatre is a presentational style of theatre; in other words the audience never forgets that what they are watching is not real life, but rather a dramatic presentation. All physical action must be imagined, as actors usually sit or stand and face the audience. Settings and costumes are limited or nonexistent.

▶ Reader's Theatre provides developing readers with an excellent opportunity to practice fluid reading. Although scripts are not memorized, always allow students time to rehearse their performances so that readers at all levels will be prepared.

Teach

Introduce students to skills related to Reader's Theatre in one or more of the following ways:

▶ Encourage students to underline or highlight the parts they read. Pauses or breaks in reading, determined through rehearsing, should be marked in some way to aid the reader. Students should decide whether they wish to use audience focus, in which all performers look at the audience while reading, offstage focus, in which performers look above the heads of the audience as if they are speaking to other, invisible characters, or (less traditionally used) onstage focus, in which performers look at one another when reading.

▶ Oral interpretation practice is important. Students need to experiment with vocal pitch, range, quality, intensity, and inflection, and learn what their voices can do. One way to do this is to present students with a simple nursery rhyme, such as "The House That Jack Built." Challenge students to say the rhyme and resist speaking in a sing-song fashion. Have them focus on the verbs and find different, appropriate ways to say them. For example, how might the verb in the line "that *kissed* the maiden all forlorn" be said differently from the verb in the line "that *killed* the rat"?

▶ Actors in Reader's Theatre often play more than one part, and doing so presents interesting challenges in vocal characterization. Have pairs of students select, adapt, or write a script containing four or more characters to perform as Reader's Theatre; challenge them to divide the roles and find ways to use their voices and facial expressions to indicate each character. They may wish to rewrite some of the descriptions of action so that they may be read by a narrator.

Reflect

Have students consider either of the following questions that apply to their exploration of Reader's Theatre:

▶ Was it challenging to act through voice and facial expressions? Why or why not?

▶ How did the Reader's Theatre performance help you better understand the reading selection?

Theatre Technique Tips
Script Writing

Focus

Writing a play allows students to directly connect skills in language arts with skills and knowledge about theatre. In this program *script writing* is defined as, "creating improvised dialogue for a monologue, short scene, or play and formalizing that dialogue by recording it or writing it in a script format."

Related Concepts

► Playwriting involves mastering the steps of the writing process, including inventing characters and plot situations, writing drafts, presenting readings, revising, and publishing or producing the finished work.

► Unlike writers of novels or short stories, a playwright's work is not fully finished until it is performed. Playwrights often revise scripts based on problems or ideas that arise during rehearsals and production.

Teach

Introduce students to skills related to script writing in one or more of the following ways:

► Younger students may not be able to write their own scripts. Script writing in this case should involve creating characters, improvising and refining dialogue, and recording this dialogue using audio or video recording. After reviewing their recorded dialogue, have students discuss whether their dialogue told a story with action and a beginning, a middle, and an end. Was their dialogue appropriate? Allow students to revise and replay their scripts.

► Encourage students to write character sketches, story ideas, and interesting verbal phrases or overheard dialogue in notebooks or journals. These ideas can be very useful when working on a script in which they are creating new and imagined characters.

► Encourage students working on script ideas to decide on a through line, or major action of the play, and conflict early on. What will be their story's Major Dramatic Question? What is its five *W*s? Who are the protagonist and antagonist(s)? Improvising scenes as invented characters can help students develop both character and plot ideas.

► Remind students that character dialogue should fit the characters. Their words and phrasing should match their personalities, times in which they live, social and economic situations, and emotional state. Students should also consider how easily their scripts can be staged.

► Have students use traditional script formatting. Characters should be introduced in a list form at the beginning of the script. When a character speaks in the play, his or her name should be set to the left of the line and be followed by a colon or period. Stage directions and descriptions of a character's attitude when speaking should be set in parentheses and italics (or should be written in a different color of ink if handwritten).

Reflect

Have students consider any of the following questions that apply to their exploration of script writing:

► Did your scene, monologue, or play have a clear beginning, middle, and end?

► Who was your protagonist or main character? What did he or she want to achieve? What obstacles made this goal difficult to pursue?

► How would you like to stage your play? Who would you cast as your characters?

Theatre Technique Tips
Storytelling

Focus

Storytelling is one of the most ancient theatrical art forms. In our program *storytelling* is defined as "the art of sharing stories with other people."

Related Concepts

► Throughout history, storytellers have served an important purpose. In preliterate cultures a storyteller was the keeper of a culture's history, beliefs, and traditions. Stories had to be passed from one generation to another, and thus traditional stories were often structured in a way that made them easier to remember, such as creating groups of three characters or events or repeating certain phrases over and over within a story.

► Storytelling in America has experienced a revival in the last hundred years. In the early twentieth century, American libraries first began to offer story hours for children. A few professional storytellers from England and Europe came and taught storytelling techniques to librarians, teachers, and many other interested people. In 1903 Richard T. Wyche organized the National Story League at the University of Tennessee, which began a revival of the art of storytelling in the South. Today there are many ways to experience American storytellers through live or recorded performances.

Teach

Introduce students to skills related to storytelling in one or more of the following ways:

► Storytelling is closely related to acting. A storyteller should use vocal and facial expressions to create characters and engage an audience. Give students time to practice telling stories they plan to share with others, working in groups to give each other constructive feedback to help improve each story. Storytellers should focus on making eye contact with the audience. They should focus on the audience's responses, slowing down, speeding up, and emphasizing parts of their stories so that the audience fully engages with and understands a story.

► Stories explaining how something in nature came to be are told throughout the world. Have students select a phenomenon or object in nature, such as the rainbow or the sun. Allow them to make up stories explaining its beginning, such as where the first rainbow came from or why the sun seems to cross the sky.

► Students may find it helpful to create outlines of stories they plan to tell. They do not need to memorize stories, but they should have a clear understanding of the order of events.

► Storytelling in the classroom can provide students with a way to share personal stories or stories from their heritages. Have students share such stories.

► There are many interesting storytelling traditions from other cultures, such as the "call-and-response" tradition in some parts of Africa. Have students research different storytelling traditions from cultures around the world and restructure a familiar story to match each of these styles.

Reflect

Have students consider either of the following questions that apply to their exploration of storytelling:

► How did you change your voice when you spoke as different characters? Were you able to keep each characterization consistent?

► What memory techniques could you use to help you remember the sequence of events in a story?

Theatre Technique Tips
Creative Movement

Focus

In this program *creative movement* is defined as "nonrealistic, expressive movement that allows a performer to communicate a concept or idea, such as joy or struggle, or to become a natural force or object, such as the wind."

Related Concepts

► *Creative movement* is a term constructed to cover a variety of movement styles that involve elements of dance. Rather than being realistic character movement, creative movement allows students to express themselves through improvised, free-form movement.

► Exploration of movement is an important tool for actors. It can be used as a valuable warm-up to get creative ideas flowing, and it can help actors overcome their inhibitions.

Teach

Introduce students to skills related to creative movement in one or more of the following ways:

► Choose pairs of contrasting ideas or emotions, such as freedom and bondage or terror and peace. Have students move around the room in a way that expresses one of these ideas; for example, they could stretch out their arms and then contract their bodies while looking around to show terror. When you use a signal such as a sound or word, they should change their movements to express the contrasting idea. Discuss the different types of movement that best showed each concept.

► Creative movement can be useful as a warm-up when portraying unusual fantasy characters. Have students choose a fairy tale or myth in which natural forces are personified, such as "The Rat Bride" from Japan. As a class, explore different creative movements that could show the force of the wind or the movement of waves. Work to incorporate these movements into actors' performances as these characters.

► Have students attempt to show an idea or emotion using controlled, repetitive movement of isolated body parts, such as their arms or feet alone.

► Discuss plays or performances in which abstract movement could be used. For older students, connect creative movement with presentational theatre, or theatre in which actors do not seek to emulate real life but rather are clearly presenting a performance.

Reflect

Have students consider either of the following questions that apply to their exploration of creative movement:

► How did using creative movement affect the way you felt while performing?

► What types of movements did you use? How did you use isolated body parts? How did you use rhythm and repetition?

Theatre Technique Tips
Dramatic Movement

Focus

When students use dramatic movement they practice showing characters through their posture and movement. In this program *dramatic movement* is defined as "a characterization exercise in which the focus is on revealing character through movement."

Related Concepts

► In the context of acting, dramatic movement can be very useful in building a character. Actors often use movement exercises, such as moving as their characters performing everyday tasks like getting dressed, to explore particular characters and to help them make choices about the way they will move onstage.

► Dramatic movement differs from pantomime in that it is not concerned with plot or conflict, but instead focuses wholly on physical characterization.

Teach

Introduce students to skills related to dramatic movement in one or more of the following ways:

► Choose a time period students have been studying in social studies. Discuss the types of dress worn by people in that time and culture, how people may have related to one another, and daily activities they probably performed. Have students use prop or costume pieces to help them understand the way people in that time would have moved; for example, they could simulate bustles by tying pillows onto themselves. Have students each select one character from this time period and act as this character getting dressed or preparing a meal.

► Have students all move as the same character performing a simple task, such as setting the table for supper. Call out different characters, such as a ballet dancer, a baby, or a penguin, and have students show the way each character might perform the activity.

► Have students choose animal characters. Assign each student a different emotion, and then have students move as their animal characters would move when affected by each emotion.

Reflect

Have students consider any of the following questions that apply to their exploration of dramatic movement:

► How did you hold your body when acting as your character? Compare and contrast this movement style with the way you usually move in real life.

► How did motivation and emotion influence the way you moved as your character?

► How did you keep your characterization consistent? Was it challenging to do so? Why or why not?

Theatre Technique Tips
Sound Effects

Focus

Creating and using sound effects in a theatrical performance is an important element of production. In this program *sound effects* are defined as "sounds and music created and used onstage to motivate action, communicate setting, or create mood."

Related Concepts

► Sound effects are an essential element of production. Sound effects used in live theatre may be live, or created at the time they are needed, or recorded prior to the performance. Mechanical sound effects help motivate action onstage. Environmental sound effects help create setting and mood; in radio drama these types of sound effects are vital to creating an image in the mind of the listener.

► Music in a performance can serve many of the same functions as sound effects. Music is sometimes a part of a scene's setting, as in the music played during a scene set at a ball. Transitional music plays between scenes and helps maintain the play's mood. Incidental music is another type of music used in plays; it is played in the background of a scene and also helps to create mood.

► Sound effects can be created using many common items. Crinkling cellophane paper can create the sound of a fire burning. Students can "walk" heavy boots across two layered boards or a box filled with gravel to create footsteps. Teacups and saucers can create the sound of rattling dishes. Large metal spoons clinked together sound like swords in a duel. A synthesizer can be used to create many interesting sound effects.

Teach

Introduce students to skills related to sound effects in one or more of the following ways:

► Have students watch a scene from a video and then make a list of all the sound effects. Replay the scene, and compare it with students' lists. Alternatively, have students watch a scene from a video with sound muted, and have them predict the effects used.

► Have students bring in recordings of their favorite music; select several of these and discuss the types of feelings each song evokes. Have groups of students improvise scenes that reflect each mood.

► Read aloud or discuss a story that takes place in a specific location, such as "Hansel and Gretel," which takes place in a forest, or bring in a book of age-appropriate scripts for older students to analyze. Discuss different possible sound effects, such as sounds that evoke setting (crickets chirping, city sounds) and sounds that motivate action onstage (a doorbell ringing, a car horn honking). If you wish, have groups of students create and record several of the necessary sound effects.

Reflect

Have students consider either of the following questions that apply to their exploration of sound effects:

► How does music affect your mood? How did you use music or how could you use music to create mood in a drama?

► Which sound effects were most effective? What are some of the challenges of creating and using sound effects for live theatre?

Theatre Technique Tips
Sensory Recall

Focus

Sensory recall or sense memory is a tool many actors use in the process of characterization. In this program *sensory recall* is defined as, "the use of remembered sights, sounds, smells, tastes, and textures to define character."

Related Concepts

► Sensory recall can be very useful to actors onstage. If an actor is supposed to act as though a cup of water is actually a cup of hot tea, he or she can use memories of the sensation of drinking a hot beverage to help create realistic reactions onstage.

► Characters' reactions to sensory stimuli can also communicate information about who they are or how they are feeling. When actors use sensory recall, they use their imaginations to transport themselves as their characters into particular situations, taking into account the characters' ages and physical, social, and emotional states.

► To use sensory recall, it is easiest to think about the small details of a memory. For example, instead of trying to remember how it feels to be hot by thinking about "hotness," remember how sweat feels as it trickles down the back of your neck or the sticky feeling of a sweaty shirt clinging to you. As an actor, using this memory and then physicalizing actions that one would take in response to it—for example, pulling at the clinging shirt or wiping the sweat off of your neck—will help recreate the sensation.

Teach

Introduce students to skills related to sensory recall in one or more of the following ways:

► Discuss with students the importance of imagination when acting. Pass around concrete objects, such as a coin, a brittle leaf, and a heavy book. Then have students pretend to pass around these same objects. Encourage them to use their memories of their previous interactions with these objects to help them imagine them.

► Have students choose a particular character and scene from a book they recently read as a class. Discuss physical sensations the character experiences in that scene. Have students identify experiences of similar sensations they have had, and have all students simultaneously move as that character, using those remembered sensations to help them act as the character.

► Discuss ways in which students could use details of sense memories they have when playing a character in a fantastic or unusual situation, such as a character who is experiencing life on another planet. How could they identify with that character's physical experience?

Reflect

Have students consider either of the following questions that apply to their exploration of sensory recall:

► How vivid or concrete was your memory of smells, tastes, and other physical sensations? Was it difficult to transfer the memory to the character's experience? Why or why not?

► How could you use sensory recall to help you better create a character who seems realistic?

Theatre Technique Tips
Emotional Recall

Focus

Emotional recall is another tool many actors use in the process of creating a character. In this program *emotional recall* is defined as "the technique of using emotional memories in the process of characterization."

Related Concepts

▶ Emotional recall is closely associated with a type of acting known as "the Method." The Method involves acting techniques advocated by Constantin Stanislavsky, one of the cofounders of the Moscow Art Theatre in 1898. Stanislavsky rejected acting methods of his day that seemed stilted and unnatural and wrote three famous books describing what he considered to be a more naturalistic approach to acting.

▶ Actors use emotional recall to help them enter the lives of the characters. If an actor cannot identify with a character's emotions in the given circumstances, he or she can find a memory that evokes that emotion. For example, if you cannot imagine the feeling of terror of a character in unusual danger but hate going to the dentist, you might use the memory of sitting in the waiting room of a dentist's office to identify with the character. Emotional and sensory recall are related, as specific physical details of a memory often help create that feeling. The feeling should then be applied to the characterization; actors do not think about their own memories in performances but rather make their experiences synonymous with the characters' experiences while in rehearsals.

Teach

Introduce students to skills related to emotional recall in one or more of the following ways:

▶ Discuss the ways students' memories of situations evoke emotions for them. How do specific details of those memories, such as sounds or smells they remember, make each memory seem more real?

▶ Have students close their eyes and recall a common event, such as arriving at school on the first day. Ask questions to help them remember details of that event, such as, "What was the weather like that morning? What clothes were you wearing?" and so on. After a few minutes, have students open their eyes and write journal entries describing any emotions the exercise evoked and what remembered details seemed to evoke the emotions. Explain that actors often use such details to help them experience and understand a character's feelings in a play.

▶ Have students choose an emotionally charged scene from a story or book. Discuss the way each character is probably feeling, using evidence from the text. Have students consider what memories from their own lives might help them empathize with each character's emotions.

Reflect

Have students consider any of the following questions that apply to their exploration of emotional recall:

▶ What remembered details most strongly evoked an emotion?

▶ Why do you think the concrete details of a memory help recreate feelings you had long ago?

▶ In what various character situations could you use this specific memory?

Theatre Technique Tips
Settings

Focus

Settings in live theatre are created visually through a combination of scenery, props, and lighting. In this program *setting* is defined as "the visual elements that combine to show when and where a play takes place and to evoke mood."

Related Concepts

▶ In professional theatre, setting is created visually through a set and lighting. Students have an opportunity to experience some of the elements of theatrical production when they create or design settings or sets for dramas. In a classroom environment, settings do not need to be very complex; the important thing is for students to consider the time and location in which a play takes place and utilize available resources to suggest that time and location. For example, students can drape blankets over chairs or desks to create scenery that evokes mountains or waves. Students might paint or draw a scenic backdrop, hang it, and then dramatize or improvise a scene in front of it.

▶ Although props are a part of the creation of setting, the use of props is covered separately on page T20.

Teach

Introduce students to skills related to settings in one or more of the following ways:

▶ Have students each make a list of every visual detail they can remember that is related to a familiar setting. Discuss their lists. What elements would be essential when communicating that location to an audience? What elements would not be necessary? Discuss choices that set designers must make when creating limited or streamlined sets.

▶ Sets are not always realistic. Sometimes scenery or props may be used symbolically to show a central theme of a production or to create mood. Older students may enjoy the challenge of creating set designs that show the theme or mood of a familiar book. You might also challenge them to create an abstract, symbolic setting for a play version of a favorite film.

▶ Discuss how details of setting affect characters in a scene. How can actors show setting through movement alone? Have students move as a character from a story with which they are familiar. Call out changes to the character's setting and have students adjust their movements. For example, if the story takes place in a desert, change the setting to a ship at sea and have students adjust their movements.

Reflect

Have students consider any of the following questions that apply to their exploration of settings:

▶ How did you create setting through your design, set creation, or movement?

▶ If you created scenery, how did it help show time, place, mood, and/or theme?

▶ Do you think sets are an essential element of theatre? Why or why not?

Theatre Technique Tips
Costumes

Focus

Costumes are an important part of play production. They help show who a character is and when and where a play takes place, and they are part of the overall visual design of a play. In this program *costumes* are defined as "the clothing and accessories worn by actors in a drama."

Related Concepts

▶ For students to fully explore the details of theatre it is important that they begin to identify and experiment with the role of clothing in characterization. In professional theatre other factors beyond characterization must be considered when costumes are designed. The costumes must both reveal characters and relate visually to the overall design and tone of a production.

▶ In classroom drama students should begin by experimenting with simple costume pieces, such as hats or scarves. For simplicity's sake, students can create costume pieces using materials such as paper grocery bags or posterboard. Make sure that all available materials are age-appropriate, and help younger students by performing tasks such as stapling or cutting through thick board.

▶ Although makeup and masks are a part of costume, their use is covered separately on page T19.

Teach

Introduce students to skills related to costumes in one or more of the following ways:

▶ Have students each choose one character from a book with which they are familiar. Tell them to imagine they must reveal this character through one costume piece only. What would be essential for that character? Have students each describe the costume piece and explain why it best shows who that character is.

▶ Have students attend a live amateur or professional theatre performance; alternatively, have them view a recording of such a performance. Discuss the ways in which costumes related to the style and color of the scenery and props. How did they help reveal who each character was?

▶ Have older students do further research on clothing related to a culture or time period they are learning about in their social studies curriculum. You may wish to have them do image searches using an Internet search engine as well as use printed resources such as encyclopedias and other books. Have each student use his or her research to create a costume design for a character from that time period. Discuss choices a costume designer might make that could depart from strict authenticity and why he or she might make such choices.

Reflect

Have students consider any of the following questions that apply to their exploration of costumes:

▶ How did the five *W*s of the story relate to your design of costumes? How did your costume reflect the character and setting?

▶ How did you use color in your costume?

▶ What types of considerations must a costume designer make when he or she is designing costumes? Why do you think he or she ought to work with the set and lighting designers?

Theatre Technique Tips
Makeup and Masks

Focus

Makeup and masks help reveal who characters are. Makeup may merely accentuate an actor's features. It can be realistic or fantastic. In this program *makeup* and *masks* are defined as "elements used to highlight or alter an actor's face."

Related Concepts

► Masks have been used in cultures around the world. Often performers have used masks for ceremonial purposes, seeking to become, embody, or personify another person or deity. Masks change a performer's face in a drastic way—for this reason, students who are reluctant to participate in dramatic activities may find mask work freeing, as masks can allow them to perform while feeling "hidden."

► Actors in professional, live theatre often design and apply their own makeup. Makeup skills are therefore essential for actors who perform in plays. Although students may learn a few of these skills, students in younger grades should feel free to experiment with makeup elements without focusing on complex, technical skills.

Teach

Introduce students to skills related to makeup and masks in one or more of the following ways:

► For the purposes of safety, do not allow students to apply makeup on each other. Make sure that each student uses his or her own brush, sponge, or cotton ball to apply his or her makeup, and that each student has access to a mirror. Emphasize the importance of safety when using makeup near eyes, noses, or mouths, and always be sure to keep the activity on-level and age appropriate.

► Allow younger students to create masks and then use face paint to transform their faces into those of

animal or fantasy creatures. Compare and contrast the way masks and makeup change their faces. Which do students prefer for certain characters, and why?

► For older students who have studied principles of visual art, it may be helpful to note that realistic makeup application involves techniques that are similar to those of a portrait artist. Highlights, shading, and color value are all important in makeup application. If possible provide students with cream foundations of various shades and makeup sponges (one per student). Have students choose foundations that blend well with their skin colors and apply a thin coat of the foundations to their faces using the sponges. Explain that this acts as a blank canvas. Have them experiment with application of lighter and darker foundations to accentuate their facial features.

Reflect

Have students consider either of the following questions that apply to their exploration of makeup and masks:

► Describe the makeup or mask you created or designed. How did your mask or makeup show who the character is?

► Compare and contrast the challenges associated with the use of makeup and masks. In what situations would one be more effective than the other?

Theatre Technique Tips
Props

Focus

Properties, commonly referred to as *props,* are an essential component of a play's setting. In this program *props* are defined as "objects found or used onstage, including furniture and items used and carried by actors."

Related Concepts

▶ There are three main types of props: floor props, personal or hand props, and decorative props. Floor props are often items such as furniture, lamps, or tables. Personal props are objects carried and used by actors; they are often small objects, such as pens or money. Decorative props are props that help reveal setting, such as a portrait or painting on a wall.

▶ Like sound effects, props can serve a variety of aesthetic and functional purposes. They can help show who characters are and when and where a play takes place. They can motivate or be an integral part of a plot. They can help create mood and show a play's theme.

▶ In classroom drama props can be simple. Use objects from the classroom whenever possible or allow students to bring in objects from home. Allow students to imaginatively pretend one object is actually another; for example, a pen could be used as a microscope or as a microphone. Have students create props using art supplies such as clay, masking tape, or posterboard.

Teach

Introduce students to skills related to props in one or more of the following ways:

▶ Explain to students that stage business, which involves the use of props and parts of the set, is an essential part of acting. Actors must seem comfortable and at ease as they interact with props onstage. The correct and safe use of certain historical props, such as swords or fans, may require special training. Have volunteers act as a character writing a letter to a friend. Discuss details of such an action and how the character might interact with props such as a pen, a desk, and sheets of paper. How would the time period affect the character's actions and the props he or she would use?

▶ Explain to students that technical rehearsals are an important part of theatrical productions. They allow the technical crew to practice performing all the technical tasks related to a production, including setting (or placing) and striking (or removing) the props. When students work with props in dramatic activities, have them practice setting and striking the props in an orderly manner. If possible have some students act as the stage crew while others work as the actors. Discuss the importance of speed and consistency when placing, moving, and removing props.

Reflect

Have students consider any of the following questions that apply to their exploration of props:

▶ How do props affect the way actors move onstage? How have they affected your own performances?

▶ What was challenging about setting and striking props?

▶ How can props create both setting and mood?

Professional Development

Planning and Managing Drama Activities

by Betty Jane Wagner
Roosevelt University

Because drama can overexcite students, it is important to establish rules and signals carefully in advance. Ideally, the students and the teacher should do this together, as planning and evaluating the effectiveness of a drama afterward are crucial parts of the whole process. You will need to freeze the action from time to time to keep the drama from spinning out of control or into silliness. You can use a bell, a couple of sharp raps on a tambourine, a loud clap, or a verbal signal, such as, "Freeze." Practice responding to the signal a few times until everyone understands.

One problem that often arises in an improvisational drama is giggling. When students are shy and embarrassed, they tend to laugh instead of staying in role and playing their parts with belief and seriousness. Talk about this ahead of time. Remind the students that when they giggle and step out of role, they make it very hard for the other students to stay focused. Tell them you will stop the drama when they find it to hard to stay serious. If only one child "loses it," go over to him or her and say, "I know this is hard for you. Please take your seat until you feel you can join us without giggling." Stop the drama entirely whenever a few students do not appear to be "with it."

Take time to establish roles before the drama begins. You might start by having everyone in the class stand as if they are, for example, an elderly woman with not enough to eat. Have all the students simultaneously pantomime the posture and facial expression of that character.

Starting with pantomime is probably the easiest way to introduce dramatic activities, especially with an unruly class. You can even do this while having the students stand beside their desks. Your goal, however, should be to arrange the room—pushing aside desks or tables as needed—so that at least half of the class can work in small groups in improvising the movements of a drama.

Remember, it is not usually important that students have an audience in educational drama. The goal is to have the *experience* of role-playing, not of evoking a response in an audience. Thus, simultaneously acting out the part of each of the characters in turn while a story is being read aloud is a good way to help students focus on each of the characters before they work in small groups to assign roles and each play a different character.

Drama Terminology

by Betty Jane Wagner
Roosevelt University

The drama activities presented in this curriculum encompass both informal drama in the classroom and the more formal theatre performance for an audience. The purpose of informal drama is to enlarge and deepen vision and understanding for the *participants*. The purpose of theatre, on the other hand, is to present an enactment of human experience in order to enlighten and entertain an audience.

When a teacher conducts an informal drama, it may be termed either *creative drama, educational drama* (or *drama in education*), or, more recently, *process drama*. The goal of all of these is an educational one: to help students come to understand human interactions, empathize with other persons, and internalize alternate points of view. There is no emphasis on training actors for the stage. Brian Way describes the goal of this type of drama as leading "the inquirer to moments of direct experience, transcending mere knowledge, enriching the imagination, possibly touching the heart and soul as well as the mind" (Development Through Drama, New York: Humanities, 1972, p. 1).

Creative drama is the older term for informal classroom drama. The action in creative drama is often suggested by a story, poem, original idea, or music provided by a child or adult. Both creative drama and educational drama may include pantomime. Both are developed through improvisation and role-playing, but educational drama is less likely than creative drama to have a beginning, a middle, and an end and to begin with a warm-up and end with relaxation exercises.

In educational or process drama, as in creative drama, the action may be introduced with a story. More commonly, however, the students are asked to confront a situation lifted from history or contemporary life. When a problem or conflict is introduced from an area of the curriculum, the students are expected to respond in role, usually as persons of authority. There is less emphasis on story and character development and more emphasis on problem solving or living through a particular moment in time. Through ritual, dramatic encounters, pantomime, writing in role, reflection, and tableaux, students enter the lives of imagined characters and play out their responses to challenges and crises. Experienced educational-drama teachers often initiate the drama or move this along by assuming a role themselves; in role, they can heighten tension by challenging the participants to respond in believable ways.

Unlike creative and educational drama, whose focus is process, the focus in theatre is on *product*— a finished, polished production for an audience. Whenever students work together to prepare a drama for an audience, they are engaging in theatre. Theatre experiences build confidence and awareness of the power of theatre elements such as movement versus inaction, sound versus silence, and light versus darkness. Students who are rehearsing in preparation for a theatre performance need to be aware of the need to project their voices so all can hear, to keep their bodies facing the invisible "fourth wall," and to use gestures and actions more deliberately in order to communicate with the audience. In theatre performance the students, as actors, must accommodate for the audience and calculate the effects of their actions on that group.

Both informal drama and formal theatre have their place in the activities of the classroom. Both share the excitement and challenge of working imaginatively in role to construct contexts, events, and interactions, and both allow participants to expand their understanding of real life and the content of the curriculum.

Developmental Stages in Educational Drama

by Betty Jane Wagner
Roosevelt University

Students who are challenged or struggling readers often shine in drama activities. Often the confidence they build in drama carries over to their approach to other school tasks. Drama teachers who meet with children only for drama sessions are often surprised to find that some of the leaders in drama work are actually having difficulty in their regular academic program. Classroom teachers report that after experiencing success in drama, students improve in other areas.

It is ironic to talk about development from a more primitive to a more advanced stage of dramatic activity given the fact that drama theorists agree that preschool and primary students are the most spontaneous and uninhibited in dramatic improvisations. As they get older, students tend to lose their belief in their roles and feel self-conscious, especially if the teacher focuses too much on performance.

In R. W. Colby's 1988 groundbreaking longitudinal study of growth of dramatic intelligence, he described developmental growth as a U-shaped trajectory. His theory is that successive reorganizations of understanding account for, for example, growth from the preschool stage of *being* a character to the middle childhood stage of *playing* a character, and from that to the adolescent stage of a return to the "notion of *being* a character, but on a higher level and with the discoveries of the previous stages available" (183). In other words, both young children and teenagers can share with accomplished actors the capacity to identify with and believe that they are the characters they are performing, but in between these stages, students resort to learning from the outside rather than from the inside of the character. It is as if they perceive acting as a "game with rules," and they are trying to figure out just what the rules are. Colby characterizes this middle-childhood stage as that of *playing* a character, or pretending to be that character and glomming onto themselves whatever attributes they think their role demands. At this stage they get better at refining their register and diction for their parts, and they learn how to create gestures and actions that an audience can respond to. In the process they often lose the spontaneity that characterizes younger children.

Cognitive psychologists in their study of the spontaneous play of early childhood have found that the proportion of time spent in symbolic pretend play declines as children grow. Of all the types of play young children engage in, symbolic play decreases as games with rules increase. Jean Piaget claimed that functional (exercise or practice) play occurs during the sensorimotor stage from birth to two years. Symbolic pretend play then takes over and reaches its height between two or three and five or six years of age. By the time a child is seven or eight, games with rules that are socially transmitted become the dominant play or ludic activity, along with constructive play. Piaget's theory could account for the change in children's involvement with drama. If by seven or eight, children then treat drama as a "game with rules," they are looking for ways to learn how to *do* drama rather than simply immersing themselves *in* a role. Only later do they return to the engaged emotional identification with a character, and by then they have internalized what they have learned at the bottom part of their U-shaped trajectories.

Howard Gardner, famous for his theory of multiple intelligences, sees growth in dramatic intelligence as critical in the development of interpersonal intelligence, an art that is in much demand in our fractured and stressful society. Students who develop diverse potentials can contribute uniquely to democratic life and appreciate the differing gifts of others. No other activity teachers can foster in the classroom contributes any more to this goal than improvisational drama.

How to Respond to Classroom Drama

by Betty Jane Wagner
Roosevelt University

Do

► Ask the children to explore a story by acting it out together.

► Respond to students in role in their drama.

► Stop the drama whenever a group of students is acting silly, and ask them if they want to continue; if so, be sure the problem doesn't recur.

► After a noisy and exciting session, have the students lie on the floor as if in their beds, and reflect on how they felt and what they thought as their characters.

► Think of ways for students in role to write diary entries, letters, or news articles for the press.

► Enter the drama yourself in role as a person who heightens the tension by introducing a problem.

► After a drama is over, congratulate the whole group for staying in role and helping the drama along.

► Talk about a drama after it is over, reflecting on whether or not persons in real situations would act the way they had.

► Create dramas that bring literature or other curricular areas alive.

► Give students opportunities to depict dramatic action through drawing, dancing, or writing.

► Reflect as a class on the drama after the lesson is over and talk about what did and didn't work.

Don't

► Imply that the goal of the drama is to perform for an audience.

► Give directions to the group in your usual teacher stance.

► Ignore the behavior of a group of students who are having trouble believing their roles and are therefore giggling, rolling their eyes, or acting foolish.

► Keep a high-action drama going so long that the students stop thinking about their roles and instead get into heightening the conflict and "hamming it up."

► Separate drama from other areas of the curriculum, such as writing or reading.

► Let the drama lose focus by letting it continue without dramatic tension and therefore become boring.

► Stop the drama to congratulate a particular student, thereby creating competition rather than encouraging teamwork.

► Tell students what to do and how to do it before they act out a story, thus confusing them with too many directives.

► Set up dramas that have no relation to what students are reading in other classes.

► See dramatization as the end point of exploring a piece of literature or curricular area.

► Grade participation in a way that singles out good performers and thus sets up competition among students.

Research That Supports Educational Drama

by Betty Jane Wagner
Roosevelt University

A solid body of research shows that informal educational drama, as presented in this curriculum, is effective in improving students' oral language, reading, and writing proficiency. For a summary of the results of studies of the effects of educational drama on language arts, see Educational Drama and Language Arts: What Research Shows (cited on page T30).

Research indicates that participation in drama leads to improved listening, comprehension, understanding of sequence, and internalization of the grammar of a story. Moreover, when students role-play in a social studies, science, or math lesson, they comprehend the subject matter better. When students are just on the edge of understanding a topic, the pressure to talk in role as if they know it will help in the forging of meaning. Because students usually feel compelled to respond in a dramatic situation, they bring to bear all they know about a person in his or her imagined shoes and often connect their recent new knowledge with their previous experience, and in the process construct new perceptions. Once they have expressed their new understanding orally, they are more prepared to write about a topic. As students assume a variety of roles in educational drama, they develop a wider range of strategies for dealing with conflicts and understanding others in the real world.

When young children play dramatically, they put themselves under pressure to use language in a more flexible and mature way. They learn very early to differentiate their voice register when talking with an imagined baby, younger child, or person in authority. In teacher-led dramas, the teacher can introduce into the drama precise vocabulary that may be unfamiliar, and the students pick up the words naturally. For example, in a drama about a hospital, young children will need to use words or phrases such as *stethoscope, urine analysis, blood test,* or *CAT scan*—all of which the teacher can supply naturally in the context of the drama. They not only expand the range of their voice register and vocabulary, but they also acquire standard dialect in an effortless way. In the process they are laying down a foundation for the acquisition of literacy because both drama and reading are symbolic acts.

Because drama is a social art, students learn that unless they cooperate and support others, the game is over. Drama also prepares children for symbolic thought. In an informal drama, real objects have to be imagined and seen in the minds of all the participants in the same way—for example, the imagined table has to be in the same spot for all of the players. In other words, the role players need to be engaging in symbolic behavior if the drama is going to work. Since all of literacy is symbolic, drama is a valuable activity to facilitate reading and writing.

Thus, although students may enjoy drama very much, it is more than fun and games. By working hard at improvisation students gain insight into the social world that surrounds them and improve their comprehension at the same time.

Theatre Arts and Students with Disabilities

by Mandy Yeager
Art Educator, Ph.D. Student
The University of North Texas at Denton

Teacher Attitudes Towards Inclusion

Any discussion of the benefits of theatre arts for students with disabilities must begin with considering teacher attitudes regarding disability and inclusion. With over six percent of all school-aged children in the United States experiencing some type of disability (United States Census, 2000), the likelihood is that students with disabilities are present in every classroom. As a result, disability becomes one of the many perspectives and voices represented in classrooms. The teacher who pays heed to diverse voices and perspectives will choose instructional methods and materials that align with the abilities and experiences of all of his or her students.

Benefits of Inclusive Theatre Arts Experiences

Students with and without disabilities have much to gain from inclusive theatre arts experiences. Research studies of students with disabilities participating in theatre arts programs report a demonstrated relationship between dramatic activities and increased academic and social skills such as oral language, on-task and courteous behavior, and conflict resolution. Positive changes in student attitudes and feelings about learning and self are most pronounced for students with disabilities.

The inclusion of students with disabilities in theatre arts programs also serves to remind teachers and nondisabled students that disability is a normal experience. Numerous studies have been conducted that prove that personal interactions with persons who are disabled are the most effective way to dispel stereotypes about disability and build equitable relationships with persons who are disabled. A curriculum and a classroom that does not ignore disability, but rather honors and addresses it, is one that prepares students for social responsibility and equity.

Practical Strategies for Inclusion

Successful adaptations for students with disabilities begin with proper attitudes towards inclusion. These attitudes should be accompanied by a willingness to obtain information about students' abilities. The Internet offers a number of resources for understanding students with disabilities. Each student with an identified disability also has an Individualized Education Plan (IEP) that details information about student learning styles, strengths, needs, and goals. The Individuals with Disabilities Education Act (IDEA) guarantees all educators of students with disabilities the right to view and receive help in implementing this plan. Other useful information about students with disabilities can be gathered through collaboration with special educators and related service personnel at the school level. These individuals can give art educators useful insight regarding successful instructional strategies and modifications for students with disabilities.

Accommodations for students with disabilities should be made in the physical space of the classroom or stage, making sure that students with mobility impairments have access to class activities. Use the principles of differentiated instruction to present material in such a way that students with cognitive disabilities can readily comprehend and apply knowledge. Provide all students opportunities to think about issues of disability through thoughtful selections of scripts and classroom activities.

Conclusion

Theatre arts have a powerful role in the education of all students, especially students with disabilities. A carefully designed program will address multiple learning and social needs of students, as well as provide them with an empowering experience.

Tips for Putting on a Class Play

✔ **Choosing a Play Script** Consider the audience and the occasion. Check for royalty fees and permission requirements. Choose plays with minimal lighting and sound. Make sure the plays require a simple set.

✔ **Young Students** It can be effective to develop a play through creative drama with five- to eight-year-olds. Begin with a good story, replay it in several different ways, and then write it down to create a script.

✔ **Director's Book** Create a director's book by cutting apart a script and photocopying the pages onto larger sheets of paper so there is space to write notes and plan blocking.

✔ **Reawaken Creativity** If a scene becomes stagnant, give students a new and unusual intention or focus, such as playing the scene in slow motion or in an angry manner.

✔ **Technical Preparations** Have students use real or temporary props in rehearsals as soon as possible. Always hold a technical rehearsal so lighting and sound technicians can practice. Practice the curtain call with actors.

✔ **Work as a Team** Encourage students to help each other out; if one student forgets a line, another should cover or ad-lib; if a sound effect is missed, students should improvise to keep the scene going.

Ideas for Cross-Curricular Theatre Activities

Social Studies

► Divide the class into two groups. Have one group reenact a historical event while the other group acts as a film crew presenting a message biased toward a particular viewpoint of this event. Let the tensions between the two groups mount as the drama unfolds.

► Have small groups of students re-create the daily family life of a tribe. At some point you should enter the scene and act as a government representative who tells them they have to leave their sacred lands. Each group should decide which object they will take with them on their journey and explain why. Allow them to confront the governmental official.

Math

► Any story problem in the curriculum has the potential for dramatization.

► Role-play a situation in which making change with play money is a natural part of the drama, perhaps taking place at imagined cash registers.

► Role-play restaurant visits and have students calculate the tips in their heads.

► Whenever a drama calls for an interior space, discuss square footage. For example, have students calculate how large a hospital must be if it has 100 rooms of 9' by 10'.

Science

► Have one group of students discover a negative, environmental impact of a development in a community, such as a factory or housing. Unfortunately the community is dependent on this development for its economic well-being. Allow the first group to confront other students portraying town leaders with the facts they have discovered.

► In small groups, have one student assume the role of an important scientist, such as Jonas Salk. Allow the others to portray people who question the validity or safety of this person's work. How does the scientist present his or her case to the larger community?

Reading/Writing

► Have readers write a diary entry for a character from a scene they have acted out.

► Have students write letters in role as one character addressing another, perhaps several years after the events in the story.

► Have students tell or write the story of what happened long ago in a certain building in the role of stones from that building.

An Overview of the History of Theatre

Western theatre is considered to have begun with the Dionysia, a huge dramatic festival that first appeared in fifth-century B.C. Greece. The festival was held in honor of Dionysus, the Greek god of wine and nature; it contained competitions for the best dramas. The first competitions were for tragedies, which were based on Greek mythology and told of the struggles and downfalls of central heroic characters. Tragedies were written in groups of three. Each could stand on its own, but together they formed a larger unity. The great Greek tragedy writers include Aeschylus, Sophocles, and Euripides. Soon a separate competition was added for comedies, which were also rooted in ritual and mythology, but concluded with happy outcomes and featured political or literary satire. Comic playwrights include Aristophanes and Menander. Both styles included musical accompaniment, and most plays had a chorus. Greek theatres were semicircular in shape and built into hillsides so that the seats rose up from the ground-level stage area, similar to a modern arena.

Roman theatre developed from the Greeks, who they conquered in the third century B.C. Many early Roman plays were translations and adaptations of Greek plays. However, while the Greeks preferred tragedy, comedy was more popular in Rome and was of a more vulgar nature than the satiric Greek comedy. Theatres were built on level ground instead of a hill and contained a raised stage with elaborate backdrops. Eventually the chorus was eliminated and a curtain was used for the first time. Entertainment in the first century A.D. turned to gladiatorial and nautical spectacles, and by the fifth century, Christian opposition to theatre virtually eliminated all forms of drama in the declining Roman Empire.

Western theatre appeared again in the Middle Ages when the Christian church that had originally opposed drama began using liturgical plays during Mass. In the eleventh century, medieval guilds began producing plays, which remained biblical. These plays were performed outdoors. Miracle plays (dramatizations of Christian miracles), mystery plays (which included bible stories), and morality plays (in which characters were personified virtues such as Truth) were all common.

A high point of European theatre came around the sixteenth century, when Renaissance drama developed and England experienced the Elizabethan period and the rise of William Shakespeare. The increasingly professional theatres could accommodate multiple plots and stage actions. The Globe Theatre (where Shakespeare's plays were performed) was an open-air octagonal theatre, with a large elevated stage, permanent backdrop, and roofed galleries for the audience. Shakespeare wrote tragedies, comedies, romances, and historical plays, including *Hamlet, Romeo and Juliet,* and *Henry V.*

After the Elizabethan period, enclosed theatres were built and European theatre became a more elite entertainment. Female actors appeared in legitimate English theatre for the first time. Professional acting companies developed throughout Europe, and by the eighteenth century, these companies were also in America.

The nineteenth-century Romantic era produced the melodrama, an emotional, excitement-driven play featuring the courageous hero, the innocent heroine, and the evil villain. In response to Romanticism, the French "well-made play" developed, which contained a tightly structured plot with a predictable beginning, middle, and end.

In the early twentieth century, modernist playwrights abandoned past dramatic traditions. Modernist plays followed the new style of realism, in which an invisible "fourth wall" was erected between stage and audience, and theatre strove to present a "slice of life." American drama today encompasses all eras, as theatre-goers can sample everything from modern adaptations of Greek tragedies to realistic Shakespearean reenactments.

Eastern theatre began much the same as theatre had in the West, with religious rituals. According to an ancient theatre handbook, Indian drama began when the creator god Brahma brought together song, dance, and recitation to please all social classes. Indian drama was reflexive, and not bound to the western idea that a play must have a set plot with rising action, climax, and resolution. The oldest surviving plays of this kind are the highly stylized Sanskrit plays from the first century A.D., which involved stock characters whose movements and physical responses were emphasized over speech. Sanskrit declined after the tenth-century Muslim invasions, and folk dramas became the popular theatre form. During the fifteenth-century Hindu cultural revival, regional dance dramas developed, as well as historical hero plays and social satires. These all play a role in modern Indian theatre.

Chinese drama also grew from religious roots, centering around gods and ancient ancestors. Other similarities to Indian drama include stock characters and the emphasis on physical performance over literary aspects. The height of Chinese drama came in the thirteenth and fourteenth centuries with the Zaju drama, a multi-act musical play in which all conflicts are resolved and peace is restored in the final act. During the sixteenth-century Ming Dynasty, most popular theatre was looked down upon by intellectuals. The exception was Kunqu, which took place in real time to bamboo flute music and took days to perform. Modern Chinese theatre began with the eighteenth century Peking (now Beijing) Opera. As in early Chinese traditions, the Peking opera used mythological and historical subject matter and focused on music and dance performances, but it added high-speed acrobatics and duels.

Ancient and modern Japanese theatre draws inspiration from Chinese legends, but its greatest influence is native culture. Unique to Japan is Noh drama, which dates from the fourteenth century. Noh features two actors, a singing chorus, and musicians. It has little or no plot or conflict and has no ties to realism. The Kabuki theatre of the seventeenth century catered more to the growing Japanese middle class. Kabuki, which means "singing-dancing-acting," features more individual acting roles and innovative stage machinery, such as the revolving stage, which was developed in Japan years before it was seen in the west.

Early African theatre, similar to its western and Asian counterparts, took form in religious rituals that included dancing, drumming, and mask work. Communal dancing and ceremonial performances were special events that involved all tribe members. Storytelling was another dramatic form in which spoken narration and dialogue was joined by music and dancing.

In the sixteenth century, African slaves brought their traditions to America, and a unique African American dramatic style developed from the original rituals. For example, clapping and foot tapping replaced African drums and eventually evolved into early American tap dancing. Many prominent African American playwrights appeared in the twentieth century, especially during the Harlem Renaissance. Today's theatre reflects a renewed interest in early African heritage.

Further Resources

Books and Articles

Arts Education Partnership (2002). <u>Critical links: Learning in the arts and student academic and social development.</u> Washington, D.C.: Arts Education Partnership.

Booth, D. H. (1987). <u>Drama worlds: The role of drama in language growth.</u> Toronto: Language Study Centre, Toronto Board of Education.

Booth, D. H. (1994). <u>Story drama.</u> Markham: Pembroke Publishers.

Byron, K. (1986). <u>Drama in the English classroom.</u> New York: Methuen.

Bailey, S. D. (1993). <u>Wings to fly: Bringing theatre arts to students with special needs.</u> Woodbine House.

Erion, P. & Lewis, J. C. (1996). <u>Drama in the classroom: Creative activities for teachers, parents, and friends.</u> Lost Coast Press.

Gardner, H. (1985). <u>Towards a theory of dramatic intelligence.</u> In J. Kase-Polisini (Ed.), <u>Creative drama in a developmental context.</u> New York: University Press of America.

Heathcote, D., & Bolton, G. (1995). <u>Drama for learning: Dorothy Heathcote's mantle of the expert approach to education.</u> Portsmouth, NH: Heinemann.

McCaslin, Nellie. (1999). <u>Creative drama in the classroom</u>. Pearson, Allyn, & Bacon.

Miller, C. S. & Saxton, J. (2004) <u>Into the story: Language and action through drama.</u> Portsmouth, NH: Heinemann.

Moffett, James & Wagner, Betty Jane. (1992). <u>Student-centered language arts, K-12.</u> Portsmouth, NJ: Boynton/Cook, Heinemann.

O'Neill, C. & Lambert, Alan. (1990). <u>Drama structures: Practical handbook for teachers.</u> Stanley Thornes Pub. Ltd.

Shah, A., & Joshi, U. (1992). <u>Puppetry and folk dramas for non-formal education.</u> Sterling Pub. Private Ltd.

Stewig, J. W. (1983). <u>Informal drama in the elementary language arts program.</u> New York: Teachers College Press.

Wagner, B. J. (1998). <u>Educational drama and language arts: What research shows</u>, third book in the <u>Dimensions of Drama</u> series. Portsmouth, NH: Heinemann.

Wagner, B. J. (1983). The expanding circle of informal classroom drama. In B. A. Busching & J. I. Schwartz (Eds.), <u>Integrating the language arts in the elementary school</u> (pp. 155–163). Urbana, IL: National Council of Teachers of English.

Wagner, B. J. (1990). Dramatic improvisation in the classroom. In S. Hynds & D. L. Rubin (Eds.), <u>Perspectives on talk and learning</u> (pp. 195–211). Urbana, IL: National Council of Teachers of English.

Wagner, B. J. (1999). <u>Dorothy Heathcote: Drama as a learning medium</u>, 2nd ed. Portland, ME: Calendar Islands Publishers.

Wilhelm, J. D., & Edmiston, B. (1998). <u>Imagining to learn: Inquiry, ethics, and integration through drama</u>. Portsmouth, NH: Heinemann.

Wolf, S., Edmiston, B. W., & Enciso, P. (1996). Drama worlds: Places of the heart, voice and hand in dramatic interpretation. In J. Flood, D. Lapp, & S. B. Heath (Eds.), <u>Handbook of research on teaching literacy through the communicative and visual arts</u> (pp. 492–505). New York: Simon and Schuster, Macmillan.

Web sites

American Alliance for Theatre and Education: **www.aate.com.** Offers opportunities for educators to get advocacy information and collaborate with other educators

Drama Education: A Global Perspective—Learning in, with and through Drama: **members.iinet.net.au/~kimbo2.** Contains lists of drama education resources, including downloadable lesson plans and class activities, compiled by a theatre educator

VSA arts: **www.vsarts.org.** Offers a number of free resources for arts educators

National Dissemination Center for Children with Disabilities (NICHCY): **www.nichcy.org/index.html.** Offers information on special education law (IDEA), agencies and resources for educators and parents (both national and state) and specific disabilities.

Scope and Sequence of Theatre Concepts

Plot	K	1	2	3	4	5	6
A Plot Is Events in a Story	U1OP, 1.1, 1.6	U1OP, 1.1, 1.6	U1OP, 1.1, 1.6	U1OP, 1.6	U1OP, 1.6	U1OP, 1.6	U1OP, 1.6
Plot and Sequence	U1OP, 1.1, 1.2, 1.3, 1.4, 1.6	U1OP, 1.1, 1.2, 1.3, 1.4, 1.6	U1OP, 1.1, 1.2, 1.4, 1.6,	U1OP, 1.1, 1.3, 1.5, 1.6	U1OP, 1.1 1.6	U1OP, 1.1	U1OP, 1.1
Beginning/Exposition	U1OP, 1.2,	U1OP, 1.2, 1.6		U1OP, 1.3, 1.6	U1OP, 1.1	1.1	1.2
Presents a Problem	U1OP, 1.3,	U1OP, 1.3,	U1OP, 1.3,	U1OP, 1.4, 1.6	U1OP, 1.3, 1.6	U1OP, 1.3, 1.6	U1OP, 1.3, 1.6
Presents a Major Dramatic Question						U1OP, 1.3, 1.6	U1OP, 1.3, 1.6
Complications			U1OP, 1.3	U1OP, 1.4, 1.6	U1OP, 1.4, 1.6	U1OP, 1.4, 1.6	U1OP, 1.4, 1.6
High Point/Climax				U1OP, 1.5, 1.6	U1OP, 1.5, 1.6	1.5, 1.6	1.5, 1.6
Problem's End/Resolution	U1OP, 1.4	U1OP, 1.3, 1.4, 1.6	U1OP, 1.4	1.5, 1.6	U1OP, 1.5, 1.6	1.5, 1.6	1.5, 1.6
Asking "What If?"	U1OP, 1.5	U1OP, 1.5	U1OP, 1.5	1.6	1.6	1.2	1.6
Plot and the Five *W*s				1.2, 1.6	1.2, 1.6	1.2, 1.6	

Character	K	1	2	3	4	5	6
What Constitutes a Character	U2OP, 2.1, 2.2, 2.3, 2.6	U2OP, 2.1, 2.2, 2.3, 2.6	U2OP, 2.1, 2.6	U2OP	U2OP	U2OP	U2OP
Character and the Five *W*s	U2OP			U2OP			
Actions and Feelings	U2OP, 2.4, 2.5, 2.6	U2OP, 2.4	U2OP, 2.2, 2.3	U2OP, 2.1, 2.4, 2.6	U2OP, 2.1, 2.3, 2.4, 2.6	2.3, 2.4, 2.6	U2OP, 2.1, 2.2
Motivations			U2OP, 2.4, 2.6	U2OP, 2.1, 2.6	U2OP, 2.3, 2.6	2.1, 2.6	2.1, 2.2, 2.6
Actions Produce Reactions		U2OP, 2.5, 2.6	U2OP, 2.5, 2.6	2.3, 2.6	2.3, 2.4, 2.6	2.1, 2.3, 2.6	2.1, 2.6
Characters Interrelate				2.2, 2.6	2.2, 2.6	2.4, 2.6	2.1, 2.2, 2.6
Protagonist and Antagonist						U2OP, 2.2, 2.6	U2OP, 2.2, 2.6
Characters Solve a Problem				U2OP, 2.5, 2.6	2.5, 2.6	2.5, 2.6	2.5, 2.6
Internal Characterization							2.3, 2.6
External Characterization							2.4, 2.6

Sound and Voice	K	1	2	3	4	5	6
Sound Can Tell a Story	U3OP, 3.1, 3.6	U3OP, 3.1, 3.6					
Sound Shows Setting	U3OP, 3.2, 3.4, 3.6	U3OP, 3.2, 3.4, 3.6	U3OP, 3.1, 3.6	U4OP, 4.1, 4.4, 4.6	U4OP, 4.2, 4.6	U4OP, 4.1, 4.4	U4OP, 4.3, 4.6
Sound Evokes Feelings			U3OP, 3.4	4.1, 4.6	U4OP, 4.4	U4OP, 4.1	U4OP, 4.1, 4.6
Music Evokes Feelings			U3OP, 3.2	U4OP, 4.2, 4.6	U4OP, 4.4	U4OP, 4.2	U4OP, 4.2
Voice Shows Emotion	U3OP, 3.3, 3.5, 3.6	U3OP, 3.3, 3.6	U3OP, 3.5, 3.6	U4OP, 4.5, 4.6	U4OP, 4.5, 4.6	4.5, 4.6	U4OP, 4.5, 4.6
Voice Shows Character	U3OP, 3.5, 3.6	U3OP, 3.5, 3.6	U3OP, 3.3, 3.6	4.3, 4.6	4.3, 4.6	4.3, 4.6	4.4, 4.6
Sound and Silence Communicate							4.1
Sound / Voice and the Five Ws				4.1	4.1	4.1, 4.3	

Visual Elements	K	1	2	3	4	5	6
Physically Showing Setting	U4OP, 4.1, 4.2, 4.6	U4OP, 4.1, 4.5, 4.6	5.1	3.1	5.3	5.1	5.1
Physically Showing Invisible Objects	U4OP, 4.3	U4OP, 4.2	5.5	3.1			
Creating Costumes	U4OP, 4.4, 4.6	U4OP, 4.3	U5OP, 5.2, 5.6	U3OP, 3.3, 3.6	5.4, 5.6	5.3, 5.6	5.2, 5.6
Creating Masks / Makeup		U4OP, 4.4, 4.6	5.6	3.4, 3.6	5.5, 5.6	5.4, 5.6	5.3, 5.6
Creating Setting	U4OP, 4.5, 4.6	U4OP, 4.5, 4.6	U5OP, 5.4, 5.6	U3OP, 3.5, 3.6	5.1, 5.3, 5.6	5.2, 5.6	5.4, 5.6
Creating Puppets			U5OP, 5.3	1.6, 5.3			
Choosing Props	U4OP, 4.6	4.6		3.2	5.2, 5.6	5.5, 5.6	5.5, 5.6
Visual Elements and the Five Ws				3.1, 3.6	5.3, 5.6	5.1, 5.6	

Scope and Sequence

Movement	K	1	2	3	4	5	6
Realistic Movement	U5OP, 5.1, 5.6	U5OP, 5.2, 5.6	4.4, 4.6	U5OP, 5.1, 5.5, 5.6	U3OP, 3.2, 3.5, 3.6	U3OP, 3.2, 3.5, 3.6	U3OP, 3.1, 3.3, 3.5, 3.6
Abstract Movement						U3OP, 3.3	U3OP, 3.3
Rhythm	U5OP, 5.3, 5.6	U5OP, 5.1, 5.3, 5.6	U4OP, 4.1, 4.6	U5OP, 5.4, 5.6	3.4, 3.6	U3OP, 3.4	U3OP, 3.5, 3.6
Repetition	5.3		U4OP, 4.3	U5OP, 5.4, 5.6	3.4, 3.6	U3OP, 3.4	3.5
Shape and Form				5.3	3.3	3.1	3.1
Action and Inaction	U5OP, 5.5	5.4		5.2	3.1, 3.6	3.5	3.4
Action and Reaction		U5OP, 5.3	U4OP, 4.2	5.5, 5.6	3.5, 3.6	3.5	3.4, 3.6
Movement Communicates	U5OP, 5.1, 5.2, 5.4, 5.6	5.2, 5.5	U4OP, 4.4, 4.5, 4.6	U5OP, 5.1, 5.6	U3OP, 3.2, 3.6	3.2, 3.6	U3OP, 3.2, 3.6
Movement and the Five *W*s				5.1	3.2	3.2	

Subject, Theme, and Mood	K	1	2	3	4	5	6
Creating Stories	6.1						
Analyzing Stories	U6OP, 6.2, 6.6	U6OP, 6.1, 6.6	U6OP, 6.1	U6OP, 6.1, 6.5, 6.6	U6OP, 6.2, 6.6	6.2, 6.3, 6.6	6.2, 6.5, 6.6
Discovering Subject	U6OP, 6.3, 6.6	U6OP, 6.2, 6.6	U6OP, 6.2, 6.6	6.1, 6.6	6.1, 6.6	U6OP, 6.1, 6.6	6.1, 6.6
Discovering Theme				6.3, 6.4, 6.5, 6.6	6.1, 6.2, 6.6	U6OP, 6.1, 6.2, 6.6	6.1, 6.5, 6.6
Discovering Mood	U6OP, 6.4, 6.5, 6.6	U6OP, 6.3	U6OP, 6.3, 6.6	6.2, 6.6	6.5, 6.6	U6OP, 6.3, 6.4, 6.6	6.2, 6.6
Showing Theme				6.3, 6.4, 6.6	6.4, 6.5, 6.6	6.5, 6.6	6.5, 6.6
Showing Mood	6.4, 6.5, 6.6	6.3, 6.4, 6.5, 6.6	6.4, 6.5, 6.6	6.2, 6.6	6.3, 6.4, 6.5	6.4, 6.5, 6.6	6.3, 6.4, 6.6
Subject and Five *W*s	U6OP			6.1	6.1	6.1	
Theme and the Five *W*s				6.2	6.1	6.1	

Scope and Sequence of Theatre Activities

Creative Expression Activity Type	K	1	2	3	4	5	6
Theatre Game	1.1, 1.4, 2.1, 2.5, 3.1, 3.5 6.2	1.1, 2.5, 3.3, 4.1, 5.3	1.1, 2.2, 3.5, 4.2, 5.1	1.4, 2.3, 5.2	1.1, 4.2, 6.1	6.1	1.1
Improvisation	1.3, 2.2, 2.3, 3.3, 4.1, 5.1, 6.5	1.3, 2.1, 2.6, 3.1, 3.5, 4.2, 4.6, 6.1, 6.6	1.3, 1.4, 2.1, 3.3, 4.3, 5.5, 6.2	1.2, 2.5, 4.3, 4.5, 5.5	1.2, 2.3, 2.4, 4.5, 6.5	1.2, 1.4, 2.2, 2.4, 3.4, 4.3, 4.5, 6.5	1.2, 2.2, 2.5, 3.4, 4.5, 4.6, 6.1, 6.5
Pantomime	2.4, 4.3, 5.2	1.2, 5.2	1.2, 2.5	1.3, 5.1, 5.6, 6.4	3.5, 3.6	1.3, 3.5, 3.6, 5.1	1.3, 2.4, 3.2, 3.6, 5.1, 6.3
Tableau	4.2, 5.5, 6.4	2.4, 5.4	2.4	2.2, 5.6	1.5, 2.2 3.1		6.4
Puppets			2.6, 5.3	1.6			
Shadow Puppets				5.3			
Play Writing/Recording Dialogue	6.6	6.6	6.6	2.6, 6.6	2.6, 6.6	2.6, 6.6	2.6, 6.6
Storytelling	1.2, 1.6, 3.6, 6.1	1.4, 1.5,	1.5, 1.6, 6.3	1.1, 2.4,	1.3, 4.3,	1.1	1.4, 4.4
Reader's Theatre				1.5		4.4, 4.6	1.5
Creative Movement	1.5, 5.3, 5.6, 6.3	5.1, 5.6, 6.4	3.2, 4.1, 4.6, 6.5	3.1, 4.2, 5.4,	3.3, 3.4	3.1, 3.3, 6.4	3.3, 4.2, 6.2
Dramatic Movement	2.6, 5.4	2.2, 5.5, 6.3	2.3, 4.4, 4.5	2.1, 6.2	2.1, 3.2	2.5, 3.2, 4.2, 6.3	3.1, 3.5
Sensory/Emotional Recall						2.1, 2.3, 2.6	2.1, 2.3, 2.6
Creation of Sound Effects	3.2, 3.4, 3.6	3.2, 3.4, 3.6, 6.5	3.1, 3.4, 3.6	4.1, 4.4, 4.6	4.1, 4.4, 4.6	4.1, 4.4, 4.6	4.1, 4.3, 4.6
Creation of Setting	4.5, 4.6	4.6	5.4	3.5, 3.6, 6.5	5.1, 5.3, 5.6, 6.3	5.2, 5.6	5.4, 5.6
Creation/Selection of Costumes	4.4	4.3	5.2	3.3, 3.6	5.4, 5.6	5.3, 5.6	5.2, 5.6
Creation/Selection of Props				3.2, 3.6	5.2, 5.6	5.5, 5.6	5.5, 5.6
Creation of Makeup Designs				3.4	5.5, 5.6	5.4, 5.6	5.3, 5.6
Creation of Masks		4.4	5.6				
Script/Story Dramatization		1.6, 2.3, 3.6, 6.2	2.6, 3.6, 4.6, 5.6, 6.1, 6.4	1.6, 2.6, 3.6, 4.6, 5.6, 6.1, 6.3, 6.6	1.4, 1.6, 2.5, 2.6, 3.6, 4.6 5.6, 6.4	1.5, 1.6, 2.6, 4.6, 5.6, 6.2	1.4, 1.6, 2.6, 3.6, 5.6, 6.6
Direction of Others			6.4	6.3	6.4	6.5	6.5

Glossary

A

acting portraying a character to tell a story

action everything characters do in a play

action/reaction the interplay between characters in which the action of the plot is moved forward

actor a person who portrays a character in a play

antagonist a character opposing the protagonist, or leading character

arena stage a stage surrounded by audience seating

artistic license the idea that an author or performing artist has a right to change a story's details to fit his or her conception of the story's theme and to make it work better as a plot

audience a group of people assembled to see a performance

B

blocking traveling movement onstage planned and created by directors, actors, and stage managers

C

character a person in a story, play, or poem; can be a personified animal or object

choreographer a person who plans dance movements in dance, opera, and certain theatre productions

chorus a group of actors who narrate the action of a play

climax the point in a plot where the interest, tension, and excitement are highest

comedy a humorous genre of theatre developed by ancient Greeks

complication a new event or character in the story that makes a problem more difficult to solve

conflict the problem or struggle in a story

costume the clothing, accessories, and makeup or mask worn by an actor in a play

costume designer a person who creates costumes for the actors to wear in a play

D

decorative prop an object, such as a framed portrait, used to reveal a play's setting but not used by an actor

dialogue speech between characters in a play

director the person who unifies all the elements of a play to create an artistic production

dramaturge a consultant, often employed by a theatre, who is familiar with a play, its history, other productions of a play, the playwright's other works and so on; assists in research and evaluation

E

emotional recall the technique of using emotional memories in the process of characterization

enunciation clear and distinct pronunciation

environmental sound effects sounds that convey setting and environment

exposition information in a play or story, usually revealed near the beginning, that sets up the plot's action

external complication a physical event that occurs in a play that makes a problem more difficult to solve

F

five Ws five questions that a plot can answer: *who, what, when, where, why*

five Ws and an H six questions that a plot can answer: *who, what, when, where, why, how*

floor properties objects, such as a sofa, table, or lamp, found onstage

full back stance an actor's position onstage when his or her back is to the audience

full front stance an actor's position onstage when he or she faces the audience

I

inaction a purposeful pause in onstage action

incidental music background music used to create various moods

inflection a change in pitch and volume of a voice

integral music music that is written into a script to help motivate action, sometimes played by an actor onstage

internal complication a feeling or attitude within a character that makes a problem more difficult to solve

L

lighting the use of colored gel sheets to create realistic lighting or mood lighting onstage to reveal the *when* and *where* of a play

lighting designer a person who designs the lighting for a play, both for basic illumination and for effect

lighting director the person who is in charge of running lighting

live sounds sounds created during a performance that are not prerecorded

M

Major Dramatic Question the main question presented in drama; the action of the play serves to address and answer this question

makeup cosmetic elements used to highlight or alter an actor's face

makeup artist a person who uses makeup to change an actor's appearance

mask a costume piece that covers the face

mechanical sound effects sounds used to motivate action, such as a ringing doorbell

mime an actor who uses body movements and facial expressions to portray a character or situation

minimalism a theatrical movement in which setting, gesture, and dialogue are stripped down to essentials

monologue a speech, often lengthy, spoken by one character

mood the emotional feelings experienced by the audience and created by a performance

motivation a character's reason for speech or action

O

objective the goal a character works toward in a scene; part of a character's major goal in a play

onstage on the visible stage

P

personal prop an object held and used by a character

physicality a focus on physical movement that suggests age, emotion, or physical condition

playwright a person who writes the action, dialogue, and directions for movement in a play

plot a sequence of events that forms a story or drama

presentational theatre an approach to theatre in which it is obvious that the play is not like real life

producer a person responsible for a play, movie, or show; he or she obtains the script, raises money, and finds the theatre for the production

profile stance an actor's position onstage when he or she is turned sideways from the audience

projection speaking with enough vocal force to allow an audience to clearly hear what is said

properties also called *props;* objects found onstage

proscenium stage a stage framed by an arch, forming a box with three sides

protagonist the leading character in a play

puppet an object brought to life for an audience

Q

quarter stance an actor's position onstage when he or she is turned a quarter left or right away from facing the audience

R

recorded sound a sound effect that is recorded and played during a performance

repetition in theatrical movement, a pattern of repeated movement

representational characterization an acting technique in which actors represent characters' thoughts and feelings through movement and costumes

representational theatre an approach to theatre in which the audience "suspends disbelief" and views the performance as real life

resolution the part of the plot, usually near the end, in which the plot's problems are solved

rhythm in theatre, an orderly or irregular pattern of movements; also the pace of a character or play

rising action the part of a play, usually at the beginning, in which a main problem is introduced

role the part or character that an actor performs

S

satire an ironic, farcical genre of theatre developed by ancient Greeks

scenario the outline of action in a play

scenery painted boards, screens, or three-dimensional units that form the background of a play and enclose the acting area

scenic designer a person who develops the environment for the action of the play

script a copy of a play that provides stage directions and dialogue

sensory recall the use of remembered sights, sounds, tastes, and textures when portraying a character

set the scenery, props, and furniture onstage; also a term for placing props or scenery

set designer a person who creates scenery for many types of productions

sound designer a person who decides how and when sound effects will be used in a theatrical performance

sound effects sounds and music used onstage

sound technician a person skilled at using sound equipment to create the special sound effects needed in a play or performance

spike to mark the location of large props with small pieces of tape onstage

stage crew backstage workers, including stagehands

or grips, who handle scenery, and the prop crew, who handle properties

stage manager a person who helps the director and actors by writing down blocking, scheduling, and overseeing the technical aspects of a production

stock character a character whose feelings and actions come from cultural stereotypes, for example, a crazy scientist or a damsel in distress

storyteller a person who remembers the order of events in a story and tells it to listeners in a narrative style

strike to remove props quickly from a set

subject what a play is about, usually an abstract concept such as truth

subtext the character's inner feelings and intentions not expressed directly

synopsis a brief, general review or summary

T

technical production includes stage management, lighting, sound, stage mechanics, promotions, set design, and directing

theatre-in-the-round a type of theatre in which an audience can sit around all four sides of the stage

theme the message a play or drama communicates about its subject, such as "greed will lead to trouble"

thrust stage a low, platform stage that projects into the audience

tone the use of inflection to communicate feelings

tragedy a type of drama, created by ancient Greeks, in which a protagonist comes into conflict with a greater force or person and ends with a sad, disastrous conclusion

U

universal character a character type who appears in stories and literature throughout the world

V

visual elements the aspects of a dramatic performance that the audience sees, including costumes, props, scenery, lighting, makeup, and puppets

Program Index

Items referenced are coded by Grade Level and page number.

Notes

Notes

Notes

Notes

Notes

Notes

Notes

Notes